'Ah, here is

Louisa thought t
greet the dashing Geoffrey might not be quite
the Done Thing in polite English society. She
sat still, trying to catch a glimpse of the
approaching social butterfly.

When she did so, all pretence of good manners
was forgotten, for walking across the thick
extravagance of carpet towards their table was
none other than the man she knew as the
reclusive and dour Mr Geoffrey Redvers.

Born in Somerset, **Polly Forrester** has been writing for as long as she can remember. Her working career began with twelve years as a humble office clerk, eventually escaping to combine her love of history and the countryside in a new career as a writer. She now lives in the depths of rural Gloucestershire with a cat, a dog and a flock of very eccentric poultry.

Recent titles by the same author:

CHANGING FORTUNES

DOUBLE DILEMMA

Polly Forrester

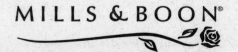

MILLS & BOON®

First published in Great Britain 1998
Harlequin Mills & Boon Limited,
Eton House, 18-24 Paradise Road, Richmond, Surrey TW9 1SR

© Polly Forrester 1998

ISBN 0 263 81076 3

Set in Times Roman 10½ on 12½ pt.
04-9808-72065 C1

Printed and bound in Great Britain
by Caledonian International Book Manufacturing Ltd, Glasgow

Chapter One

November 1910

Someone was coming. Louisa could hear the faint, uneven rattle and thrum of a motor car cutting through the wintry dusk. Here in England, she had heard, doctors regularly motored in the countryside. Everyone else must prefer the reliability of carriage horses, she thought wryly, trying to keep her seat in the tilting, crippled carriage.

As the motor car clattered past it sent a shivering vibration through the whole carriage. Louisa's gloved hands clenched convulsively on the edge of her seat, waiting for the carriage to lurch further into the ditch. Nothing happened. The carriage was stuck fast, as her driver had realised more than an hour before. It merely settled a little on its bearings.

Outside in the lane, the motor car had hissed to a halt and suddenly there was the clatter of nailed boots running back towards the carriage. For the first time in her ordeal Louisa felt a pang of nervousness.

Surely doctors did not run? Even if they did, she was
certain that an English doctor would never wear hob-
nailed boots. Both actions would show a shocking
lack of decorum.

The footsteps skidded to a halt. Louisa heard the
invisible new presence circle around her carriage,
then drop down into the ditch below and rustle
through the undergrowth around it. Cautiously, a head
appeared at the carriage window beside her.

The new arrival was muffled up in a thick coat,
scarf and heavy cap. The scarf was pulled down
quickly to reveal the face of a young man with blond
hair and a broad, friendly smile.

'A lady? Goodness, miss, are you all right? What
happened?'

'I am perfectly unharmed,' Louisa began, trying
not to sound as nervous as she felt. A lady should
never be seen to be at a disadvantage, and there were
few more awkward situations than being perched in
a wrecked carriage. She was watching the newcomer
try to open the carriage door and hoping his attempts
wouldn't make the vehicle tip still further. 'There was
a great brute of a dog blocking the road. When my
syce tried to take the horses past, the dog lunged and
sent them into a panic. The carriage landed in the
ditch, as you see, and Sami has taken the horses back
to the last village we passed on the main road to try
and find somewhere for me to lodge—'

'What ever were you doing out here in the wilds,
miss?' The young man's voice was gently chiding
and, Louisa thought, altogether over-familiar.

'There's nothing up here but Mr Redvers' place,' he concluded.

'I am on my way to Roseberry Hall. We were told in the village that it is along this lane.'

'Roseberry Hall? Why in the world should you want to go there, miss?'

The young man disappeared again before Louisa could question his impertinence. There was some more rustling, then a gentle rocking of the vehicle as he climbed up onto the side of the carriage that faced the lane. With a slight shudder of the carriage he managed to open its offside door.

'If you can try and get out this way, miss, I'm sure Mr Redvers will drive you back to the village. Your carriage is quite secure—I have checked everywhere and it will not be moving anywhere without a block and tackle.'

Louisa gathered her heavy winter coat about her and made her way with difficulty up the sloping floor of the carriage. With one hand on the door-frame and the other on the shoulder of her rescuer she made the four-foot drop to the lane lightly and without hesitation.

'Well done, miss! Oh, and I'm Higgins, by the way. Mr Redvers' gardener.'

'Really?' Louisa said without much enthusiasm. She was cold, tired and hungry, and wanted nothing more than to get to Roseberry Hall as quickly as possible. 'Could you bring my hand luggage, Higgins? I shall go and introduce myself to Mr Redvers.'

The motor car was some yards ahead, breathing some sort of steam into the chilly dusk. Louisa stepped out smartly, glad of a chance to stretch her legs after the tiresome journey and unscheduled delay. The lane was unmade and unreliable but by wielding her trusty furled umbrella now as a stick, now as an aid to balance, she managed to cut through the darkening November dusk without incident.

There were two figures in the fretful motor car. The chauffeur sat erect, his hands in their heavy gauntlets gripping the steering wheel of the car as though they were the reins of a skittish horse. His passenger sat in the rear seat, an anonymous bundle of winter clothing.

'Mr Redvers, I take it?' Louisa enquired over the thunder of the engine. The passenger looked around quickly—or as quickly as his armoury of thick clothing would allow.

Louisa was brought up short. He was *young*! She had expected some crusty old man hunched up with rheumatics, not this. A pair of clear dark eyes were regarding her keenly from a pale face, and Louisa was immediately tempted to see more. As though reading her thoughts the passenger raised one hand and pulled aside the muffler that was hiding the lower part of his face. Suddenly Louisa found herself staring at the most handsome man that she had ever seen.

'I am Geoffrey Redvers, yes,' he replied, with as much interest as Louisa had paid to Higgins earlier.

She made a mental note to apologise to the gardener for her distraction as soon as possible. It was not pleasant to be on the receiving end of chilly indifference.

'I am Mrs Algernon Hesketh,' Louisa announced,

offering her hand. Instead of taking it politely Geoffrey Redvers merely nodded his head in a perfunctory gesture, although there was a cautious interest in his eyes. Louisa tried again.

'Your man Higgins suggested that you might be kind enough to help me complete my journey, Mr Redvers. I was on my way to Roseberry Hall when—'

Her interest in Mr Redvers wavered long enough for her to notice the companion at his feet. An enormous mastiff was sitting on the floor of the motor. As she stared at it, the dog swung its huge, slack-lipped jowls up onto Mr Redvers' knee.

'That dog flew at my horses.' Louisa narrowed her usually gentle brown eyes with sudden anger.

'Grip is trained to repel trespassers.' Redvers pulled the dog's ears absent-mindedly.

'I was *not* trespassing.' Louisa made an effort to keep the growing anger out of her voice. 'I was on the public highway. On my way to Roseberry Hall.'

'No one goes there,' Redvers said as though his word was law. 'As a consequence, Grip considers this lane to be a part of my property.'

'Well, *I* am going to Roseberry Hall,' Louisa stated firmly. 'My great-aunt left it to me in her will, and now I intend to make it my home.'

A sudden smile enlivened Mr Redvers' face, but only until he managed to marshal his features back to indifference.

'Roseberry Hall has been empty for years. You will find no welcome there, Mrs Hesketh.'

'In which case, perhaps your driver would be kind

enough to take me back to the village, Mr Redvers, where my syce—'

'You have come from India?' His dark eyes gave a momentary flicker of interest.

'Indeed, sir. Now that I have no family left there, and my parents always spoke so fondly of life at Roseberry—'

'What about *Mr* Hesketh?'

Louisa looked away quickly.

Redvers cleared his throat and moved uncomfortably in his seat. To cover his embarrassment he tapped his chauffeur sharply on the shoulder.

'Get out and open the door for Mrs Hesketh, Williams.'

'Oh, but your dog…' Louisa began, remembering the thunder rolls of its barking and Sami's terrified shouts.

This concern was evidently too stupid to require a reply. Williams, the chauffeur, got out of the car, opened the rear door and hauled the mastiff out. The dog lolloped to the ground, its tail wagging the whole vast bulk of its body as it pushed a great square muzzle towards Louisa. Terrified, Louisa backed away, but the driver shoved the dog aside as though it were nothing more than a badly stuffed sack of flour. It would have to trot along home behind them.

'Grip will not hurt you, Mrs Hesketh,' Redvers said, although his weary tone told Louisa that he was thinking, Imagine being afraid of a mere *dog*!

Louisa stiffened her expression, but kept one eye on the dog as she stepped up into the car. Mr Redvers had been quick to make room for her to sit beside him, but he was now showing little interest in her other than that. Louisa was trying to think of something to say—anything that might make this vision that was Geoffrey Redvers look at her again. He was obviously not about to speak to her of his own accord. Instead, he addressed the chauffeur once more.

'Straight to Holly House, Williams.'

'Wait a moment! I am supposed to be going to Roseberry Hall!' Louisa stood up in a flurry of alarm, desperately looking for a way to get out of the car.

'The hall is a ruin, miss,' her rescuer, Higgins, called out as he arrived with the hand baggage and wedged it into the front footwell of the car. 'Leastways, it is as near to a ruin as you could get without the place actually being in pieces. Mr Redvers will drop you off in the village—'

'No, Higgins. Mrs Hesketh is coming with us to Holly House,' Redvers stated firmly.

The gardener's jaw dropped with an astonishment that he did not bother to conceal from Louisa.

'Well, *that* will be a turn up for the books, and no mistake!' He laughed, catching hold of Grip, the dog's, collar and pushing him away from the motor car before squeezing in hurriedly beside Louisa's luggage as the vehicle moved off. Higgins would have to suffer and the dog would have to walk now that there was a lady and her luggage to be carried.

Louisa was uneasy. The frosty air whipping into her face chilled her skin, but her nerves were being assailed by a much more sinister attacker. Her own dark thoughts. A lone woman, miles from anywhere, with only a gentleman and his servants as her travelling companions—what on earth would people think? If anyone in polite society heard about this she would be cut, for sure.

'Where is your maid, Mrs Hesketh? I should have thought that a well-dressed lady such as yourself would have been travelling in the company of at least one other woman.'

'Indeed, sir. The truth is that my maid, Betsy, travelled with me as far as Bristol, where she had an elderly aunt in need of a companion. Betsy stayed with her, and I intend to employ a local girl as my lady's maid when once I can take possession of my house. I thought the journey to Stanton Malreward would be an uncomplicated one. I see now that I was wrong.'

Louisa forced herself to look at her rescuers again. Redvers was first, as was only proper. Louisa could not think of his fine features now, only the suspicion that accepting his company might be the death of her reputation. In the fading light he looked austere and almost threatening, but he was staring across the fields beside the lane, not at her. If ungentlemanly behaviour was on his mind, he was not directing it towards her. Yet.

In the front seat of the car Higgins and the chauffeur were both staring straight ahead, seeming to take no notice of either of their passengers. Louisa gave them only the briefest of glances. Then she looked back for the dog. It was being left further and further behind as it trotted along, but kept its eyes on the car all the time.

Redvers cleared his throat as though to speak and

Louisa immediately transferred her attention back to
him. She realised then that he had been looking at
her, although now he looked away again quickly.
Louisa gave him a penetrating stare. If he had anything improper in mind she wanted to know in good
time, so that she might be ready to escape his
clutches. The newspapers were always carrying stories about how decent women could be robbed or
worse by rogues, and Louisa did not intend to fall
prey to anyone.

After only a moment's further study she drew her
finely arched eyebrows together a little in thought. If
Mr Redvers was a rogue he was hiding it beneath a
very heavy disguise. The strong profile visible above
his layers of warm winter clothing was the only thing
that stopped him looking like an invalid. More than
one shade of grey knitted scarf was visible above the
collar of his heavyweight overcoat, while a thick
woollen blanket in an equally dismal shade covered
him from the shoulders downwards. Despite his co-
coon and this initial appearance of fragile suffering,
Mr Redvers' face was clear, although pale. He was
feigning indifference towards her presence in the car
now, but Louisa could see that his eyes were the sort
that missed nothing. When she cleared her throat to
speak he darted a look at her that needed no explanation.

'It *is* kind of you to offer me hospitality, Mr
Redvers,' she said cautiously.

All the cool composure left him immediately, and
to her surprise Louisa saw a flash of alarm flicker
through those dark, previously unfathomable eyes.

'I have read that England can sometimes be an unfriendly place. I am pleasantly surprised to find such ready hospitality,' she finished, noticing a flush struggling to colour his face.

In the seat in front of Louisa, the gardener muttered something that was stifled by the roar of the motor car engine, but the chauffeur beside him laughed.

'What was that, Higgins?' Geoffrey Redvers leaned forward sharply, rapping out words like blows from a hammer.

'I was agreeing with the lady's surprise, sir. After all, we are always so like finches in winter up at Holly House—a real bachelor household.'

Redvers subsided in his seat, but his dark brows were still contracted with anger. Higgins must have guessed at the look his employer was giving him. Although he had not turned around, the gardener's head drooped as much as his layers of winter clothing would allow.

Louisa decided to give up trying to be polite. Conversation was not going to be easy, and would have to wait until they reached their destination. It was difficult enough trying to make oneself heard over the splutter of the engine without trying to make conversation with a man as taciturn as Mr Redvers.

The first faint stars were pricking the evening sky as the car came to a halt. Louisa immediately took a firmer grip on the handle of her umbrella, but when she saw the establishment that they were about to enter she was almost reassured. A little way ahead the country lane ended at a set of tall gates that guarded parkland beyond. Large trees studded the landscape, but with the approach of evening they were becoming nothing but dark shapes pinned against the sky. A scatter of rooks gusted in to roost, their harsh calls ringing through the frosty air.

It was all so different from life in India. Louisa felt the excitement at the great plan she had been devising rise up within her until she could hardly contain the secret.

'Is your home anything like Roseberry Hall, Mr Redvers?'

'Hardly.'

There was a soft cadence in his single word, and Louisa was quick to sense mockery.

'Roseberry Hall has been left untended for several years, Mrs Hesketh. I do not believe that time has been kind to it. I, on the other hand, always ensure that my house is tended economically, thus retaining its value.'

Mean as well as miserable, Louisa concluded.

Holly House came into view around a bend in the drive. It was a solidly built manor house of pale grey stone that glowed like moonlight in the growing dusk. It must have been extended many times over the years, Louisa realised, for the silhouette was jagged with additions to the roof line and profile. It had character, as an old English house should. Louisa knew instinctively that she would like Holly House.

It was a pity that the same could not be immediately said for Mr Geoffrey Redvers, she reflected. He certainly had the air of a gentleman, and those looks…

The car shuddered to a halt. Higgins, the gardener,

immediately leapt out and opened the passenger door for Louisa. She stepped down, then turned to watch Geoffrey Redvers do the same. He was to surprise her again. Taller than she had imagined, he moved with purpose, walking around to where Higgins was now unloading Louisa's luggage. Redvers' smooth, measured stride was a revelation. Louisa had half expected him to be a shuffling invalid after all.

Throwing his discarded travelling rug back into the car, he bent to pat his dog as it eventually panted up to the group beside the car.

'Do we have any food in the house?' Redvers was muttering to Higgins in a low voice that a lady brought up in a genteel English household would have pretended not to hear.

Louisa, however, had not been brought up in an English household. She had been born into privilege and raised by native servants in the cut and thrust of life at an Indian hill station. Gossip and eavesdropping were precious commodities there, to be hoarded and traded like jewels. As a consequence, Louisa rarely missed anything.

'If you cannot entertain me, Mr Redvers, then perhaps your chauffeur could take me back to the village,' Louisa interjected helpfully. 'I should not like to put your household to any trouble.'

It was a mistake. Despite the darkness, Louisa could feel the furious glare he turned upon her. This was evidently not how an English lady should behave. At least not in Mr Redvers' presence.

'It will be no trouble at all.' His voice cut through the dusk, as sleek and tempered as Sheffield steel.

'Higgins will show you into the drawing room while dinner is prepared. I do not usually eat dinner when in residence here, Mrs Hesketh,' he finished meaningfully before stalking towards the house.

Perhaps you ought to start, Louisa thought as she watched him go. Geoffrey Redvers was slight despite his layers of clothing and looked as though he had missed out on quite a number of good nourishing meals, as her mother might have observed.

Now that all the excitement of arrival was over, Grip, the mastiff, trudged after his master dutifully, head held low.

'Is there somewhere that I may dress for dinner?' Louisa called after her unwilling host, but Geoffrey Redvers and his dog had already been swallowed up by the gloom of his house.

'I will sort something out for you, Mrs Hesketh.' Higgins set the last valise down on the gravel and slammed the door of the motor car shut. 'My sister, Maggie, deals with the food at Holly House, so I shall have to go off and ask her to rustle something up for you—but I will see you settled in first.'

Louisa showed Higgins the cases that she would require for her toilette. He carried them into the house, while she followed in his wake. Although it was too dark to see much, Louisa thought that Holly House must have a large entrance hall. The cold draughts whipping about it certainly gave the illusion of wide open space. The place smelled unloved—full of trapped air and seasoned with a touch of damp. Louisa drew herself down into her overcoat and tried not to notice the cold. The dinner dress in her case would not go well with a blue complexion, but with the rest of her luggage travelling on later by rail it would have to do.

Higgins put the cases down and lit a small gas lamp which wavered in the chill. In its hesitant pool of light Louisa could make out a door of dark wood and brass furniture which had probably once been highly polished. Higgins reached up and took a key from the lintel and unlocked the door, lighting a second gas lamp inside the room.

It was a tiled cloakroom, complete with water closet and bath. Both were garlanded with pink painted roses, an unexpected splash of frivolity for which Mr Geoffrey Redvers could hardly be responsible, Louisa decided. She went in for a closer look while Higgins gathered up the cases.

'I will fetch some hot water for you directly, madam.' Higgins was flushed and clearly distracted. 'Although it will likely take some time, as the fire has not been lit these past two days.'

'Perhaps you could show me where I might wait in the meantime?' Louisa suggested kindly. Her unexpected arrival had obviously thrown what passed for a household here into confusion, and although she was tired, dusty and hungry that was hardly their fault.

'Oh—right, madam.' Higgins brightened at once with obvious relief. 'Follow me.'

To Louisa's surprise Higgins carefully extinguished the cloakroom light and locked the door again as they left. He went through a similar ritual of find-

ing a key, unlocking an unloved door then lighting
one small gas lamp in a neighbouring room.

Louisa followed him apprehensively. Holly House
was like a house featured in a London magazine.
Sadly, something illustrating Mr Conan Doyle's sinister stories in the Strand rather than the pages of
Country Life, she thought with a grim smile.

'The drawing room, madam,' Higgins announced
gravely as Louisa peered through the enveloping
gloom which hung about the room like cobwebs.
'Sherry, madam?'

Louisa disliked sherry intensely but as she was in
an English country house she knew that she would be
expected to play by the rules.

'Thank you, Higgins.'

He began rattling through a collection of bottles on
a side table in the dim distance. Louisa tried to make
out more of her surroundings, and was drawn by a
large portrait hanging over the empty and cheerless
fireplace. Ignoring the moaning draught that was
dropping down the chimney and slicing around her
ankles, Louisa balanced on the lip of the empty hearth
and looked up into the round, self-satisfied face of the
young woman who stared down from the portrait.

Then she became conscious of Higgins clearing his
throat respectfully. She looked back at him over her
shoulder.

'If you please, madam, it would seem that we have
no sherry at the moment...'

'That is quite all right, Higgins. You concentrate
on getting that hot water ready. I may amuse myself
here quite well enough without sherry.'

It was a strange idea to have in this drawing room, as Louisa soon discovered. The young woman looking down from the portrait above the fireplace cast a chilly spell over the room, which smelled thickly of dust and disuse. Louisa could not even cheer herself up with some music. The piano, like all the doors at Holly House, was locked.

Louisa was thoroughly glad when Higgins informed her that hot water was waiting for her in the cloakroom. The tedious business of locking and unlocking all the doors had to be gone through a second time, then she was alone in the cloakroom with the key on her side of the door.

Looking at the long, deep white bath, Louisa would have loved to soak away all the dust of her journey, but there was neither time nor water for that. She washed quickly, then dressed in the rose-coloured evening gown that suited her so well. Rather too well, she reflected, looking at her reflection critically in the full-length mirror. Algy had always appreciated plenty of *décolletage* when they had been dining alone, but Geoffrey Redvers' frosty reserve was unlikely to thaw at the sight of her spilling out of this tightly cut bodice.

Retrieving a lace handkerchief from her dressing case, Louisa tucked it demurely into her bodice like a lace fichu.

It was a shame that she did not have Betsy on hand to do her hair, but simplicity would have to serve. Louisa piled her hair up and pinned it until the dark curls were smoothed into submission, then eased on her evening gloves. Holly House was proving to be a cold place. The gloves would at least keep her lower arms warm until the time came to eat.

She chose an amber necklace from her jewellery box because the catch was easy enough to manage alone. The rich golden brown of the stones was a perfect match for her eyes, especially when they flashed with her occasional bouts of wilful anger, but Louisa was quite happy at the moment. Cold, but not angry.

She left the cloakroom and groped her way across the now unlit hall to the drawing room again. Three lumps of coal, two pieces of stick and a scrap of newspaper were smouldering smokily in the hearth while Higgins tried to wheeze some life into them with a set of bellows.

'I am afraid dinner might be some time, madam—' he began, but a thunderous roar silenced him.

'Higgins!'

The servant dropped his bellows and dashed out into the entrance hall. From there, Louisa could hear the voice of Geoffrey Redvers rising and falling in a series of staccato mutters. Higgins was getting his fortune told about something and no mistake, she decided.

'I am sorry about that, Mrs Hesketh.' Redvers strode into the drawing room, clicking his tongue with impatience. 'Staff these days! Leaving lights burning and clothing scattered all over the cloakroom.'

In the normal course of events Louisa would have apologised immediately for forgetting that she no longer had her own maid to tidy up behind her. Now she could say nothing. She had been temporarily struck dumb. Geoffrey Redvers had undergone a transformation, and it left her speechless.

The hunched figure in thick layers of sensible outdoor clothing was now immaculate in full evening dress. Although Geoffrey Redvers was tall enough to carry off the severe black of the suit, it hung on his slender frame as though he had lost a considerable amount of weight since it had last been worn. The unmistakable smell of mothballs confirmed that the suit had been prised out of some distant wardrobe, and he was further ruining the effect of easy elegance by continually fiddling with a set of silver cuff-links at the wrists of his starched white shirt.

'I hope that Higgins has supplied you with a drink, Mrs Hesketh?' His voice was as brisk as the irritable movements of his fingers. 'Oh—I suppose there isn't any left.'

'That is quite all right, Mr Redvers.'

'With my—' His glance slipped from Louisa to the portrait, then back again. 'That type of thing tends to get forgotten now.' His lips were tight with the thoughts that were darkening his eyes.

'I understand,' Louisa said softly, and at that moment she thought that she did.

His taut expression relaxed momentarily into a smile that suggested quite the opposite. 'You will find me dull company as both a host and a neighbour, I am afraid, Mrs Hesketh. I have a rule never to entertain and never to accept while at Holly House.'

'Then thank you for making this exception.' Louisa sparkled graciously.

'I could hardly leave a lady in distress by the side of the road, could I?' His voice was smooth with good manners, but his eyes were watchful. Despite his veneer of easy charm Louisa had noticed that he was probably as suspicious of her as she felt about him. I hope I am rather better at disguising it, though, she thought with amusement.

He was still concerned with his cuff-links, Louisa noticed. In fact he was so absorbed that she hardly liked to interrupt him by trying to keep the conversation flowing.

An age of uncomfortable silence was punctuated only by Louisa's awkward comments about the weather. Then Higgins arrived in a clean collar and smart jacket to announce that dinner was served in the dining room.

Louisa had expected Geoffrey Redvers to offer her his arm and lead her into dinner as a matter of course. He did not. Instead, he led the way to the door then waited to make sure that Higgins had extinguished the gas in the drawing room before striding into the chilly twilight of the hallway. In the ordinary way of things Louisa might have stood her ground and cleared her throat at such dusty treatment from a host, but unusually she decided to give him the benefit of the doubt.

English country manners might well be different from those of the hill stations in India. Fashions certainly were. On the journey home she had been made painfully aware of how unfashionable all her clothes were. As she had travelled through India towards the coast, the first thing that she had realised was that

ladies from Delhi dressed in fashions and colours sub-
tly in advance of those back at Karasha. Reaching
England, Louisa had allowed herself to take a crumb
of comfort from the fact that even the Delhi ladies
were outclassed in this country. Fashion magazines
were always so out of date by the time they reached
India, that was the trouble.

There would be nothing for it but to go on a major
shopping expedition as soon as possible, Louisa
thought glumly as she followed Geoffrey Redvers
into the dining room. She hated shopping, much pre-
ferring the outdoor life to the close, dusty atmosphere
of towns and their dingy shops.

If all English country houses were like Holly
House, then Louisa wondered if she was going to like
England at all. The only thing Holly House seemed
to have in abundance was fresh air. Unfortunately, it
was all howling in around the window-frames.

The dining room was so poorly lit that it was almost impossible to make out any fine detail. It was a
large room, but lit only by a single candelabrum in
the centre of the highly polished dining table. Two
places had been set with silver cutlery and starched
white napery. Geoffrey Redvers took his place at the
head of the table, while Louisa had a long walk to
reach the other setting which was at the further end
of the long table.

Her heart sank. Conversation over dinner had always been a highlight of the day back in India. It
looked as though Geoffrey Redvers' staff had gone
out of their way to make conversation as difficult as

possible here. She would surely have to shout to be heard across these acres of mahogany.

The first course was soup. Louisa could not quite identify the flavour, but it was warm and comforting, which was more than she had hoped to get from Holly House catering. To her surprise—and relief—Geoffrey Redvers opened the conversation of his own accord by asking her about her life in India. It was only when Higgins came to remove their soup plates that Louisa realised that Geoffrey Redvers was a perfect listener, but gave nothing away himself. He had made polite enquiries whenever she'd paused, but, despite clearly having visited the place himself, offered none of his own experiences of India. Louisa resolved to talk a little less and listen a little more. She wanted to learn more about this handsome man who would soon be her neighbour.

Although a battery of cutlery lay on either side of her plate, neither game, poultry nor meat course appeared. After a long wait some scrambled eggs on toast arrived, decorated in evident desperation with whole anchovies, fresh from the tin but complete with heads and tails. The anchovies eyed Louisa balefully as she tried to swallow her hunger along with the cold, rather rubbery scramble. Then there was a single wedge of cheese, hard, waxy and straight from the cold store, but no pudding. Higgins, rather breathless, brought in a bowl of fruit when he arrived to clear the table.

'There is cream as well if you would like it, madam,' Higgins said with nervous glances at the grave, shadowed expression of his master.

'I do not think cream would go well with raw apples, do you, Higgins?'

Redvers' brows rose in amusement as he looked at the servant, whose tense smile hinted at desperate panic down in the kitchen.

'Thank, you, Higgins, I am sure an apple will be sufficient,' Louisa murmured as Higgins offered her the bowl of fruit.

'The Blenheims are just coming into their own, madam,' Higgins said as her fingers hovered over the bowl of russet, yellow and green apples nestling in a bed of wood wool. 'Those are the big, red-streaked yellow ones,' he added helpfully in answer to her unspoken question.

Louisa peeled her apple deftly with her knife and fork as Mama had taught her, then noticed that Redvers had quartered his unpeeled fruit directly onto his plate.

I suppose that is another English fashion, she thought as she ate. Throughout the meal she had been casting many quick glances in the direction of her host to see if she could learn anything of English manners from him. On more than one occasion he'd caught her eye as she'd looked down the table at him, but although he'd been quick to give her a brittle smile he had not been stirred into making conversation.

Finally, Louisa could stand the silence no longer. Touching the starched white napkin to her lips and trying not to recoil again at the strong smell of mothballs, she moved her chair back a little. Redvers immediately put down his knife and fork and rose to his

feet. After summoning Higgins again he offered
Louisa the stiff formality of a bow as she drew level
with him.

'Do you wish me to join you later in the drawing
room, Mrs Hesketh?'

And extend this *delightful* evening? Louisa
thought, but instead of putting her discomfort into
words she smiled.

'It hardly seems right to withdraw when I am the
only lady present.' Louisa offered him an escape
route. 'I was intending to retire for the night.'

'Of course. How foolish of me not to realise that
you must be tired, Mrs Hesketh.'

That smile again—winning, but it never quite man-
ages to cheer the look in his eyes, Louisa noticed. It
must be some sadness that makes him like this.

Redvers reached across again to where the bell-pull
hung sullenly beside the door.

'Higgins—wherever he has got to—will light you
to your room. I trust you will have a good night's
sleep, Mrs Hesketh.'

'I am sure I shall—as long as I reach my room
without incident, Mr Redvers. I will bring my own
dark lantern when I come visiting from Roseberry
Hall in future!' Louisa said lightly, but even as she
was speaking Geoffrey Redvers stopped toying with
his glass abruptly and stared at her. There was not
even the pretence of a smile now.

Those eyes of his…they were like pools of dark
but turbulent water…

'You intend to receive another invitation, Mrs
Hesketh?'

For once Louisa was lost for words. It had been intended as a light-hearted remark but Geoffrey Redvers' gaze and tight-lipped retort made her feel like an insolent child confronted by a schoolmaster.

'Well…I—that is, if you were kind enough to extend one, Mr Redvers…' she floundered.

'I have *never* been a man for entertaining.' He continued to stare at her, casting words into the cold air like drops of lead shot. 'Not even when my wife was alive.'

That explained a great deal to Louisa. The painted cloakroom, the portrait…

'As Higgins explained, this is a bachelor household, and we keep ourselves very much to ourselves.'

His eyes were glittering with the intensity of jet in the lamplight.

'Yes…well, goodnight, Mr Redvers. Thank you again for putting yourself to so much trouble on my behalf.'

'Please do not mention it, Mrs Hesketh,' he replied stiffly, making Louisa wish that she had not.

She inclined her head gracefully and he responded in kind. His exchange with Higgins was abrupt, and within moments Louisa was following the servant up a cold, bare marble staircase to the first floor where she was shown into a bedroom. To her amazement it was ablaze with lights.

'The master is always very strict about the matter of lights, madam,' Higgins said carefully.

'I had noticed, Higgins.'

Higgins was a loyal servant, but it obviously went against his nature to see a lady subjected to life at

Holly House without an explanation. The kindness of Louisa's smiling reply gave him the courage to speak out.

'The master is a very private man, madam. We servants know nothing, as you may imagine, but there is talk as how there was a terrible fire at his last place, so he is always concerned that no lights are left burning unattended, madam.'

He was watching her warily, caught between the rules of the house and seeing a guest properly provided for. Louisa treated him to another kind smile.

'It was good of you to arrange all this for me, Higgins. Don't worry—I shall take great care, and I will not tell Mr Redvers that you made the room look so welcoming.'

Relief flooded the servant's face and he thanked her as well as wishing her a good night before leaving.

Louisa locked the door behind him and paused to take stock. The bedroom she had been given was spacious, with a high ceiling hemmed with a cornice of plaster fruit and flowers. This must once have been white, but dust had long since dulled its features. Heavy brocade curtains in a dismal shade of old gold hung in pairs along the far wall, reaching from floor to ceiling.

Although she knew it would be dark outside, Louisa went over to look out of one of the windows. A frosty moon was rising over a wooded ridge, allowing glimpses of the parkland below. The shadows were so deep that there was little to see except the outlines of the many trees. One particularly large cedar sheltered the house, its great flat top and layers of branches making an unmistakable silhouette against the violet of the evening sky.

Louisa leaned on the sill, looking down to where a thread of light spilled from the house onto the gravel drive beyond. Her room must be almost directly above the dining room, she realised. Mr Redvers must have decided to remain there for a cigar after all.

Geoffrey Redvers was a strange man, she thought as she closed the curtains and went into the dressing room that adjoined her bedroom. He was as handsome a man as she had ever seen, and it looked as though he could be quite jolly, but something seemed to be holding him back. Those eyes…they had a haunting quality which warned off anyone who tried to get too close, either physically or conversationally. At times, he could be so abrupt in speech and so stiff in manner that Louisa wondered why she could not find it in her heart to thoroughly dislike him. Learning that he was a widower had softened her view of him. Perhaps he had been on his own for too long—like Louisa, he might be missing the companionship of marriage.

When Roseberry Hall is restored I shall be quick to invite him and let him know how delightful entertaining *can* be, Louisa thought. Then she reconsidered. It might be even more delightful if she postponed her intended entertainment until she'd had a chance to get to know all the eligible young ladies in the parish. To find Mr Geoffrey Redvers a good woman *and* give him a good square meal at the same time would be even more of an adventure.

She undressed quickly and said her prayers. Then

she slid into bed, delighted to find that a stone hot-water bottle wrapped in cloth was warming the crisp cotton sheets. The cumulative effects of weeks of travel followed by the long day and the tense atmosphere over dinner had quite drained Louisa. Sleep stole over her quickly, wiping all mischievous thoughts of eligible Mr Redvers clean out of her head.

Louisa sat up in bed with a start, suddenly wide awake in the darkness. She had heard something, but did not know what. She listened to the sound of her own racing heartbeat for a long, long time before deciding that her imagination must have been playing tricks. It must be the unfamiliar surroundings, she told herself. All houses make sounds that are unusual to a visitor's ears.

Eventually her tense nerves eased and she sank back onto the soft cloud of her pillows. Sleep began to drift around her again like a warm mist. There was nothing to worry about…whatever the sound might have been…her door was locked…she was safe enough…

A tremendous crash from downstairs catapulted Louisa from her bed, still halfway between sleep and consciousness. As she came to her senses she realised that the house had once again slipped back into tense, waiting silence.

That was as bad as the unexplained noise, especially as her mind was full of the fear of fire after the warning from Higgins. Groping for her dressing gown by the dying light of the embers in the grate, Louisa dashed to the door of her room and looked out.

The corridor outside was deserted and all in darkness, as she had expected. There was no way of knowing where the servants' wing was, so Louisa fetched her bedside candle and lit it from the remains of the fire.

Hanging her trusty umbrella over her arm so that she would be armed and ready to repel intruders, she went out into the hallway. Her bare feet made no sound as she hurried along, shielding the candle from draughts with a cupped hand around its wavering flame.

There were no sounds of commotion from downstairs, but, Louisa reasoned, those thick mahogany doors might muffle many sounds. She pressed on down to the ground floor, her ears straining to pick up any and every noise.

Then she heard it. A faint sound coming from behind one of the anonymous doors that stood guard around the dark hallway. The chill that had long since numbed Louisa's feet ran through her body and she froze.

The sound stopped. Louisa stood still for another half a dozen heartbeats, then let her breath go in a rush. This is silly, she rebuked herself sharply. If there is an emergency, I ought to find out what it is. The place could burn down around our ears, and all because I was afraid to find out what was wrong.

Grasping the cold brass candle saucer more firmly, she marched towards the door which had seemed to be the source of the noise and tried it. It was unlocked, so Louisa flung it wide open.

Geoffrey Redvers was seated behind a large desk,

directly opposite the door. He sprang to his feet with an oath at the disturbance, then stopped as he saw Louisa.

'Oh…I am terribly sorry to disturb you, Mr Redvers—' Louisa began, stepping forward automatically despite her *déshabillé*.

'Get back!' he roared at her, rounding the desk and crossing to the door in a few strides. For a second Louisa was too stunned to react, but as Redvers continued to advance towards her her muscles contracted, ready for flight. He towered above her, bearing down with a look between rage and despair. Louisa backed away, then as soon as she was out of reach turned and dashed blindly for the glass door in the large entrance hall that led to the outer lobby. To her surprise and relief the door opened: she tumbled out into the chill of the lobby, Redvers' voice ringing in her ears.

'And don't come back in! Not before—'

Louisa did not wait to hear any more. She flung herself at the great front door, wrenching it open and escaping out into the night.

Chapter Two

The escape was not one of Louisa's better ideas. A dressing gown that had been proof against the evening chills of a hill station was proving worse than useless in the face of this frosty English night.

She had stopped at the first sting of gravel beneath her bare feet, as no sounds of pursuit had come from inside the house. Now, standing on the steps of Holly House, Louisa thought quickly. All her clothes and jewellery were up in her room. She could not possibly leave this place without them. An English gentlewoman alone at night would raise enough suspicions. One clad only in her night attire would face a short trip to the nearest asylum.

'Well, I may not be a typical English rose, but I shall just have to become a climber,' Louisa said to herself, looking up at the first-floor windows of Holly House where a dim glow still showed through the open drapes of her room. She had dropped her candle and her umbrella during the escape, but at least Mr Redvers would know what to do about *them*. It did at least leave her unencumbered. Rubbing her palms

down her nightgown, Louisa approached the wall of
Holly House.

Finding footholds on the carved frame of the din-
ing-room window and the winter-bare trellis work beside it was easy. She began to climb, carefully steadying herself on a nearby drainpipe where she could.

Scaling the front of Holly House turned out to be
simpler than scrambling up a rock face after one of
Algy's botanical specimens. The only difficulty was
that there was no direct route to her own window.
Louisa had already noticed that, with the exception
of the room she occupied, each of the sash windows
on the first floor had been raised an inch or two to let
a breath of air circulate through every room. Reaching
a window close to her own, she soon managed to raise
the sash enough to wriggle through. Scrambling into
the room beyond, she landed on the floor with a gasp
of relief.

Pleased that she had not lost her climbing abilities,
Louisa stood up, brushing mortar dust from her dressing gown and congratulating herself—for as long as
it took her to remember the golden rule of Holly
House.

Thou shalt not suffer any room to remain unlocked.

She ran softly to the door, but it was as she had
dreaded. It refused to open.

Louisa stood and thought. If she went back out
through the window she would be no better off than
she had been before. She might of course stay in this
room, but it smelled damp and was much colder than
her own. Creeping back to the open window, she tried
to pull it down, but now it had decided to stick fast,

letting in great gasps of the penetratingly chilly night air.

The problem seemed insoluble. Louisa looked around the room for inspiration, and noticed a gleam of brass in the darkness. It was another door which might be worth trying, even though it would probably only lead into a dressing room which too would be locked.

Louisa made her way carefully over to the door. To her delight it was not locked, and swung towards her easily on well-oiled hinges. There was a second surprise. Instead of leading directly into another room, the open door revealed the face of a second door immediately behind it. This place gets more like Alice's Wonderland every moment, Louisa thought, trying the second door with hope growing by the minute. It too was unlocked, but proved difficult to push open more than a few inches. Then she noticed the obstruction. A heavy curtain hung down beyond the door to keep out draughts.

Louisa soon realised why draughts had to be excluded from this second room. A gust of warm air faintly perfumed with fresh polish and shaving soap enveloped her as soon as she pushed the curtain aside.

Oh, my lord—it must be *his* bedroom! Louisa thought in horror.

Her mind worked quickly. Redvers would probably have gone back into the room downstairs after their confrontation. Certainly, if he was in his bedroom now he would hardly have stayed silent while the door beyond its curtain was opened.

Louisa squeezed into the gap allowed by the heavy

curtain then stole into Redvers' room, closing the two doors behind her and rearranging the curtain as carefully as she could in the darkness. There was a chance—just a chance—that the main door to a place used as frequently as Redvers' suite would be unlocked.

In answer to her prayers a door that led into the corridor opened under her hands. With a gasp of relief Louisa slipped out, only to hear the irregular scuffle of two sets of footsteps coming up the cold bare marble staircase towards the upper landing. She looked about wildly for somewhere to hide, but there was nowhere. It was too late, in any case. An illumination of candlelight showed that Redvers and his man-servant were about to reach the top of the stairs.

Higgins saw her first. Redvers was stumping up the stairs, head down, consumed as usual by his own thoughts. The alarm in the eyes of his gardener was swiftly replaced by a frantic, wordless appeal to Louisa to get back to her room before the master saw.

At that moment Redvers raised his head.

'*Quick!*' Seizing her roughly, Higgins shoved Louisa back down the corridor and into her own room, slamming the door. 'I will be back as soon as I can, madam!' he hissed through the door as Louisa stared at it incredulously.

They are all quite, quite mad here, Louisa thought as she listened to Higgins racing back down the corridor. I am in a mad house, and the sooner I can escape the better.

She wasted no time. Dressing hurriedly, she was

putting the last few pins into her hair when there came a soft tapping at the door.

'It is only me, madam. Higgins.'

Louisa opened the door wide so that Higgins could see her packed and stacked bags. He clicked his tongue in disappointment.

'The master sent me to see what the matter was, madam.'

'Too drunk to do it himself, I suppose?'

Higgins opened his eyes wide in astonishment. His expression was as much as to say, What sort of folk is this lady used to socialising with?

'No, madam, the fact is that he was a bit wary about approaching you again. After you went dashing out into the night, which is where we both thought you were when we met you just now…'

'*Anyone* would have fled when confronted by Mr Redvers roaring like that. The man must be quite deranged.'

'Didn't you see all the broken glass on the study floor, madam? The master says that he only shouted in warning…'

It was Louisa's turn for astonishment—a feeling that soon sank into a deep well of horror. She had taken to her heels in the face of a perfectly reasonable warning. Geoffrey Redvers must be convinced that *she* was the mad one. He was probably barricading himself in his room at this very moment.

'A…a misunderstanding,' Louisa said when she could manage to speak.

It was the middle of the night. To move out of Holly House now would confirm her as a madwoman

in Geoffrey Redvers' eyes. She would have to stay,
if only to put matters right between them in the morning.

Muttering something about hasty actions, Louisa
dismissed Higgins as quickly as she could and got
ready for bed a second time.

This time sleep did not come so easily. Now that
she thought back on the scene downstairs, Geoffrey
Redvers' actions were understandable. At least *most*
of them. It did not explain how the broken glass had
come to be on the threshold of the study in the first
place, or why the main doors had been unlocked in
such a usually well-secured house, or what the noises
had been that had woken her in the first place.

Louisa lay awake for a long time, thinking. She had
misjudged Geoffrey Redvers on their first meeting.
Seeing him bundled up in the motor car had given
him the air of an invalid, when he was clearly a man
of some vitality. The way he had moved so quickly
across the room towards her just now had shown her
that only too well. She had misjudged him again on
that occasion too, hearing rage when he had been con-
veying concern.

There was definitely more to Mr Geoffrey Redvers
than met the eye. Whether he would make a good
neighbour remained to be seen. There was too much
mystery, too many dark secrets hidden in those mysterious eyes.

Louisa woke early the next morning. She rang and
rang to let the staff know that she was awake and
ready for hot water, but no one came. Finally she put

on the day dress that she had arrived in the previous evening and went in search of some breakfast. The meagre meal she had been served the previous evening was a very distant memory. If she arrived in person at the kitchens, the staff might be surprised into action where the mere ringing of the bell had failed. She had seen the rows of bells padded with felt in the servants' quarters back in India, so that they would not ring at inconvenient times. The same tricks must go on all over the world.

All the doors were locked, as she had expected, but in each case the keys had been lodged on the lintel above. It took Louisa several minutes of stealthy door-opening and peeping before she found the kitchens of Holly House, but by that time she was not in the least surprised to find the rooms deserted. The silence that hung about the great house had told her to expect as much. There *were* no staff in the house. No welcome, and no warmth.

The kitchen fire that must have been lit to prepare hot water for her the evening before had long since crumbled to embers, but it was the only hope for food or friendship in that whole unfriendly house. Louisa pulled up the sleeves of her day dress and set to work. There was at least a small pile of morning wood stacked beside the range. After clearing out some of the fine powdery ash that was choking all the life from the last few glowing coals, Louisa laid on half a dozen small sticks. A quick tour of the kitchen found a large baking tray, burnt black with age. Louisa knelt down on the rag rug in front of the hearth and held the baking tray up in front of the fire so that air was concentrated into a draught rushing in from underneath. It worked. With a whoosh the smouldering coals burst into new life, engulfing the sticks with flame. Louisa took the baking tray away and quickly fed the fire with more small sticks until it was well alight.

'You will need some coal to keep it going,' a deep voice rolled across the kitchen.

'Oh!' Louisa jumped, accidentally knocking the baking tray from its resting place on the hearth. It clattered to the flagstones of the floor with a clang that echoed around the whole room. Geoffrey Redvers winced.

'A lady lighting a fire?'

He was watching her with a quizzical smile. With a rush of embarrassment Louisa wondered how long he had been standing there in the kitchen doorway.

'Whatever next?' he continued quietly, giving her a carefully appraising look. 'What manner of a woman *are* you, Mrs Hesketh?'

'A practical one, Mr Redvers,' Louisa countered, rising to her feet. She felt warm, and not only from the effects of the fire. 'It was a choice between cold hunger in my room or doing something useful. As Holly House would seem to have no servants living in, I might as well try to repay your hospitality by doing what I can. Now, if you would excuse me, Mr Redvers, I shall go and fetch the scuttle full of coal that is beside the hearth in my room—'

'You have a smut on your nose,' he said suddenly as she passed him.

Louisa froze. Their eyes met, and they stared at

each other for several heartbeats. Then Louisa saw that suddenly, unexpectedly, the expression on his face was changing. The muscles around his finely drawn mouth tensed, pursing his lips with some difficulty. For once his eyes had lost their wintry sadness.

He was trying not to laugh. And this time his amusement was heartfelt.

Louisa burned with embarrassment. Lifting her skirts, she ran from the room, scampering up the stairs as though the devil himself were after her.

Bolting into the relative safety of her room, Louisa locked the door behind her and leaned against it, trying to catch her breath. Her reflection in the dressing-table mirror only made things worse. She rubbed the smut away furiously then closed her eyes, the fierce heat of shame washing over her again.

Hateful man! He should have told her about it long before. Or stepped forward like a true gentleman and wiped the smut away without comment.

Louisa burned with shame, wishing that she could get the vision of his smiling, beguiling eyes out of her mind.

After that disaster, Louisa would have liked to stay in her room until someone came to collect her. Eventually, though, hunger overcame her shame. There was the kitchen fire to consider, too. It would soon go out without attention. Geoffrey Redvers hardly looked the type to shift himself in that way.

Forcing herself to pick up the coal scuttle, Louisa carried it along the landing to the top of the stairs.

Voices drifted up to her from downstairs. First there was male laughter. Then there came the sound of a door opening, quick footsteps, and Higgins came into view at the foot of the stairs. When he saw what Louisa was carrying he leapt forward and soon relieved her of the heavy scuttle.

'If you please, madam, I have just brought breakfast across from the garden house—that is where it is prepared. There is hot water, too—if you would like to make use of it, I shall tell Mr Redvers that you will be joining him for breakfast.'

'Of course, Higgins,' Louisa said, but realised that she had made a mistake as soon as the servant had gone out of sight. She should have asked to take breakfast in her room. It would hardly be unexpected. Not after the horror of the night before, and the laughing-stock she had made of herself already that morning.

Louisa went down to the cloakroom and hurriedly got herself ready for breakfast with Mr Geoffrey Redvers. When she was washed and dressed she took an unusual amount of time checking her appearance meticulously in the looking-glass. Her long dark hair was drawn back simply in a knot at the nape of her neck, its glossy depths showing off the pale delicacy of her skin. The plain brown day dress was quite a contrast to the rose-pink dinner gown of the previous evening, but Louisa hoped it would give her a proper air of contrition.

Despite the simplicity of her gown Louisa looked every inch a lady, except for her expression. Her wide-set, honey-brown eyes were troubled, and she was nipping her lip thoughtfully. Geoffrey Redvers was not her only concern today. Today she must go and see her new home, Roseberry Hall, for herself.

Louisa's life in India had been a hollow shell since Algy's death. He had left her well enough provided for financially, but that was the least of her problems. She had company in Karasha, but no real friendship—not of the lasting kind that she had known with Algernon. Oh, there had been plenty of tea parties and requests for her to make up a couple for tennis, but in the end all the invitations had led to the same conclusion. She'd had to return to an empty, friendless bungalow at the end of each day.

When the idea of taking up her great-aunt's bequest had struck her, Louisa had been almost glad of the excuse to travel to England. Her parents had always referred to it as 'home' and Louisa did too, although until now she had never been away from India. She had been glad to leave the claustrophobic atmosphere of the hill station behind. Friendly concern there could soon turn into nosiness. Conversations all too often became nothing but gossip and spite. Louisa was glad of the chance to start a new life in England—or so she kept telling herself.

Now life in England was turning out to be very different from the dreams that she had harboured of 'coming home' and starting a new life, all excitement and glamour. Instead of the grand country house she had expected to find, Roseberry Hall was apparently a wreck. English people were a strange, unfathomable troupe too, if Geoffrey Redvers was anything to go by.

The mere thought of his name made a shiver run down Louisa's spine. His eyes haunted her, even now. Those dark, almost black pools of mystery missed nothing, but gave little away. Higgins might have told her something of Geoffrey Redvers' personal tragedy, but Louisa could not recall seeing grief in the gentleman's eyes. A wistfulness occasionally, perhaps, overlying a slow-burning anger, but grief? Hardly that.

Eventually, Louisa managed to gather her nerves for the coming ordeal and tried to walk confidently to the breakfast room. Whatever her own private thoughts about him, she was a guest in Geoffrey Redvers' house and he deserved her best behaviour, if not her trust.

Her host was already seated at the table and had started his meal, but stopped and rose from his seat politely as Louisa entered the room. Low slanting rays of sun slipped through the window, highlighting the spiralling dust motes that rose softly through the slightly musty atmosphere.

'Mr Redvers?' Louisa queried, surprised that he should have started the meal before her arrival.

'Mrs Hesketh,' he replied formally, then recognised the look that she was giving him. He smiled, and unwillingly Louisa felt her suspicions soften again.

'It is a general rule in English country houses, Mrs Hesketh, that one begins to eat as soon as the meal is delivered—the distance from the kitchens often being so great that the meal is stone-cold by the time one has observed all the genteel niceties. It surprised me, too, when I first arrived home from India.'

Louisa felt her face dissolve into a smile, despite

her misgivings. They did at least have two small
things in common, then. Both had been in India, and
she was not alone in finding England and its society
puzzling.

Geoffrey Redvers gestured towards one side of the
room where a long sideboard flanked by two sofa
tables held court. With a sharp intake of breath Louisa
saw that breakfast at Holly House was going to be a
considerably more lavish affair than dinner had been
the previous evening. Half a dozen covered silver
chafing dishes stood on a starched white cloth
hemmed with flounces of delicate crochet work. In
addition to the hot dishes there was a basket of bread
rolls, peeping from the crisp white folds of a napkin,
a glass dish of apples draped with grapes that had
been frosted with sugar and, in the centre of the display, an arrangement of tiny hard-boiled eggs set in
a dish of crushed ice to keep cool.

'Goodness,' Louisa whispered, not quite knowing
where to start.

'As I said, I have never been in the habit of entertaining, Mrs Hesketh, although last night you found
my household particularly wanting in hospitality. I
have been in London for a few days and hardly expected to have visitors. The provisions were therefore
a little meagre. It is amazing to see what Higgins and
his sister can do when given a little notice, is it not?'

Geoffrey Redvers looked as impressed as Louisa
felt. She went to the sideboard and lifted each silver
lid in turn. Kedgeree, crisp, curling rashers of bacon,
eggs, chops, kidneys, sausages and vegetables all released their delicious perfume into the air. Louisa

chose bacon, an egg and some scalloped potatoes before returning to the table. When she had said a murmured Grace she was immediately offered a silver cruet lined with Bristol Blue Glass and a crystal dish of redcurrant jelly. This was a considerable advance on the previous evening.

'Had you intended to visit Roseberry Hall today, Mrs Hesketh? If so, I shall put Higgins at your disposal. He will drive you over there in the dog cart. I shall be using the motor myself.'

'Oh, Mr Redvers—but you have been so kind already!'

Privately delighted that Geoffrey Redvers seemed to be thawing a little, Louisa thought that a little genteel protest might give him some encouragement. It worked rather more successfully than she had anticipated, for as she spoke he smiled. Actually, genuinely *smiled*. The result was devastating. Already handsome, the easy smile with its good white teeth made him look absolutely irresistible. With growing alarm Louisa had to stop herself wondering what it would be like to be kissed by him. Despite her inexperience in such matters, she knew that thoughts like that must be far too shocking to be allowed in polite society.

'Nonsense! It is the least that I can do for a potential neighbour,' he said cheerfully. Then suddenly his expression became guarded again. 'You have no inkling of the condition of Roseberry Hall, Mrs Hesketh?'

'No, but I am beginning to wonder if coming to England was such a good idea when you appear so concerned, Mr Redvers.'

Louisa looked down and studied her breakfast to avoid meeting his eyes.

'Mrs Vernon—the lady that I assume was your great-aunt—was a lady who kept herself very much to herself. That is why we got on so well as neighbours—a greeting in passing was as much as ever went between us, although I did pay a courtesy call to Roseberry Hall when I first moved in here. The place was in a pretty poor state of repair then, and that was nearly six years ago. I cannot think that time has been very kind to it, Mrs Hesketh.'

'Please—call me Louisa,' Louisa said quickly, unused to the English type of formality. All her other thoughts had been paralysed by his words. Roseberry Hall sounded worse and worse with every mention. What on earth was she going to find there?

'I would rather not,' Geoffrey Redvers said mildly, touching a napkin to his lips before taking a sip of water. The conservative cut of his dark business suit, brightened only by the gold loop of a fine watch chain, emphasised his quiet formality. 'I shall instruct Higgins to accompany you everywhere today, so that there can be no question of you coming to any harm. Although of course that rather depends upon you, Mrs Hesketh. Higgins is a sensible fellow. As long as you do as he says…' He left the warning hanging in the air.

It is almost as though this Geoffrey Redvers knows me as well as I know myself, Louisa thought, and risked another glance at him across the breakfast table. He had been studying her again, but now he looked away almost guiltily. If he was feeling guilty then perhaps it was the time to resurrect her own feelings along that line.

'I am so sorry about what happened last night, Mr Redvers. I misunderstood…and thought that you were angry with me for disturbing you.'

'That is quite all right, Mrs Hesketh.'

Refusing to use her Christian name kept a gulf between them. Louisa took that as a bad sign.

'I heard a noise and thought it might be intruders—'

'So you went into the attack armed with nothing more formidable than an umbrella? You must be a remarkably confident woman, Mrs Hesketh!'

'You must know yourself, Mr Redvers, that life in India breeds a particular sort of woman. Those who cannot fend for themselves do not survive for long.'

'Indeed I do,' he sighed, and the sound was not a happy one. 'It will need someone of mettle to take on Roseberry Hall, too, I think.'

The rest of the meal passed in silence. Louisa was too immersed in her own thoughts to provide the spur to conversation that Geoffrey Redvers seemed to need. When he had finished his meal he sat staring across to the great windows, apparently lost in thought. When at last Louisa put down her napkin he immediately rose from his seat. Only then did she realise that he must have been waiting for her.

'I am afraid that I must excuse myself from your company, Mrs Hesketh. My business in London was not completed, it seems, and I must return to the city. Please make yourself at home in my absence. Higgins and his sister will take care of everything.'

'Then you are what is so mysteriously called "something in the city", Mr Redvers?' Louisa roused herself from her thoughts for one last attempt at pleasantries. She was glad for the prospective patients of Stanton Malreward that this stiffly formal and taciturn man was not their local doctor, despite his motor car.

'Indeed.' He gave her a slight and rigidly formal bow.

'I have often wondered what gentlemen get up to in the city,' Louisa went on as she followed him from the table. She had expected him to tell her more, but he said nothing. Although Geoffrey Redvers stepped back after opening the breakfast-room door to let her pass through first, his manners did not, apparently, extend to small talk. Louisa decided that life was too short for any more subtle pleasantries.

'What do you actually *do* for a living, Mr Redvers?' she enquired brightly as she passed him, and saw his usually closed face open with astonishment for a split second. Persistence was obviously not expected in a guest, but he regained his composure quickly.

'My business imports…things, Mrs Hesketh.'

Louisa stopped and turned to look at him closely. Her first reaction had been to say, Ah, what *sort* of things? But then instinct made her hold her tongue. Geoffrey Redvers was not the sort of host with which she might comfortably take that sort of liberty. Whether her host worked in the field of bells, bicycles or bright blue ribbons would have to remain his secret, at least until she had got to know him better.

Privately, Louisa began to hope that he might be

something to do with the bicycle business. She had seen several ladies riding bicycles since she had arrived in England, and could hardly wait to try this latest craze for herself.

Geoffrey Redvers had told Louisa to make herself at home, and she intended to do exactly that. He would be well out of the way, travelling to London, and there was no knowing if she would ever get another invitation into such a bachelor household. Holly House needed to be explored at leisure, and by his own admission Geoffrey Redvers was not the sort of man to hold parties.

Louisa began on the ground floor. The entrance hall was indeed large and high-ceilinged, although the general air of underuse made it feel cold and unwelcoming rather than light and airy as a well-loved house would have done. There were six doors leading off the entrance hall. Four of these rooms she knew already: the cloakroom, the breakfast room, the dining room and the drawing room, where she had been left to wait the previous evening. The doors to the other two rooms remained locked, as Louisa had expected, but, unlike the kitchen wing, the door keys were not lodged in the usual hiding places on their respective lintels. One was in a cache pot, slipped in beside the dusty, compulsory aspidistra. Another had been hidden among the curlicues of an ornate china clock housed beneath a glass dome on a hall table.

Finding the keys did not do Louisa much good. The rooms must have been closed up and undisturbed for a very long time. Wooden shutters had been fastened over each of the long windows, allowing only the narrowest rays of light to infiltrate around their edges. Through the gloom Louisa saw that furniture had been stacked in the centre of each room and covered with white dust sheets. Her walking boots tapped across bare floorboards, as not even the carpets had been left to provide a bit of comfort. Although curious, Louisa knew better than to poke around any further and left the rooms hiding their secrets.

It was the same story on the first floor, although here most of the keys remained in their locks and had not been hidden away. The room Louisa had been given was by far the best of the three that had not been closed up and dust-sheeted. It had the same fine view across parkland that was enjoyed by the dining room, and with a fire burning in the grate it was just the place where an English lady might be closeted quite happily all through a late autumn day with her embroidery.

Louisa was not an English lady. She preferred the outdoor life to the production of antimacassars and samplers to join the endless circulation of Christmas and birthday presents. If forced to stay indoors she preferred to read, but Geoffrey Redvers did not appear to possess any books. At least, Holly House had no visible library.

Inspecting the rooms of Holly House took Louisa the rest of the morning. Then she remembered the kitchen fire, which would be the only source of warmth downstairs and would have to be kept going at all costs.

Hurrying down to the kitchen, she was surprised to

find the room warm and bright. The fire was well tended and Higgins was busy pouring hot milk onto coffee essence. He smiled as Louisa walked in and went to fetch a china cup and saucer from a cupboard. Sitting them on a tray, he added a silver teaspoon to the saucer, precisely in line with the handle.

'Laying a tray must be a rare skill to find in a gardener, Higgins!' Louisa observed with a smile.

'With only me and Maggie and Mr Williams, the chauffeur, working here we all have to be able to turn our hands to anything, madam.' Higgins smiled, but he was noticeably uneasy. 'If you would like to go back into the breakfast room, madam, I shall serve coffee there in two minutes.'

It obviously was not the done thing for a guest to come visiting the kitchens. Louisa wondered what Higgins would say if he knew that she had lit the fire that morning.

Leaving the kitchen and heading back to the breakfast room, she heard Higgins following her only a few yards behind. As she took her place at the table he arrived beside her with a heavily laden tea tray.

As well as the coffee pot and the delicate bone-china cup and saucer, there were three china plates on the tray which Higgins set down on the table in front of Louisa. One plate held a selection of tiny pastries, the second had been laid with slices of home-made cake, while the third was piled high with chocolate biscuits. Louisa felt the bones in her day dress creak in awful warning.

'Goodness, Higgins. I thought Holly House was not used to entertaining!'

'We don't get the chance—with no mistress in the house.' Higgins frowned slightly, adding as though to divert Louisa's attention from what he had just said, 'Maggie likes the chance to show off her baking. She was up late last night and then early again this morning.'

'Did your sister make these chocolate biscuits, too?' Louisa enquired, wondering how soon she could disturb the pile without seeming indiscreet.

'Oh, no, madam. I bought them up in London yesterday—'

Louisa was immediately curious and interrogated Higgins with a stare. '*You* bought them, Higgins? Surely this does not mean that you have to buy provisions for Mr Redvers as well as doing his gardening, acting as his companion and serving about the house?'

'Oh, no, madam.' Higgins was squirming under Louisa's angry expression, but he was not about to get his master in trouble as well as himself. 'They were a sort of…present. For Maggie. My sister. She is mad keen on the Royals, see, and the shop had a sign up saying that these were the favourite snack of the late King.'

'I don't doubt it.' Louisa transferred her gaze to the plate of delicious-looking biscuits and recalled illustrations of the very well upholstered King Edward from the *Bombay Times and Herald*. Her expression had softened as she'd listened to the story—but she still took a biscuit from the plate.

'Very well, Higgins, although I have to say that chocolate biscuits are not a particular favourite of

mine.' She tried to lie convincingly. 'And you had
better take them away before the smell of so many
puts me off the rest of my refreshments.'

'Yes, madam,' Higgins said with more than a trace
of relief. 'Will you be requiring me for anything else
today?'

Roseberry Hall. The thought of it interrupted
Louisa's contemplation of the morning tray and
brought her quickly back to earth.

'Indeed I shall, Higgins. I should like to be driven
to Roseberry Hall as soon as possible, to inspect my
inheritance for myself.'

Louisa had prepared for the worst when packing
for England. She had heard those returning to India
after home leave talking about the cold and rain, and
had been determined to be ready for anything that the
English weather could throw at her. As well as taking
her trusty umbrella she dressed for the afternoon in a
good thick skirt, a woollen blouse and stout tweed
jacket beneath her overcoat. Walking shoes would be
more practical than button boots in case she wanted
to try pacing around the estate, and she put on an
extra pair of stockings against any chill.

Rather than wait in the entrance hall for Higgins to
bring the cart around to the front door, Louisa went
outside to wait on the gravel turning circle outside
Holly House. It was a beautiful day, bright with cold.
The sky was high and blue, and traces of frost still
lingered in the shadow of the trees surrounding the
house. The countryside around it was so peaceful. It
was quite unlike India, where the rustle and chirrup

of birds, the chatter of monkeys and the incessant chorus of insects meant that total silence was a rare treat.

As she stood in the shelter of the main doorway, watching brittle sunshine shaft through a copse of beech trees on a nearby hillside, Louisa gradually realised that the English countryside was not so silent after all. A distant cawing of rooks was disturbed by the rattle and cry of bird scarers. A little nearer, a gaggle of women on their way to work in the fields straggled past her crippled carriage, which was still wedged in the ditch outside the grounds of Holly House. Although the carriage was several hundred yards away, Louisa heard the women discussing it and she wondered how long it would be before the villagers discovered that Mr Redvers had a house guest. A *female* house guest, at that!

Louisa could not help but smile to herself at the thought. If Mr Geoffrey Redvers was as sharp with the villagers as he was with his staff and occasionally with his guests, her arrival would certainly set everyone talking. They might think that he was softening in his old age.

Louisa stopped short at that thought. Geoffrey Redvers might never say two words when none would do, but yet there was still something strangely compelling about him. On the few occasions that she had seen his usually austere expression softened by humour, those strong, regular features had been transformed into something that ignited long-buried thoughts within Louisa. And when his usually measured stride had been fired by concern the night be-

fore Louisa had been able to recognise a further un-
settling transformation.

There could be no doubt that there was far more to
Mr Geoffrey Redvers than there appeared at first
glance. With a flush of shame Louisa realised that she
might have wanted to explore those hidden depths,
too. If only she had not been such a well brought up
young lady, and Mr Redvers such a perfect gentleman.

It came as a relief of sorts when another noise came
crackling through the still morning air to distract her
thoughts. Higgins brought a dog cart around from the
carriage yard at the back of the house. It was drawn
by a grey pony, which, although it looked well
groomed, had evidently been living out in the fields
rather than in the pampered surroundings of a stable.

Louisa was glad that she had pinned her hat down
well, for Higgins set the pony off down the drive at
a smart trot. As they passed her carriage, he told
Louisa that some men from a neighbouring farm
would be over that afternoon to prise it out of the
ditch and take it off for repairs.

'Your boy Sami has settled in well down at the
Crown, madam. I informed the publican that you were
staying here until Roseberry Hall was in a fit state to
live in.'

'Oh, you did, did you?' Louisa looked at the gardener quizzically, but he returned her stare innocently.

'That is only what the master—Mr Redvers—said
to tell him,' he countered, as though hurt by the
thought that Louisa might have been accusing him of

speaking out of turn. 'The master reckons that should put paid to any gossip.'

I would not like to count on it, Louisa thought privately. Although this Mr Redvers seemed to be taking a lot upon himself where she was concerned, Louisa was privately relieved that she would not have the headache of trying to find trustworthy lodgings as well as worrying about Roseberry Hall.

Suddenly the note of the pony's hooves on the lane changed. Higgins was slowing the dog cart down, and that could mean only one thing. They were about to arrive at Roseberry Hall.

Chapter Three

'Here we are, then, madam—Roseberry Hall.'

Louisa had been staring fixedly at her walking boots, but as the sound of the pony's hooves slowed to a walk she knew that the time of reckoning had arrived.

'After what your master has told me, Higgins, I can hardly bear to look.'

'It is really not that bad, madam. Leastways, not from the outside.'

Louisa had been gripping the edge of the dog cart and now managed to transfer her stare to her gloves as the cart racketed up the drive. When at last she steeled herself to look up she saw that Higgins was right. The exterior of Roseberry Hall looked almost intact—apart from the small sapling thrusting out through a broken pane in one of the downstairs windows.

Roseberry Hall was built of the same soft grey stone as Holly House. At first Louisa was surprised at how small the house appeared, half hidden behind the lowering branches of an ancient cedar. The face of the house showed only one large bay window, with two smaller plain windows breaking up the rest of the house front. Only when Higgins turned the dog cart to go along the side of the house did Louisa realise that Roseberry Hall stretched back for a considerable way. It was as though the house had been built the wrong way round, with visitors approaching the side of the house rather than the front.

Higgins took the dog cart around to the back of the house where there was a cobbled stable yard garlanded with swags of traveller's joy and wild honeysuckle. It was as though nature was trying to smother everything made by man with her own handiwork.

Higgins handed Louisa down from the cart and she prepared to look around. She had intended this as a brief visit to satisfy her curiosity, as she had not yet been to pick up the keys from the agent. Higgins had other ideas.

'Look—that window isn't fast, madam. Do you want me to get in and unfasten the back door from the inside?'

Louisa looked at the little window beside the servants' door of Roseberry Hall. Ivy hung over it like a living green curtain, and as Higgins moved towards it a tiny bird flew out with a scolding churr.

This is *my* house now, Louisa thought with a sudden rush of unexpected pride in ownership. I suppose it is my duty to find out the worst.

With a speed and agility that Louisa could only envy, Higgins prised open the window and squeezed inside. He was gone for some moments before the back door of Roseberry Hall finally opened and he stood aside to let her in.

'This door leads into the kitchens, madam. The floors are flagged so they are safe enough, but the poor old place is pretty run-down, I am afraid.'

Louisa wrinkled her nose at the smell of damp and decay that struggled out as she went cautiously into the house. Shawls of cobwebs were draped around the cornices and dust lay thick upon every horizontal surface.

'Do you know anything about houses, Higgins?' Louisa asked after she had stood in the hall for some time, hardly daring to explore further.

'Enough to know that what looks bad at first sight might be easily enough repaired. Although there must be more guano here than there is in the Chincha Islands—' he paused to shoo a pigeon out through a broken window-pane '—a lot of this might soon be put to rights if the rot hasn't gone too far. Done by the proper sort of workmen and with the right care taken, of course.'

'Of course,' Louisa echoed. Roseberry Hall could be put right. It *would* be put right. She had decided.

'May we go a little further, Higgins?'

'I had better go before, madam. Just in case.'

Louisa looked up at the faded and fly-spotted map of the house that hung above the great kitchen fireplace. While Higgins went on into the main body of the house she counted up—fourteen rooms on the ground floor, fifteen rooms on the upper floor and a block of three rooms set a little apart from the others and marked 'Servants' Quarters'.

A bit of a change from the five-roomed bungalow at the hill station—however grand that had seemed at the time, Louisa thought with a catch of apprehension. What on earth was she going to do with all that space?

'I shall hold a party,' she decided aloud, remembering the idea she had thought up the previous evening. 'A Christmas party.'

'Yes...I don't see any reason why the old place should not be up to it well before this time next year, madam,' Higgins said, hands on hips as he surveyed the inner hall.

'No—*this* Christmas,' Louisa said, deciding that a transformation could be brought about in at least as many rooms as were habitable in Holly House.

Higgins stared at her, frankly disbelieving.

'I admit that the breakfast you laid on this morning was spectacular, Higgins, but your master did not offer me any hospitality last night that could not be laid on here, once the place is made safe and decorated.'

'Yes, but madam—what about builders? Repairs? How will you find anybody to do the work at such short notice?'

'I shall instruct my agent,' Louisa said loftily. Now that she had seen Roseberry Hall for herself, all that she could see were its possibilities. And there were plenty of those.

Geoffrey Redvers did not return to his house for over a week. When he did, it was late in the evening and Louisa was already at dinner. He strode into the dining room, casting slightly suspicious glances at the bowls of fresh flowers set around the room and the freshly laundered white damask tablecloth. He looked as though his trip to London had not been a success.

'Mr Redvers! What a pleasant surprise!' Louisa said as an attempt to try and lighten his heavy expression.

'Higgins told me that you were in here,' he said gruffly as the servant quickly laid a second place at the end of the dining table remote from Louisa. 'Although he never informed me of all *this*...' Redvers threw a hand dismissively at the small flower arrangement in the centre of the dining table which trailed garlands of fine green smilax across the pristine white tablecloth.

'You told me to make myself at home, Mr Redvers,' Louisa said evenly. 'Although Holly House was about as welcoming as a church hall at the time. All I have done is to instruct Higgins to brighten the place up a little. In my opinion he has talents that are sadly going to waste in your employment, Mr Redvers.'

She smiled at Higgins as he added a little to the glass of wine that she had barely touched. Geoffrey Redvers said nothing until Higgins was safely out of the room, but the rigid set of his body and his thunderous expression were enough to tell Louisa that her opinion was not something that he either looked for or appreciated.

'Do not make too free with my staff, Mrs Hesketh. This is not India,' he reminded her coldly.

The nerve of the man! As if she could ever forget that she was in cold, formal England now, instead of the warm and colourful place where she had been born.

'How was your trip to London, Mr Redvers?' Louisa enquired with sweet venom as Higgins brought in roast mutton and vegetables for his master.

'It seems that I had best return there as soon as possible, Mrs Hesketh.'

Fired by his words, Louisa missed their implied intention.

'Oh, Mr Redvers—might I be so bold as to ask if I may travel up to the capital with you?' Louisa put down her dessert spoon and fork, treating him to her most winning smile. 'I should dearly like to do some shopping there.'

'What about Roseberry Hall? Should you not be concentrating upon that?' Geoffrey Redvers proved to be an equal master of the cutting reminder.

'That is part of the reason why I need to go shopping.' Louisa was warming to her theme now, candle-light dancing in her dark eyes and casting delicate shadows across the creamy smoothness of her skin as she moved. 'I am determined to have a few rooms there habitable by Christmas, Mr Redvers. My agent has put me in contact with a reputable builder. The men have already started work, clearing the place out and making preliminary estimations. I have not been idle in your absence, Mr Redvers.'

'Indeed you have not, Mrs Hesketh.' Her host was frowning at the flower arrangement again. An earwig had dropped from one of the chrysanthemums and was insinuating its way across the tablecloth towards the cover of a trail of maidenhair fern. 'It is like dining in the midst of an herbaceous border.'

He looked around the room glumly, then rallied a little as he realised something.

'Naturally, I would be pleased to offer you transport to the railway station, Mrs Hesketh, but of course there can be no question of doing so. A lady could not possibly travel about in London alone. It would be most improper.'

Louisa had thought of that.

'Maggie Higgins would be coming, too. She has agreed to act as my maid.'

'Indeed?' Geoffrey Redvers raised one eyebrow in disapproval. 'Not only do you give Higgins ideas above his station by praising him in front of me a moment ago, but you now inform me that I must look for a new cook-general because you have decided to requisition mine!'

'Not at all, Mr Redvers. Maggie has agreed to act as my maid only for the duration of my stay at Holly House. I have told her that her work for you must always take precedence.'

'It is a shame that you did not think to tell *me* of all these arrangements.' Geoffrey Redvers was pushing his rapidly cooling mutton chop around his plate irritably. 'Our association has been a brief one so far, Mrs Hesketh, but I am beginning to feel that nothing you do should surprise me.'

'Then you will allow us to accompany you to London?' Louisa's eyes were bright with the thought of a new adventure.

'On the understanding that my motor car leaves this

house not one minute later than half past seven tomorrow morning, Mrs Hesketh. I will not be kept
waiting.'

Louisa was ready and waiting outside the main entrance of Holly House by twenty minutes past seven
the following morning. Maggie Higgins, a plump,
pretty girl in her twenties, was in charge of the bags
and stood guard over them until the puffing shape of
Mr Redvers' motor car chugged around the corner of
the house towards them. At the same moment the
owner himself came out through the front door behind
the two women.

'Where is your luggage?' he enquired sharply after
the usual curt formalities of greeting had been exchanged.

'This is all that we are bringing, Mr Redvers. I
thought you would not wish us to overburden your
motor.' Louisa and her temporary maid exchanged a
look of secret amusement.

'Hmm.' Geoffrey Redvers sounded slightly taken
aback, but as the sun had not yet risen above the ridge
sheltering Holly House it was difficult for Louisa to
gauge his expression.

Maggie seated herself in the front of the motor car.
Geoffrey Redvers himself held the passenger door
open for Louisa to step up and take her seat while
Williams, the chauffeur, loaded the cases into the
storage trunk of the car.

Before he got up into the car himself, Geoffrey
Redvers turned to his dog, Grip. The animal followed
him almost everywhere, except, Louisa had noticed,

when she was about. The dog's wrinkled muzzle was usually drawn back in the canine equivalent of a grin, but this morning was different. Grip had sensed that his master was going away. Everything about him drooped—head, tail, smile. As Geoffrey Redvers bent to pull the creature's ears, the dog lifted one great paw the size of a saucer and dropped it down heavily onto Redvers' arm. The good-tempered ear tugging became a caress in another brief show of softening in her host's iron exterior.

He may yet prove to be human after all, Louisa thought with a small smile, but she was careful to look away quickly before he realised that she had been watching him.

'I am really looking forward to this trip, Mr Redvers,' Louisa shouted over the roar of the motor car engine as they bounced along towards the railway station.

'You will not find the streets of London paved with gold as so many imagine, Mrs Hesketh,' her host countered.

'Ah, no—I intend only to make the best use of the money I have, Mr Redvers. My financial advisor, Mr Willis, has allowed me a little spending money, so I am determined to enjoy myself.'

'Willis? Not Henry Willis of Dunston?'

'Why, yes. Do you know him, Mr Redvers? I believe his father acted for my great-aunt.'

Geoffrey Redvers looked shocked.

'Then you are not dealing with old Mr Willis direct?'

'No—his son. Both are called Henry, I believe,' Louisa replied.

Redvers muttered something that Louisa could not hear over the engine noise, but his face was grave.

'Do you not approve of the Willis family, Mr Redvers? I thought that it seemed reasonable to entrust my affairs to a local firm which has at least some connections with my family—however tenuous. Mr Willis was sure to have all the details of Roseberry Hall's accounts easily to hand, I thought. Don't you agree?' she asked suspiciously.

'This is hardly the time or place for such a discussion.' Geoffrey Redvers gave a meaningful look at the chauffeur and maid seated before them. 'Never in front of the servants, Mrs Hesketh.'

Louisa pursed her lips. This Mr Redvers evidently knew the proprieties inside out, and she should try to learn from him. Folding her hands primly in her lap, Louisa decided to be a model of propriety from then on.

Louisa found herself a seat in a first-class carriage of the London train while Maggie took her chance further down the carriages.

Louisa had thought it would be odd but inescapable that she would be travelling in one part of the train while her host studiously ignored her in another part of it, but Geoffrey Redvers had other ideas. He chose instead to ignore her at close quarters—getting into the same carriage where Louisa was sitting.

Before taking his place on the opposite seat and in the furthest corner of the carriage from Louisa, he handed her a copy of *The Times*, muttering that it would relieve the tedium of the journey.

'Goodness, Mr Redvers! What *will* the village of Stanton Malreward say when they hear of us travelling alone together?' Louisa said, startled.

'Maggie Higgins is already safely on the train, and too wrapped up in the novelty of the situation to have noticed anything, I fancy,' he said firmly, shaking out the folds of his own newspaper.

He did not look to have any sinister motive in choosing to sit with her for the long journey. Louisa wondered why on earth he should have decided to share her carriage at all. Conversation obviously was not the reason, but she did not mind. She was content to look out of the window as the train drew out of the station. The English countryside was still fresh and novel to her, despite the leaden hues of November.

After an hour or so, Louisa thought she had better make use of the newspaper that Redvers had given her. The front page of obituaries was too depressing, so she turned instead to the letters page. The correspondence was learned, and with a sigh Louisa decided that the readers of *The Times* could have no sense of humour at all.

The court articles were far more interesting. Louisa pored over details of what the ladies had worn and the delicacies that had been served to royalty on their travels. As soon as I get Roseberry Hall in order I shall have restrained tea parties like these, she thought, wondering to whom she could send invitations—which should be engraved, she learned, and on fine white card.

At this point her eyes strayed towards Geoffrey Redvers. He was studying his newspaper intently, but as though becoming aware of her scrutiny he looked up. His level stare soon softened, and the corners of his eyes lifted as he smiled.

'Travelling by train is *such* an experience, Mrs Hesketh.'

Louisa continued to stare at him, uncertain of this sudden relaxing of his manner.

'Most women are obsessed by their appearance. Your lack of absorption in that department does you credit, Mrs Hesketh.'

What on earth could he mean? Louisa had a sudden, almost overwhelming urge to check her appearance in her hand mirror, but she fought against it. She was not about to give him the satisfaction.

Still smiling, Redvers' gaze returned to his newspaper. When she was sure that he was not looking at her, Louisa drew out her hand glass, hiding it beneath the handbag in her lap until she had taken another quick look at Redvers to make sure that he had not noticed what she was doing. Then she lifted the glass—and saw the black smudge on the tip of her small nose.

'Oh!' The exclamation jumped out before Louisa could stop it. Redvers looked up, smiling openly now. Louisa ignored him pointedly, trying to pull a handkerchief out of her handbag. In her struggles the bag slipped off her lap, scattering its contents over the floor of the carriage. Compact, lip colour, hairpins, hat pins and travel sweets rolled and bounced across the carpet, dancing merrily to the rattle of the train. Louisa was far too busy trying to rub away the smut on her nose with the wisp of lace masquerading as her handkerchief to do anything about them, but Geoffrey Redvers immediately dropped his news-paper on the seat beside him and set about gathering up the escaped articles.

'No—please don't bother—I shall manage...' Louisa began, then remembered the way that he must have been laughing at her privately. 'I would rather that you had told me about the mark on my nose,' she snapped, stinging for the second time after he had caught her at a disadvantage.

Her tone had been harsh, but Geoffrey Redvers leaned forward with an almost mischievous twinkle in his eyes.

'Do not concern yourself, Mrs Hesketh. It was no worse than the smut you gained from the fire last week,' he said in a low voice. There was no one else in the carriage to hear, but Louisa's cheeks still burned with shame.

'All the same, it was hardly the act of a gentleman to allow me to be seen in public like that, Mr Redvers.'

'It must have been printer's ink from the news-paper, Mrs Hesketh. Not soot. There was no trace of it as we left the station,' he confided, picking up the last silver hat pin from the carpet. 'And you did not open the newspaper until long after the train had pulled away from the platform. Your secret is safe, Mrs Hesketh.'

They spoke little for the rest of the journey. After yet another shaming at his hands Louisa was determined never to acknowledge him privately again, but it was not long before that resolve ebbed away. She found herself looking across at him covertly from beneath her long dark lashes. There was no doubt that he was extremely good-looking, despite the dark, sober grey of the business suit which made his good, clear skin look even paler than usual.

As the train wheezed to a standstill in Paddington station, Redvers stood and opened the door for Louisa. After stepping down she turned to thank him, but he had already been absorbed into the milling throng of people jostling along the busy platform. She had to make do with the chatter of Maggie Higgins as they found themselves a cab and headed for the shops.

Shopping in the metropolis was a totally different experience from the hot, dusty duty it had always been in India. For the next few hours Louisa discovered a new pleasure in the act of being indulged and fêted as she sat and inspected the finest upholstery, napery, rugs and chinaware that the grand shops of London had to show her.

Before leaving Stanton Malreward Louisa had decided how much money she would spend, and when she was within five pounds of her budget she decided to stop for tea. Sending Maggie off to enjoy herself until it was time to catch the train home at six o'clock, Louisa set off for the Lethbridge Hotel. Many of the old stalwarts in India had spoken of the place with longing, and she had heard that she was bound to get an excellent meal there in good company.

It was the company that almost proved Louisa's downfall. She had not given it a thought until she was within fifty yards of the impressive façade of the hotel. It was ten minutes to four—a popular time for tea, and several couples appeared through the dusk and then disappeared into the welcoming oasis ahead of her. Then she noticed a single, distinguished, expensively dressed woman being engaged in conversation by the doorman. With a polite but firm smile, the lady was turned away from the door.

An uncomfortable thought struck Louisa. Back in Karasha, everyone knew everyone else, and a lady forced to dine alone through circumstance would have hardly rated a second glance. Here in England, those wretched proprieties evidently called for more restraint.

Louisa's footsteps faltered and paused. The Lethbridge Hotel was the only establishment in London that she knew she could trust for certain, by reputation. A lady could not afford to make a mistake by entering the wrong place, or by being turned away from a place such as the Lethbridge.

Then suddenly the clouds lifted.

'Well—if it isn't Louisa!'

A loud, cheerful voice threw out a conversational lifeline which Louisa grabbed thankfully. Turning round with a smile, she recognised Charles Darblay-Barre, a friend of her late husband.

'Mr Darblay-Barre! How lovely to see you!' Louisa responded to the prosperously rounded gentleman with genuine feeling. 'I did not know that you were in London.'

It was a lucky meeting, as Charles Darblay-Barre immediately invited Louisa to tea at the Lethbridge Hotel, solving her problem at a stroke. She confided as much to him as they walked up the front steps, and his ready laugh filled the lobby.

'Actually, you will be doing *me* a favour too, Louisa. I and my business associate, Mr Stephen Allington, are supposed to be taking tea with an excellent customer and his wife, but to tell you the truth they are rather heavy going, conversationally speaking. A bit limited. You will be just the woman to keep our spirits up!'

When Louisa learned that the customer for Charles Darblay-Barre's fine teas and blends was Sidney Tonbridge, she was even more relieved. Sidney and his wife Edna were friends of her parents from a long way back and conversation, she was sure, would be easy.

Charles and Louisa had barely taken their seats at a discreet little tea table in a private alcove than the Tonbridges bustled in. They were delighted to greet Charles and meet Louisa again after such a long time.

The Tonbridges were quick with their condolences.

'We heard that poor Algernon had been killed, of course, but never imagined that you were the brave little wife to whom the papers referred. Dear Louisa— you must have been through so much!' Mrs Tonbridge cooed sympathetically.

Louisa hid a grimace and murmured the usual platitudes about doing her duty that people always wanted to hear. Fortunately the Tonbridges were quick to change the subject with news of Charles Darblay-Barre's business associate, who had been held up outside.

'Not by a pretty face, for a wonder!' Sidney Tonbridge said with a chuckle. 'A clip between an omnibus and a cart—he offered to act as arbitrator. You know Geoffrey—or at least you soon will, Louisa, when he starts working his charm upon you in a few minutes' time!'

'Geoffrey? But I thought you said his name was Stephen, Charles?' Louisa's brow creased as she turned a puzzled look on her host.

'I certainly do not think that a respectable widow like Louisa will want to be paired off with Geoffrey *too* readily,' Mrs Tonbridge reprimanded her husband sharply, but she turned to Louisa with a twinkle in her eyes. 'Geoffrey is an excellent businessman, Louisa, but he does have an irredeemable eye for the ladies!'

Louisa laughed lightly as she listened to tales of the incorrigible Geoffrey's philandering. She wondered if her intended matchmaking with Stanton Malreward's Geoffrey would ever turn *him* into a ladies' man. That, given his long, difficult silences and stilted conversation over dinner, seemed highly unlikely.

Charles Darblay-Barre and the Tonbridges were good company, despite Mrs Tonbridge's eagerness for the dashing Geoffrey to arrive. Louisa took little notice of this thinly disguised attempt at matchmaking. All the women at Karasha had started scheming in that way on her behalf within months of Algernon's death. At the time, Louisa had considered it to be not only upsetting, but the height of bad taste, too. As the months had gone by she had learned to let the concern of others wash over her, and to ignore their best efforts at finding her a new partner.

Marriage to Algy had been a revelation. He had encouraged Louisa to have faith in herself. 'You never know what you can do until you try,' had been one of his favourite phrases, enticing her into leaky boats on the Ganges, onto fraying, swaying rope bridges across ravines and through seemingly impenetrable jungle. All in the name of his plant-hunting expeditions.

It would have to be a remarkable man to take the place of Algernon Hesketh, Louisa knew, and she would be highly unlikely to meet him over tea in a grand London hotel. Safe in that knowledge, she even accepted an invitation to a house party at the Tonbridges' the following weekend—despite warnings that the devastating Geoffrey would no doubt make it his business to pursue her unmercifully if she attended.

'Of course, we shall be enjoying grapes from our own vinery during the weekend, and indeed until well into the new year,' Sidney Tonbridge was telling Louisa proudly as he described their house and grounds. 'Our man Chivers is an absolute treasure. I simply do not know what we would do without him. All I have to say is, Saw a fine pineapple at the Westmorelands', Chivers! and blow me down, for nothing more than the price of a new greenhouse and a few tons of coal the man will have the same on our table within a matter of months!'

'Goodness,' Louisa said with proper awe.

That single word hid a multitude of thoughts. How long would it be before the gardens of Roseberry Hall produced as much as a lettuce leaf? Algy had taught Louisa a great deal about the flora and fauna of India, but her knowledge of English cultivated plants was sketchy in the extreme. It did not take a mind like Charles Darwin to realise that producing anything from the bramble-choked wilderness that was supposed to be Roseberry Hall's kitchen garden would take a long time. It certainly would be a case of survival of the fittest. Louisa's intended household would be sending out for many things, and not simply pineapples, for some considerable time to come.

Suddenly Mrs Tonbridge's voice broke through her gloomy thoughts with a tinkling laugh.

'Ah, here is Geoffrey now!'

Chuckling, Sidney Tonbridge acknowledged the arrival of the fifth member of the party. 'Now we shall have some fun. Prepare to repel boarders, my dear Louisa!'

Louisa thought that to turn around in her seat to greet the dashing Geoffrey might not be quite the Done Thing in polite English society. She sat still, smiling at Charles and merely inclining her head a little to try and catch a glimpse of the approaching social butterfly.

When she did so, all pretence of good manners was forgotten. Oblivious for once of her stays, she turned in her seat to stare openly at the new arrival.

For walking across the thick extravagance of carpet towards their table was none other than the man she knew as the reclusive and dour Mr Geoffrey Redvers.

Chapter Four

He recognised her a split second after she had seen him. His regular stride hesitated momentarily, then unguarded surprise was immediately replaced by a studied curiosity. That single moment convinced Louisa that there was something very strange going on. Charles was not a man to make a slip in conversation, yet he had called his associate Stephen Allington. Not only that, but the Tonbridges' excitement would never have been sparked by the taciturn man Louisa was lodging with in Stanton Malreward.

'Edna—Sidney—how lovely to see you,' Geoffrey was murmuring politely. He was smiling, too, as Sidney and Charles Darblay-Barre shook his hand in turn and Mrs Tonbridge leaned forward to kiss him lightly on the cheek. But he was not only smiling at his host, his customers or the offered handshakes. Part of that slow, measured amusement was reserved especially for Louisa.

The look in his eyes seemed to say, Well, that's it. I have been caught out, fair and square! But his smile told another story. That was almost predatory—as though he was daring Louisa to give his little game away—whatever that game might be.

'Louisa, I would like you to meet Mr Geoffrey Redvers of Darblay-Barre Tea Traders.'

'My grocery shops will stock nothing but Darblay blends…' Sidney Tonbridge began, but Louisa only half heard his glowing testimonials. The transformed vision that was standing beside their table—totally at ease in the social situation—moved forward to take her hand. Louisa was conscious that staring was not acceptable, even in these bizarre circumstances, so she forced her mouth to smile and make the appropriate polite sounds of welcome.

'Have we not met somewhere before, Mrs Hesketh?' He was raising those fine dark eyebrows, daring her to expose him.

Louisa's false smile faltered. If ever there was a moment to denounce him, then this was it. Oh, but surely you *must* remember me, Mr Redvers! Louisa rehearsed the words inside her head. I am the lady who is disrupting your dour bachelor life back in Stanton Malreward. I am the woman who is sharing your house. We travelled up to London together, alone together in a carriage. Wasn't it jolly?

If any of these words tumbled out it would shatter every convention of polite society. With Edna and Sidney Tonbridge already in awe of their associate's skill with women, Louisa could imagine their reaction to that. Her good name would be ruined for ever, and the reputation of Geoffrey Redvers would rise to even headier heights.

Louisa hesitated, then gave him an open, innocent smile.

'I do not think that I have ever had the pleasure, Mr Redvers,' she said carefully, as he must have calculated that she would. She treated him to a smile as brittle as hoar frost, and was trapped by his sardonic smile in return.

'Geoffrey claims a prior acquaintance with all the eligible young ladies!' Edna Tonbridge giggled from behind her fan.

'Sit there opposite Louisa, Geoffrey, while I order some more tea.' Sidney Tonbridge snapped his fingers imperiously at the nearest waiter.

'Yes, you two young people can get to know each other.' Charles Darblay-Barre winked at his business associate in what Louisa took to be a very arch fashion.

Little chance of *that*, Louisa thought. She found herself looking at the transformed Mr Redvers far more carefully than she would ever have dared to look at any other stranger at a first meeting. This man—hermit or rake, whatever he might be—deserved careful, if unobtrusive, scrutiny.

Living in the English countryside must definitely be ageing, Louisa decided. She had previously guessed that her host, Mr Redvers, must be approaching forty. Here, under the bright, unforgiving lights of the Lethbridge Hotel's drawing room, he looked to be only a few years older than herself, and probably no more than thirty. His smart business suit and perfect manners over tea were completely at home here in the Lethbridge, where the loudest sound was the chink of silver teaspoons against fine bone china.

The only false note in the whole of Geoffrey's performance was his expression. He was so watchful that Louisa could only study him properly when the formal starch of his collar meant that he had to turn to emphasise a point of business to either Charles or Mr Tonbridge.

If ever she caught his eye by mistake, he would treat her to a feral smile, knowing that the time for revelations had passed and that the secret of his other life in Stanton Malreward would stay a secret. For the moment, at least.

'I know that look in your eyes, Geoffrey!' Mrs Tonbridge teased, tapping him on the knee with her folded fan. 'Louisa has only recently arrived from India, and we do not want her falling under your spell. At least give the girl a chance to meet everyone else first!'

'As if I would force myself upon a lady,' Geoffrey said slowly. 'I dare say that you and Sidney will be able to think up plenty of amusements for her, Edna?'

'Of course we will!' Mrs Tonbridge simpered like a girl.

The idea of amusements being laid on in her honour was news to Louisa. She did not need a social life organised for her. She was quite capable of doing that for herself, if she put her mind to it.

'Although you need not think that we are going to abandon poor Louisa to you as easily as that, Geoffrey!' Mrs Tonbridge continued, much to Louisa's embarrassment. 'Do not worry, Louisa, dear—we shall make sure that you are always properly chaperoned!'

'Perhaps it is Mr Redvers who should be watched. Perhaps he is even more of a dark horse than you imagine,' Louisa said innocently, pausing to sip her tea as her words took effect. She sensed a subtle but immediate change in the vision sitting at the opposite side of the small walnut tea table. Geoffrey continued to smile, but although his expression was still as bright the muscles on either side of his finely drawn mouth had tensed. He was waiting to hear what she would say next.

'He is obviously *such* a danger to women!' Louisa concluded sweetly, transferring her attention to the plate of tiny cress sandwiches that Charles offered her. The sandwiches were cut into novelty shapes and Louisa chose a tiny heart to nibble delicately as she turned her attention back to Mrs Tonbridge. The older woman gave a little chuckle of agreement.

'It is to be hoped that you apply as much energy to your work as you do to your pursuit of the fairer sex, Geoffrey!'

'More, I would say,' Charles Darblay-Barre said quietly.

Sidney Tonbridge joined in the laughter but his tone was more appreciative. 'There cannot be many men who work as hard as Geoffrey does, nor can strike a harder bargain, as I know to my cost!' He laughed.

'There, Charles! My work in England is appreciated. You need not have travelled all the way over from India to check up on me!' Geoffrey said archly.

Louisa was astonished. If Charles was only visiting England, surely he would expect to be entertained at Holly House? With Geoffrey's reputation carrying all before it, any business partner would be horrified to find him housing a lady lodger. The conclusion would be obvious—Mr Redvers had been busy with pleasure when he should have been working. It would be interesting to see how her host would wriggle out of that confrontation.

'The tea trade must be an interesting one,' Louisa began, hoping to keep the conversation on the subject of his work. 'Tell me, Mr Redvers, do you know India at all?'

The question clearly unsettled him, but he was quick to cover his true feelings with another easy smile.

'I was there for a while, but that was years ago. I stalk clerks now, rather than tigers. They are much easier to handle when at bay!'

Mr and Mrs Tonbridge exchanged a horrified glance. Sensing the unspoken alarm, Geoffrey looked from Louisa to Charles and back again in amused bewilderment.

'Have I said something out of turn?'

Neither Charles nor the Tonbridges could speak. Their frantic glances flicked towards Louisa, but then went straight back to Geoffrey and stayed there. Louisa could imagine the frantic grimaces that they would be making and decided to capitalise upon them.

'My late husband was killed by a tiger, Mr Redvers,' she said succinctly.

He went white.

'Oh…then I am truly very sorry, Mrs Hesketh.'

'Not as sorry as I was, Mr Redvers.'

'An accident…' Mr Tonbridge plunged in, trying to make things better but instead making them much worse.

'I hardly think that Mr Hesketh would have been killed on purpose,' Geoffrey spat coldly. Sidney Tonbridge withered under the blast and Louisa felt that she had to come to the rescue of her old acquaintances.

'The tiger killed my husband. Then I killed the tiger. That is all there is to say upon the matter,' she said firmly, picking up the teapot to help herself to another cup of tea. A waiter appeared miraculously at her elbow and meekly Louisa put down the teapot again so that he could pour for her. This minor distraction in the tea ceremony had given everyone a chance to think of safer topics of conversation and once the waiter had poured the tea and reversed away from the table both Mr and Mrs Tonbridge began to talk at once.

'You will be coming to our little house party, won't you, Geoffrey? You must come too, of course, Charles.'

'We shall be having *so* much fun next weekend, Louisa!' Mrs Tonbridge leaned towards her through a haze of English Lavender.

'Then…Mr Redvers and I are *both* invited to your house party?' Louisa asked slowly.

'There is no need to look so horrified, Mrs Hesketh,' Geoffrey said in a low, silky voice. 'To ruin your debut into society is the very last thing on my mind. How may I make amends? Shall I refuse Edna and Sidney's kind invitation?'

The Tonbridges looked alarmed.

'No! No...' Louisa looked at each of them in turn, but had to lower her lashes before looking across the delicate arrangement of little iced cakes towards Geoffrey.

'Surely *you* will not be refusing our invitation, Louisa?' Mrs Tonbridge looked genuinely disappointed.

'Er...' Louisa was caught on the horns of a dilemma. It seemed that there was nothing else to do but try and push her suspicions to the back of her mind.

'Of course I shall not refuse.' She smiled at Mrs Tonbridge kindly, although her mind was working on more than party manners. 'I would like nothing more than to see the pretty house and garden that you have told me so much about, Edna.'

She would look forward to the party, but seeing King's Folly was not the only reason that Louisa steeled herself to accept the invitation.

She was determined to find out more about this Geoffrey Redvers—hermit or scamp. And a weekend in an English country house would prove an ideal setting for her studies.

Louisa was not at all surprised when Geoffrey Redvers made the excuse of pressing business elsewhere in town. He left Charles and the Tonbridges at the very next lull in the conversation.

As soon as he had gone, Louisa listened more carefully to the idle gossip about him. All she learned for certain was that Mr Geoffrey Redvers was in sole charge of the English arm of Darblay-Barre Tea Traders. The visit of his partner in the business, Charles Darblay-Barre, meant that there was often an extra man at social events, and Louisa's arrival had eased this problem at a stroke.

Louisa now knew the secret of her host's trips to London, but she was still not satisfied. She wanted to know what his glittering London friends thought of the grim surroundings of Holly House, and how her presence there would be explained when the time came for him to host his own social events.

'Mr Redvers must be an old hand at house parties,' she said carelessly when Edna Tonbridge paused for breath in her list of Geoffrey's accomplishments. 'I suppose that you and Sidney must be regular visitors to his home.'

'Oh, *indeed*!' Mr Tonbridge puffed out his chest importantly like a pouter pigeon. 'The Dorchester Hotel is never so jolly as when Geoffrey is holding one of his soirées.'

'His country house must be very dull after such city excitements,' Louisa persisted gently, spooning a little jam onto her plate beside a fresh warm scone.

'Aha! I do believe that you are smitten, Louisa!' Mrs Tonbridge leaned against her with a conspiratorial whisper. 'But you do not need to worry about Geoffrey owning anything so dull and ordinary as a country house. No, Louisa. He much prefers city life and lives here nearly all of the time. Apart from the times when he is sampling country life "at second hand", as he likes to call it, by attending house parties such as ours!'

A picture was beginning to form in Louisa's mind about the lives of the strange man who was so close at his home yet so expansive away from it. It was not a very clear picture, as yet, but she felt that she was beginning to get somewhere. With the Tonbridges exchanging grimaces of delight at the progress of their matchmaking, Louisa quickly changed the subject. It would not be the done thing to pursue the matter of their mutual acquaintance. The Tonbridges might get quite the wrong idea about her interest in Mr Geoffrey Redvers.

She must not be suspected of any attraction of that kind. Geoffrey's good looks and charm could evidently be turned on and off at will. While Louisa had to admit that they were very appealing, she felt that he was tinged with something far more sinister now.

Why on earth would any *honest* man wish to run two entirely different and separate lives?

To Maggie's great astonishment, Louisa paid for her temporary maid to travel home with her in a first-class railway carriage. Louisa announced that as the winter afternoon was already pitch-black between the wavering pools of gaslight glow it would be better for them to travel together rather than separately. Privately, she was hoping to learn more about the 'country mouse' side of her host's double life.

Maggie Higgins was a talkative girl, but although she said a lot she did not actually tell Louisa very much. Louisa gradually learned that Maggie and her brother had been living in the Big House for eight years, working first for the local squire, then being inherited with the house when Mr Redvers had bought it five years ago. Sam Higgins did the garden and worked about the house while she did the cooking and Williams, the chauffeur, took care of the cars, the horses and helped Sam with any heavy work.

Mr Redvers kept himself to himself when he was at home, but though he never said much he could be very good to them at times. He was always generous at Christmas, and only a couple of weeks ago he had taken Sam up to London. It had happened because Sam had said in passing that he would love to see one of the fancy flower shows that were held in London each month. The next thing he knew, Mr Redvers had paid for him to go up on the train. This had amazed them at the time, and Maggie's eyes still shone with the wonder of it.

'Your master does not go in for a lot of entertaining at Holly House?' Louisa asked to break Maggie's dream.

The girl burst into fits of laughter. 'Why, bless you no, madam! It is the talk of the parish that he has taken a lodger, even one as respectable as yourself!'

That put Louisa in her place. She was not at all sure that she wanted to be the talk of the parish. Especially if it meant that her name was linked with a man with two identities.

The best thing to do was to move out of Holly House as soon as possible, Louisa decided. That would dampen village gossip. Roseberry Hall might even be ready to take her. The old house was proving to be less of a problem than she had first imagined, although it was proving quite a drain on her supply of ready cash.

Louisa was delighted with the progress that had been made on the house. As the builder showed her around, the day after her return from London, it was clear that the kitchen and old Mrs Vernon's suite had needed very little work to get them put to rights. Those parts of the house were very nearly finished.

Louisa alarmed the builder by announcing that she would be moving in as soon as she had returned from the Tonbridges' house party the following weekend. Maggie Higgins was staggered, too.

'But Sam says that the place is like a building site, madam! How on earth will you manage?'

'A good warm kitchen and a tidy bedroom will be enough to begin with,' Louisa asserted firmly. 'Besides, with the lady of the house in residence, the builders will be inspired to work twice as hard. You will see!'

Sam and Maggie Higgins were such an ideal pair of servants that Louisa wished she could harden her heart and lure them away from Holly House. To entice them to work at Roseberry Hall would not be playing fair. Instead, she asked them to put the word about for good, reliable staff. She could already call on Sami, the young man who had accompanied her from India. He was steady, honest and reliable. A dedicated butler could wait until she was more settled.

At the present time, a plain cook-general and a maid of all work would be sufficient to help Sami.

Louisa was particularly proud at her idea of employing a maid of all work rather than separate house and lady's maids. A girl of the right sort could soon be trained up to become a good lady's maid, while a lady's maid would never demean herself by black-leading grates or picking up a feather duster. Besides, said Louisa's practical streak, a lady's maid would cost an extra twenty pounds a year.

All these arrangements were very exciting. The days leading up to the Tonbridges' house party flew by, until Louisa almost began to wish that she had refused their invitation. The only reason she did not cry off from the party with a fictional dose of influenza was a growing curiosity about her host at Holly House.

Louisa had not seen or heard anything of Mr Geoffrey Redvers since he had walked out of the Lethbridge Hotel. During the daytime, Louisa was always too busy to have time for anything but thoughts of Roseberry Hall, but at the end of each day there were those few idle moments just before sleep.

Lately, the enigmatic Geoffrey Redvers had developed a maddening habit of infiltrating her thoughts. Louisa would find herself wondering what he was doing and with whom. Then those thoughts would begin to crowd in upon her. She began to feel that the next time they met she would simply have to march straight up to him and confront him over this infuriating duplicity. To get everything out in the open. And to break the spell that he seemed to have cast over her.

The following Friday morning dawned crisp and

bright. It was ideal weather for travelling, with the roads dry and clear. The pony's hooves rattled a rapid tattoo on the way to the station as Higgins drove Louisa to Gloucester in the trap. She was so excited at the prospect of going to the Tonbridges' house that the spectre of her host turning up at the same party had been pushed conveniently to the back of her mind.

'I hope that Maggie will not be too disappointed at being left behind,' Louisa said as they turned into the station approach. 'As I explained to her, if Mr Redvers were to return home during my absence, he would not thank me for spiriting away his excellent cook-general!' she added, hoping to continue the fiction of solitary curmudgeon that Geoffrey Redvers had spun for himself.

'No, madam,' Higgins said shortly, bringing the pony and trap to a halt outside the station.

Louisa could see how tense Higgins was by the set of his jaw as he unloaded her cases from the cart. He even snapped at a surly porter. Louisa raised her eyebrows in disapproval of that, but she was glad when he bullied the porter into finding her a good seat on the train. With the prowling menace of Higgins close by her luggage was dealt with quickly and efficiently, too.

'Goodbye, Higgins,' Louisa said, pressing a two-shilling piece into his hand. 'I shall be returning on the morning train, on Monday. Please meet me here then. *And I hope that you do not look like that when you are working for Mr Redvers!*' she added in a low voice, looking at him disapprovingly. At once his furious glower dissolved into apologies.

'I'm sorry, madam…it is just that Maggie was so looking forward to a trip away from home. She had never travelled further than the next village before you came, see, and thought that with you needing a lady's maid—'

'I have explained to her that Mrs Tonbridge is lending me a lady's maid for the weekend,' Louisa said firmly. She felt sorry for Maggie, but if Geoffrey Redvers did not approve of giving his servants ideas above their station he certainly would not relish the thought of Maggie Higgins travelling halfway across the country. The chance of Maggie coming face to face with her employer at the Tonbridges' would have been a disaster. It would have been unlikely, as not even a lady's maid would have mingled with the guests, but there was always a chance that Maggie might have stumbled upon the secret of her master's double life.

Louisa wondered who she was trying to protect—Geoffrey Redvers or Maggie Higgins. She had the uncomfortable suspicion that Geoffrey Redvers might not continue employing Maggie if he thought she knew too much.

Sam Higgins accepted the finality in Louisa's voice and turned away to start off for home. Louisa had dealt with servants all her life, but it never made disappointing them any easier. She decided then and there that, if she spoke to Geoffrey at all during the coming weekend, it would be to persuade him to make it up to Maggie Higgins in some way.

Louisa told herself that the business of Maggie Higgins was the reason why she was looking out for Geoffrey Redvers from the moment the train wheezed into Paddington station. To find him among the milling throng of London with its hordes of newspaper sellers, flower girls, businessmen and itinerant workers all seeking their fortunes—together with the occasional lady on her way to a fashionable house party—would be impossible. Louisa found her connection for the Surrey countryside and travelled on in hope and expectation until she reached the Tonbridges' country home.

King's Folly was a large house which had recently been attacked by the craze for everything mock Tudor. The brick walls of its gables had recently been painted white, and black laths had been nailed up in an effort to make the house look like a relic from Olde Warwickshire.

Louisa was not impressed by the alterations, but the deep flower borders of newly turned earth beneath each window gave her an idea that she could copy back at Roseberry Hall. Perhaps Sam Higgins would know of a suitable gardener whom she might employ.

Louisa tried hard to concentrate solely on her plans for Roseberry Hall. Despite that, her heart was beating very quickly as the carriage that had collected her from the station drew up outside the grand front entrance of King's Folly. It was not the thought of meet-

ing many strangers that had put Louisa on edge. It
was the thought of one stranger in particular.

Resplendent in black bombazine and pearls, Edna
Tonbridge met her on the steps of the large house.
Louisa greeted her warmly, and her hostess ushered
her quickly into the warmth of the house.

A bright fire crackled in a sparklingly black-leaded
grate within the large entrance hall of King's Folly.
Its brilliance was picked up by the glitter of a large
chandelier hanging high above the stairwell. Several
guests had already arrived. They were enjoying some
hot punch as they sat on expensively upholstered
cream settees drawn up around the fire.

'Oh!' Edna Tonbridge sounded disappointed.
'Well—where has Geoffrey gone? He was here only
a minute ago, Louisa. Never mind—I shall seat him
next to you at dinner. Make sure that you mingle well
with all the other guests before then—I am sure that
dear Geoffrey will not give you the chance to make
any other acquaintances once he has set his mind
upon you!'

Louisa could not imagine that would be the case,
but tried to laugh off the suggestion easily. If he has
not put himself out to be devastating when we have
been living under the same roof, he is hardly likely
to begin now, she thought darkly.

While her luggage was taken upstairs and unpacked, Louisa was introduced to the knot of guests
around the fire by Edna Tonbridge. Mr and Mrs
Brigstone, the local bank manager and his wife, were
both severely efficient in black. He was wearing a
crisp suit while his wife was rigid in black silk and

jet beads. The Tonbridges' nearest neighbour, George Andrews, was a large, florid man in an expensively uncomfortable jacket and tie. He talked in large amounts of money to Mr Brigstone, but his huge gnarled farmer's hands rather ruined the gentlemanly effect he was trying to make.

His daughter, Victoria, was a tall, serene girl who had recently completed her education at Cheltenham Ladies' College, Mrs Tonbridge told Louisa with a smile of pleasure at such an achievement. Victoria's hair was dressed up into a mass of tiny curls on the top of her head, giving her a striking look of Queen Mary. She had Queen Alexandra's cool beauty, and Louisa almost began to wish herself taller and more classically pretty, like Victoria Andrews. Louisa already knew the final guest at the fireside.

Charles Darblay-Barre approached, smiling, offering her a cup of punch. 'Yes, that is right—the tea man bringing something a little stronger! Did you travel all the way up from the country on your own, Louisa?' he enquired kindly.

'Yes,' Louisa nodded. 'Mrs Tonbridge is lending me a maid for the duration of the party,' she said, grateful of the opportunity to remind her hostess without seeming to do so directly.

'Of course, Louisa. I shall go and sort the matter out right now. Charles can keep you entertained until Geoffrey returns.'

Charles Darblay-Barre was a large man, prosperously padded around his waist and dressed with expensive understatement. His grey hair was thinning, and even if she had not known that he had travelled

from India Louisa would have guessed from the
brown weathering of his hands and face. He must be
a real working man, she had always thought, as a
mere pen-pusher would never have gone out in the
heat without gloves and a hat. She liked him, especially as he had a fund of amusing new stories about
the place that Louisa still considered home, despite
her uneasy new love of England.

As he talked about his work and his invaluable
partner Geoffrey Redvers, Louisa suddenly thought
she knew why Charles Darblay-Barre had looked so
relieved when she had told him that she had travelled
up to the party alone. Perhaps he knows, she thought
to herself as he chattered on in the light, bright way
of older men in conversation with pretty young
women at respectable events. He might have guessed
that bringing a servant here from Holly House would
compromise his business partner.

'I think that any reputation Stephen—I mean
Geoffrey—might have as a ladies' man is always
rather inflated by hopeful hostesses,' Charles Darblay-
Barre was saying with a smile.

'Even when he does something like that?' Louisa
sipped her punch, watching Geoffrey Redvers insinuate his way back into the company. He had immediately cornered Miss Victoria Andrews into conversation.

'Geoffrey! Come over here at once. You have not
been introduced to the latest, and most delightful, arrival!' Mr Darblay-Barre called across the hall with a
laugh.

Louisa took another sip of punch to steady her

nerves, but carefully. She had already felt the wicked glimmer of alcohol behind its sweetness of berry fruits and lemonade. Alcohol at teatime? She would have to watch the Tonbridges, that was certain.

Geoffrey Redvers did not look at all happy at the summons. Making his apologies to Miss Andrews, who simpered prettily, he crossed the hall in a few strides. The meaningful look he trained on Charles Darblay-Barre barely softened as he greeted Louisa.

'Mrs Hesketh. What a delight to make your acquaintance again.'

It sounded as though it was an annoyance rather than a delight.

'Oh, come *on*, Geoffrey! You can do better than that!' His friend baited him light-heartedly.

At this point, the Geoffrey Redvers of Stanton Malreward would have turned and stalked away in silence. Louisa expected him to do the same here. He did not.

'Indeed. I hope that we shall have plenty of opportunities to get to know each other better over the course of this weekend, Mrs Hesketh,' he said in a low, well-modulated voice. Despite its charm, his voice lacked the silky, veiled insincerity that a seducer in action would use. Louisa was not fooled for one moment.

Geoffrey Redvers had his heart set upon Miss Victoria Andrews, and Louisa's presence at this house party was nothing but an inconvenience. Made all the more irritating by the thought that she could, at any time, expose his double life.

'I feel as though I know you quite well enough

already, Mr Redvers.' Louisa smiled sweetly, watching a cloud of uncertainty pass across his dark, mysterious eyes. 'So I should hate to drag you away from the delightful Miss Andrews. Please—return to your conversation. Mr Darblay-Barre and I will find plenty to amuse ourselves in your absence.'

'Not *too* much, I trust!' Geoffrey countered with a smile rather more in keeping with his reputation. 'But perhaps you do not know me as well as you think you do. Although I am sure Charles will delight you with his many stories of my antics!'

The words might have been spoken by any wanton with a sense of humour, but the tone in which they were said was quite different. As he spoke, Geoffrey Redvers fastened a vivid look upon Louisa. Together with the warning note behind his words, he was telling her to be careful.

Louisa regarded him keenly, the honey-brown glow of her eyes now set as hard as the amber necklace around her throat. If this man thought that he could frighten her into silence, then he had another think coming.

'My word, Mr Redvers. You *do* have a mighty high opinion of yourself! I doubt if a thought of you will cross our minds, much less our conversation!'

Mr Darblay-Barre burst out laughing, the old-gold silk of his waistcoat stretched dangerously taut across his generous waistline. 'Well, that is telling you your fortune, Geoffrey, and no mistake about it!' he laughed. 'Perhaps you would have better luck courting Miss Victoria Andrews after all!'

'It looks as though I am not destined to soften Mrs

Hesketh, that is for sure,' Geoffrey said through clenched teeth. Taking his leave of them both with a slight, formal bow, he went back to join Miss Andrews and her father on the other side of the hall.

Louisa watched him go. Back to study the charms of a woman who would appreciate his sort, she found herself thinking.

'It was the best day's work that I ever did, making Geoffrey the head of the English arm of Darblay-Barre Tea Traders,' Mr Darblay-Barre said with considerable satisfaction. 'At first I was worried that he would be working too hard, burying himself in ledgers and accounts and order books, but now I can see that he has plenty of time and energy left for more gentle pursuits, too!'

'A little *too* much time, I would say,' Louisa observed stiffly, watching Geoffrey Redvers bearing down on his victim, Miss Andrews, like spring sunshine.

'Every man should be allowed a little licence.' Charles Darblay-Barre took her glass with the intention of refilling it at the punch bowl.

'Are you quite convinced about your friend Mr Redvers? I have heard you call him Stephen on two separate occasions, Charles!' Louisa began as Charles ladled a dangerous quantity of punch into her glass.

'An oversight, I assure you.' Charles smiled easily, holding out the punch glass to take her mind off his associate. Louisa was saved an early overdose of Tonbridge hospitality by the arrival of her hostess with news that her room was ready. That gave her the chance to refuse the punch politely.

Louisa escaped gratefully. The first thing she did was to enjoy a long, leisurely bath to ease away the travel and trials of the day. A light tray of refreshments was sent up, and when she had enjoyed tea and hot buttered crumpets before the fire in her dressing room she rang for the maid to help her get dressed, ready for the evening's entertainment.

Edna Tonbridge had announced that there were to be 'diversions' before dinner, and Louisa was excited at the thought of wearing the new dress that had been made for the occasion. It was cut from heavy silk in a beautiful shade of pale parma violet, with deep ruffles of cream lace around the scooped neckline and the short, puff sleeves. The skirts of the gown fell from the narrow waist of its closely fitted bodice in rich folds to a small train. Louisa loved it.

Mrs Tonbridge's maid laced her into a new corset, then lowered the violet gown reverently down over Louisa's head. With all the hooks and ribbons fastened, Louisa felt every inch the lady. A pair of satin slippers, just right for dancing, had been dyed to match the colour of her dress, and full-length evening gloves had been made from the same lace that cascaded from her bodice.

The maid brushed Louisa's hair to a lustrous shine, then dressed it up to show off the clear pale skin of her neck and shoulders to the best advantage. A filigree necklace of diamonds that Algy had given her as a twenty-first-birthday present added a touch of glitter.

When Louisa looked at her reflection in the long cheval-mirror, she was delighted with the skill of her

dressmaker and with the way that she had been prepared for her big adventure into society. Victoria
Andrews might be more than a head taller than me
and have all the classical beauty of a Greek statue,
but I am at least a thing of flesh and blood, Louisa
told herself.

Rather too much here and there, she thought with
a rueful smile, looking critically at the voluptuous
curves of her hourglass figure. She was hoping against
hope that there would not be any chocolate biscuits
on offer during the weekend. She would never be able
to resist them, and her new dressmaker back in
Gloucester would have to start working to a whole
new set of measurements.

Thinking of chocolate biscuits made Louisa remember the finishing touch for her ensemble. Maggie
Higgins had been treated to a look at the dress when
it had been delivered to Holly House. She had suggested that a posy of real Parma violets would set it
off a treat. They were Maggie's favourite flower, and
Sam always forced a few for her in the Holly House
greenhouse through the winter, encouraging them to
flower weeks ahead of plants out in the open garden.

Maggie had packed a bunch of the special violets
in moist moss for the journey, and now Louisa had
them set into her silver posy holder. The lady's maid
then pinned this to the shoulder of Louisa's gown. A
few dabs of Devon Violets at the pulse spots on
Louisa's wrists and neck completed the vision.

Even Mrs Tonbridge's maid remarked on how well
Louisa looked, giving Louisa a boost to her confi-

dence that was welcome when she had to walk down
the long staircase into the hall of King's Folly.

Making an entrance always made Louisa nervous.
She had to concentrate hard upon what her mama had
always told her. Head, up, take a deep breath and *keep
smiling*.

It worked. The low murmur of conversation in the
entrance hall below became ragged, and then stopped
altogether. All the guests who had already changed
for the evening's entertainment were waiting below
and turned to appreciate the latest arrival. Edna
Tonbridge, resplendent in a taffeta gown as pink as
her rouged cheeks, rustled to the foot of the stairs to
meet Louisa as she descended.

'Louisa, my dear, you look ravishing! Perhaps it
was a mistake to seat you next to Geoffrey at dinner
after all, when you are looking so beautiful!'

'Oh, I do not think Mr Redvers will be paying the
slightest attention to *me*,' Louisa said, watching the
spectacular fuss Geoffrey was making of Miss
Victoria Andrews.

The farmer's daughter was a vision in white satin
and gold lace, as cool as fresh frost against the cream
of the settee where she sat. Geoffrey Redvers was
evidently on sparkling form. He was smiling and talking to her with animation. In fact, Geoffrey was so
absorbed that he was the only person in the room who
was not making a long and detailed study of Louisa
in her new dress. She, however, took a covert interest
in his appearance.

The moth-balled evening suit he had prised from
some hiding place in Holly House on her first evening

there was now nothing but a faint memory. Tonight, he was wearing a new and extremely smart black suit with a crisply starched white dress shirt. His clothes were so plain and so well tailored that they were obviously very expensive. He looked like what he was—a prosperous young businessman. One with an eye to advancing his position in his private life as well as his public one, Louisa thought suspiciously as Edna Tonbridge told her about the riches that Farmer Andrews lavished on his only child, Victoria. Who could blame Geoffrey for making such an obvious play for her? Edna confided. It was such a pity that George Andrews had such humble beginnings.

Louisa only half heard the prejudices of her hostess. She watched Geoffrey while she could, secretly wondering what it would be like to be the focus of such lavish attention.

Edna Tonbridge seemed to have a much better match than a farmer's daughter in mind for her dear Geoffrey. She went out of her way to try and put Louisa's thoughts into reality. The company played a few hands of bridge before dinner, and Louisa found herself paired with Geoffrey rather more by the design of her hostess than by any accident. Used to the light-hearted merriment and open cheating of bridge parties in Karasha, Louisa was puzzled to find that Geoffrey Redvers was impossible to goad or hint. She had to rely on picking up his suggestions through bidding, which took concentration rather than wit and guile.

They lost all but their final game, by which time Louisa had started to realise what was expected of

her. By then it was too late. The dismal gloom of
Holly House was threatening to engulf their table.
Geoffrey Redvers was plainly a man who liked to
win.

Louisa was greatly relieved when the soft rumble
of the dinner gong sounded and they were summoned
from the card tables.

Making a supreme effort to speak through her
shame, Louisa apologised for her poor showing.
Geoffrey did not wave it away with indulgences, but
pursed his mouth into a narrow line as though biting
back a caustic comment.

'I would offer to escort you in to dinner, Mrs
Hesketh,' he said, despite the frantic fluttering of
Edna Tonbridge between them, 'but unfortunately I
have already agreed with Mr Andrews that I should
escort his daughter.'

The fine narrow line of his lips curved up into a
slow smile, but his eyes remained enigmatic and
watchful.

Louisa wondered why he had bothered to pause and
give the rebuff, unless it was to rub salt into any
wound he thought he might have caused by abandon-
ing her. She returned his look, and with interest. She
had no intention of letting him think that he had disappointed her. If he had not excused himself and
turned away to find Miss Andrews, Louisa might have
said as much to his face.

Instead, Louisa accepted the arm of Charles
Darblay-Barre for the short walk in to dinner. As they
approached the table, talking about the supposedly
friendly bridge tournament, Louisa discovered the

Edna Tonbridge was not a woman to give up easily. Geoffrey Redvers had already discovered from the place cards where he was sitting.

'So—I am to have the best of both worlds. A charming young lady to take my arm on the way in to dinner, and then I find that I am placed as the thorn between two beautiful roses at the table!' Geoffrey smiled to the company as he pulled back the chairs on either side of his place at the table, seating first Victoria Andrews then Louisa before sitting down himself.

'At least I shall have the chance of some interesting conversation.' Louisa smiled at Charles as he took his seat on the opposite side of the table from her.

'You do not appreciate my company, then, Mrs Hesketh?' Geoffrey turned his lustrous dark eyes full upon her, causing Louisa to wonder once again what was going on behind that enigmatic, teasing expression.

'I appreciate the company of anyone who has plenty of interesting conversation. About a wide range of subjects,' Louisa added, with a meaningful look past him at the vision that was Victoria Andrews.

'Ah, but then we do not all share your cosmopolitan interests, Mrs Hesketh,' Geoffrey said mildly before turning back to concentrate upon the views Miss Victoria Andrews held about the latest fashions and hairstyles.

Louisa decided to enjoy herself that evening if only to spite Mr Geoffrey Redvers for the way he had snubbed her. Over dinner she traded lively reminiscences with Mr and Mrs Tonbridge and Charles

Darblay-Barre about their experiences in India. This seemed to exclude Mr and Mrs Brigstone, the bank manager and his wife, so Louisa made a point of asking them if they had any views on house renovation in general and what she should do about Roseberry Hall in particular.

'First and foremost—get yourself a good and trustworthy financial advisor!' Geoffrey Redvers quipped unasked. Louisa had not even been aware that he had been listening to the conversation. He had been turned aside from her, apparently absorbed in the wisdom of Victoria Andrews and her father.

'Oh, really, Mr Redvers? I did not know that you were interested in matters as dry and dusty as financial advice.' Louisa turned a penetrating smile upon him, but he simply reflected it with charm.

'Rest assured that I am red-hot where large amounts of money are concerned, Mrs Hesketh!' He leaned towards her cheerfully.

Louisa pointedly moved away, keeping a respectable distance between them.

'Do you always show such delightful reticence to a prospective financial advisor?' he enquired with a teasing tone that succeeded in making Victoria Andrews giggle, but not Louisa.

Louisa hardened her expression.

'Of course I do, Mr Redvers. Although most gentlemen know their place. As a matter of fact, I shall be dining with Mr Henry Willis, my new financial advisor, next week. I doubt that any lady who wanted to retain her reputation would ever agree to dine alone with *you*, Mr Redvers.'

He stopped laughing abruptly. Now his expression became cat-like, almost menacing in its minute study of her face.

Suddenly, Louisa remembered the quiet, restrained dinners they had shared alone together back at Holly House. A terrible flush of embarrassment rose from deep within her to colour her cheeks with shame.

He must know what I am thinking because he must be thinking the same thing himself. Louisa blushed again furiously.

'No,' he said slowly. 'I do not suppose that a lady with a spotless reputation *would* dine alone with me, would she?'

Chapter Five

Edna and Sidney Tonbridge were so keen to keep abreast of fashion that King's Folly even had a small ballroom. With a sprung floor, as Edna was keen to say at every opportunity. After dinner, the ladies withdrew to let the gentlemen enjoy their port and cigars. The hostess showed her lady guests into the drawing room, or salon as she liked to call it, and over tea and petits fours told them all about the improvements that had been made to the house. When the gentlemen had been given enough time to enjoy their own company, Mrs Tonbridge led the ladies to the new ballroom. The gentlemen straggled in soon afterwards.

Watching Geoffrey Redvers was an education for Louisa. One moment he was in the thick of male conversation, the next he was at the side of Victoria Andrews. Requesting the first dance, naturally, Louisa guessed.

It did not give her any pleasure to be proved right. As he led Victoria out onto the dance floor, the delighted company laughed knowingly at his tactics. Louisa did not laugh. She felt her heart darken to-

wards Mr Geoffrey Redvers still further. He would
have two good reasons for keeping so close to Miss
Victoria Andrews, and both were equally sinister.

The first reason goes without saying, Louisa
thought frostily as she watched Geoffrey gazing down
at his partner, for all the world lost in admiration. The
second reason interested Louisa rather more. He is
avoiding *me*, she thought. Society will surely shun us
both if it is discovered that we are sharing a house—
although there would be more scorn for me and more
envy for him, she guessed. At least while we keep a
formal distance between us here the proprieties are
maintained. There can be no whiff of scandal. Yet
Louisa found that it was hard to enjoy the evening
when he was virtually ignoring her.

Without the trio of musicians installed in the corner
beside the potted palms, it would have been very difficult for Louisa to follow her mother's advice about
never scowling. As the musicians struck up the 'Gold
and Silver' waltz she could not help but smile, despite
the way that she was feeling. Her parents had always
called Edna and Sidney the 'Two Tune Tonbridges'
as the 'Gold and Silver' waltz and 'The Blue Danube'
were the only tunes they had ever requested at dances
back in Karasha.

Charles Darblay-Barre immediately asked Louisa
to dance. She accepted in the spirit in which the request was made, and even began to enjoy herself.
Like many large men, Charles was very light on his
feet and propelled Louisa around the dance floor with
cheerful accuracy. He laughed when she wondered
aloud whether the next tune would be 'The Blue

Danube', seconds before the trio broke into the first bars.

'I think I shall sit this one out, and let you younger ones indulge yourselves!' Charles subsided into the nearest chair and summoned a drink. Then he called for Geoffrey.

'Here you are, Stephen. Keep my delightful partner entertained until I have caught my breath, would you?'

Without warning he caught hold of Louisa's wrist and handed it to the man she knew as Geoffrey Redvers. Once again he had called him Stephen. This was far too much of a coincidence to be sheer absent-mindedness. There was something very strange going on between Charles and this Mr Redvers, but Louisa had been too stunned by the sudden gesture to ask. To judge by the expression on the face of her new partner, he was stunned too, but far too respectful of his senior partner to refuse the command.

'It would seem that we have no choice in the matter, Mr Redvers,' Louisa managed as sweetly as she could for the benefit of their hosts. The Tonbridges had been thrown into new delights by this development, but Victoria Andrews was looking Louisa up and down with a cold, critical stare. Louisa smiled, but not at either her new partner or Miss Victoria Andrews.

'I can only hope that your business associate is as good a dancer as you are, Charles.' Louisa smiled at the older man with genuine warmth. 'He is unlikely to be as good at conversation, that is for sure!' she added, hooking the loop of her train over her fingers as Geoffrey led her out on to the dance floor.

His face was grim, and showed none of the vacuous charm that he had been showering so lavishly on Miss Victoria Andrews. Gripping Louisa's hand far too tightly, he swept her into his arms.

'I know what you must be thinking, Mrs Hesketh.'

'I doubt that,' Louisa countered crisply. 'If you did, you would hardly be gracing this assembly. Unless, of course, you are even more of a bounder and cad than I have started to think you are.'

'It does not sound as though that would be possible,' he murmured through a polite smile, trying to lighten the atmosphere between them. It did not work. Louisa stared up at him stonily. He had made her suffer with silence on several occasions back at Holly House. Now it is his turn, Louisa thought.

'Why does Charles keep calling you Stephen?'

He was gazing at a point somewhere over the top of her head as they danced, and did not reply.

That confirmed Louisa's worst fears. An honest man would have come straight out with a stumbling explanation—forgetfulness, another colleague of that name—while a bounder would do one of two things. He would either explain deftly with the skill of forethought and long practice, or he would remain silent.

Her partner said not a word.

'Are you going to give me the courtesy of an explanation, Mr—?' Louisa paused theatrically, her eyes wide with feigned concern. 'Goodness! I do not even know what to properly call you!'

'Either name will suffice,' he spat suddenly, sweeping her into a turn as they passed the trio. 'My full baptismal name is Stephen Geoffrey Redvers Allington. Geoffrey Redvers would be better here, if we are not to throw the company into utter confusion.'

Louisa's look of scorn relaxed, but only by a fraction. The fact that his alias was at least part of his own name had punctured her wilder suspicions about him. It was a tiny saving grace, but it did not explain his reasons for using it.

Instead of the rapt attention that he had beamed down upon Victoria Andrews, Louisa found that Geoffrey was looking about the ballroom with a distracted air, as though he would have preferred to be anywhere else in the world rather than dancing with her.

Good, she thought, preparing to twist the imaginary knife a little more.

'I think that you owe me rather more of an explanation than that, sir.' She smiled up at him with glacial charm. 'If you are such a sparkling, feckless guest, Mr Redvers, why are you such a dour if dutiful host back at home?'

'Sometimes a man needs to escape,' he muttered, showing every sign of wanting to do exactly that.

'From what?' Louisa enquired, her eyes narrowing with renewed suspicion. Then she caught sight of the look that Victoria Andrews had trained upon her. 'Or should I say from *whom*?'

'I would rather not say.' Geoffrey cut her short by guiding her into several turns in quick succession. With each manoeuvre he drew her a little closer to him. 'Until we know each other a little better, Mrs Hesketh.'

'*I am living in your house, Mr Redvers Allington!*' Louisa hissed.

'Where you are a delight and an ornament!' he countered in loud, smiling delight as they drew close to Mr and Mrs Tonbridge.

'You are looking radiant tonight, Mrs Hesketh,' he went on, obviously intending their hosts to hear every word. 'Tell me: is the fragrance of Parma violets as fleeting as that of their wilder cousins?'

'You must surely be the man to find out, Geoffrey!' Sidney Tonbridge chuckled, glancing at the posy clipped to Louisa's shoulder by its silver vial.

'Now you come to mention it, Sidney...Edna...it is growing a little warm in here. Have you seen the conservatory here at King's Folly, Mrs Hesketh?'

'Oh, but you must!' Edna burst out before Louisa could refuse. 'Louisa loves flowers, Geoffrey. Her late husband was a respected botanist, and Louisa did much to help him in his work in India. Perhaps you will be able to tell us the names of some of the ones that we brought back from our travels, Louisa! We have plenty of lights in the conservatory—go out there now and take a look—the place is a regular treasure house!'

'If Mr Redvers is finding it warm in here, Edna, I dare say that he will find a conservatory heated enough to grow tropical plants even more uncomfortable,' Louisa said, looking up at her partner.

Then it happened—a double bump of her heart made Louisa catch her breath. Geoffrey suddenly looked…irresistible. The smooth plane of his freshly shaved jaw, the clear, pale skin illuminated by those dark, desirable eyes…

'Oh…'

'Are you quite well, Mrs Hesketh?'

'Yes…I think perhaps you were right, Mr Redvers. It is a little hot—'

'Geoffrey!' Edna clucked in alarm. 'Take Louisa aside until she has caught her breath! The conservatory! At once!'

Geoffrey was all gushing concern until he had drawn Louisa away from the Tonbridges and they had reached the side of the dance floor. Then his voice sliced like a knife.

'I suppose this is all the fault of your dressmaker, Mrs Hesketh, barricading you into whalebone stays a size too small? And all in the name of fashion. Be sure to have them made the right size next time,' he finished scornfully.

Louisa gasped with indignation, but felt her head swim infuriatingly as though in agreement.

'You are fortunate that I think far too much of the Tonbridges to slap your face for that remark, Mr Redvers. You certainly deserve it!' Louisa snapped, flicking out the folds of her fan and using it desperately.

'I am sure that it was no less than any other man would have thought. The difference is, Mrs Hesketh, that I am never afraid to make a helpful suggestion. Someone like young Henry Willis would simply let you suffer.'

'Mr Willis? My financial advisor? What on earth

has he got to do with this?' Louisa shot him a look of stony suspicion.

'I believe that young Mr Willis spends far more time entertaining eligible women than he ever does in the office. That is why I removed my business from the offices of Henry Willis of Dunston, I am afraid.'

'It sounds more like a severe case of envy.' Recovering a little, Louisa continued to look up at him sharply.

'Not in the slightest, Mrs Hesketh. I have nothing to prove,' Geoffrey said loftily, as though daring her to deny it. When she bridled defensively, Geoffrey looked pointedly over the top of her head in the direction of Miss Victoria Andrews.

'Oh, you are the most *insufferable...*' Louisa struggled for words as he began to laugh in that light, musical tone that she had heard him lavish on Miss Victoria Andrews. 'It is no wonder that you keep a low profile when living in the country, Mr Redvers. Your busy social life when mingling in society must quite exhaust you!' She lowered her voice to a hiss as the music came to an end with a flourish. As the dancers paused and clapped appreciatively, Edna Tonbridge rustled towards them, a determined smile on her face.

'How delightful to see that you two are getting on so very well together,' she gushed, barely pausing for breath before adding, 'I could see that whatever it was that you had to say soon had Geoffrey smiling, Louisa!'

'Oh, to manage that is not very difficult, Edna.

Geoffrey seems to laugh easily at everything, however unamusing it might seem to us ordinary mortals.'

'Oh, come, Louisa!' Edna Tonbridge nudged her playfully, an action which Louisa disliked. Despite that, she kept smiling. 'You are delightful company and you know it, Louisa!' her hostess persisted. 'Now, come along to the conservatory, the pair of you. I want Louisa to tell me all about my plants.'

'Shameless matchmaking, I call it,' Charles Darblay-Barre murmured to Louisa as she and the other guests dutifully trooped out into the conservatory in the wake of their enthusiastic hosts. 'I am quite mad with jealousy, Louisa!'

He was laughing, and Louisa hoped that he was joking. She gave him only a weak smile. Charles Darblay-Barre might be an excellent dancer and a charming dinner companion, but Louisa could not bring herself to think of him as a partner in any other respect. If he did consider paying too much attention to her, it would be a difficult task to harden her heart and destroy his hopes.

The Tonbridges' conservatory was almost as hot and humid as the Indian subcontinent. Louisa was relieved that she had recovered from the dancing, and told herself that she was glad that Geoffrey Redvers had taken the opportunity to drift back into the orbit of Victoria Andrews.

The new conservatory ran along the entire south side of King's Folly. Any available sunshine during the day was trapped by the thick glass of the structure and absorbed by the stone and plaster façade of the house. This natural warmth was increased by a network of four-inch iron pipes running around the walls of the conservatory. These circulated hot water around the building. The climate had been made even more tropical by adding a large formal fish pool, where goldfish gasped and water lilies stewed gently. Artificial water lilies, each holding a small night light, floated among the real plants with an eerie glow.

'The perfect place for a little bit of billing and cooing,' Mr Tonbridge said to no one in particular, and the whole company laughed.

Not if I can help it, Louisa thought, edging away from Charles Darblay-Barre as carefully as she could while pretending to study the plants wilting in their artificial home. Although she did not realise it at the time, this movement brought her closer to Geoffrey. Louisa was too busy pretending to study the plants that Chivers, the head gardener, had so artfully arranged in pots and beds around the conservatory. She recognised plenty of the plants: tiny star orchids wired to dead apple boughs that had been half buried in the conservatory border among azaleas and camellias. The plants were all very small at the moment but with time they would each make large, noble specimens— if they survived.

Louisa had seen plenty of crazes among the ladies at Karasha come and go in her time, and most of them—unlike bicycles, she hoped—were short-lived. One day it would be shell gardens, decorated with beads and bits of broken pottery. Sewing boxes and the results of kitchen accidents would be hoarded and traded. The talk in the 'hen house' would be of little else. Then the fashion would disappear as suddenly as it had appeared. Someone would happen to mention their pet bird, and before long all the ladies would be training mynah birds to sing and talk in cut-throat competition.

Louisa hoped that the plants in Edna and Sidney's conservatory would be loved for a lot longer than the few weeks of a passing craze.

She did not want to be considered a show-off, so she told Edna Tonbridge only as many plant names as she thought polite. Her hosts and their guests were delighted, but their obvious pleasure only made Louisa blush.

Geoffrey had watched the unwilling display and was one of the first to speak up. 'You should not be so coy about your talents, Mrs Hesketh. You obviously know a great deal about your subject, and should be proud to exhibit it,' he observed drily, then rather spoiled the effect by adding, 'Besides, the beautiful shade of your blush does nothing whatsoever for the colour of your exquisite gown!'

This prompted a ripple of amusement, and another furious blush from Louisa. The cheek of the man! How *dare* he embarrass her in front of all these people?

Louisa tried her best to avoid him for the rest of the evening, but it was impossible. His fascination with Miss Victoria Andrews meant that he was never far from the refreshments table or, later, the supper buffet. As soon as Louisa moved towards either, he was ready to hand her a glass of lemonade, or cutlery, napkins or hot savouries. If it had been anyone else Louisa might have been flattered, but, as Edna

Tonbridge had said, no woman was safe from Geoffrey's blandishments, and no woman under twenty-five was safe from him at all.

Every time he turned to offer her some assistance, with that mischievous smile never far from his lips, Louisa felt the strange, novel surge within her that had affected her so badly during their waltz together.

'Time will tell whether he is quite so attractive outside of the party season,' Louisa said obliquely to Charles Darblay-Barre as they ate hot cheese pastries during a pause in the dancing.

'I think that Geoffrey merely needs to find the right woman,' Charles announced. 'Then he would settle down, I am sure.'

'I would not like to count upon it, Charles,' Louisa said quietly as Geoffrey strolled across the dance floor after parking Miss Victoria Andrews between her father and a plate of iced fancies.

'Would you give me the honour of the next dance, Mrs Hesketh?'

If Louisa had been expecting his invitation, she might have had time to think up a suitably cutting response. As it was, the totally unexpected request took her by surprise. There could be no quick refusal—and no considered one, either. Not when Geoffrey was smiling at her in that particular way. Louisa felt as though she had turned into a blade of quaking grass.

'As long as it will not keep you away from your friend Miss Andrews for too long, Mr Redvers,' she managed, trying to concentrate upon finding her gloves and pulling them on rather than looking into his beguiling eyes again.

'If you would rather not…'

She had wrong-footed him, and he began to turn away—until a loud cough from Charles Darblay-Barre stopped him in his tracks.

'I really do think that you should stop trying to monopolise Miss Andrews, Geoffrey!' he said almost irritably. 'Give the rest of us a chance. I rather fancied cutting in there myself, as a matter of fact.'

'Oh…of course, Charles.' Geoffrey gave his senior partner a polite if mocking bow, but Charles had not yet finished speaking.

'As long as I may leave Mrs Hesketh in safe hands, that is.'

'Of course, Charles,' Geoffrey repeated with a shrug, returning to offer his hand to Louisa. Louisa was not impressed. As the band struck up variations on a theme of 'The Blue Danube' again and Geoffrey led her out on to the dance floor, she felt like a parcel passed from one partner to another. And just in time for the longest piece of music in the trio's repertoire.

She might as well have been a parcel, too, for the silence that descended over the first long moments of their dance together.

'Shall you be hunting tomorrow, Mrs Hesketh?' Geoffrey managed at last, although he was concentrating on guiding her around the other dancers rather than looking her in the face directly.

This was a new line of attack. Louisa had steeled herself against flattery, but such an ordinary opening gambit was another total surprise. After her humilia-

tion at the bridge table, Louisa no longer had any
confidence in her knowledge of things English.

'I...don't know, Mr Redvers,' Louisa said carefully. 'I enjoy riding very much, but with regard to
the famous blood lust of hunters in England—'

Geoffrey made a contemptuous noise. 'The last
time the Tonbridges' local hunt caught something, it
was influenza. You will be in absolutely no danger of
seeing anything untoward, Mrs Hesketh, if you are
brave enough to come out with us tomorrow.'

That did it. Brave enough? Of course she was.
Braver than a man who felt he needed concealment
behind two names, that was for sure.

She would show him.

Louisa was up and about before it was light the
next morning. Revelling in the indulgence of an experienced lady's maid again after what seemed like
an eternity of 'making do', she was bathed and
dressed before half past seven. She dismissed the
maid, but then lingered in her room for a while longer
before going down to breakfast. Louisa could never
be described as vain, but she wanted to study her
reflection in the looking-glass before making an entrance downstairs.

Nothing must go wrong. She had to make a good
impression on Geoffrey Redvers. It had sounded as
though he had expected her to refuse the risk of the
hunting field, but she was determined to show her
mettle to this shadowy imposter.

He must have something to hide, some shadow in
the past, to keep up this pretence of one persona and

manner in the country and a completely different one
for his fashionable friends, Louisa decided. Somehow,
she would persuade him to confide in her. The problem was in deciding how to do it.

It would be a laughably simple matter if she flattered him with fluttering eyelashes and simpering
smiles, as the other females in the party did—but
Louisa was determined to do things differently. Any
information she managed to tease out of Mr Stephen
Geoffrey Redvers Allington would be on her own
terms. The effect that his look had on her and the
confident feel of his hands when they danced together
had unnerved her the evening before, but on this clear
winter morning Louisa's resolve was as firm as an
icicle. She was not going to let herself fall for his
charms.

Certainly not.

Louisa looked at her reflection in the full-length
glass critically, then allowed herself a small smile.
When she looked like this, she would surely have no
trouble in getting Geoffrey's attention. The black riding habit that had been made for her up in London
had been worth every penny. The tight-fitting jacket
emphasised the slenderness of her waist as well as the
feminine swell of her bosom, while the full, soft folds
of the calf-length apron rippled around to conceal her
legs like the skirt of an elegant gown. The boots she
wore were not new—only the *nouveaux riches* sac-
rificed comfort for the sake of being seen riding out
in a totally brand-new fig—but the boot boy had done
wonders with them and they glowed with the light of
quality.

Let our friend see this and not be impressed, Louisa thought with a twinge of justifiable pride. Her only problem today was likely to be how to keep Geoffrey at bay, not the poor unfortunate fox.

Her amber eyes twinkled at the thought of how she would keep Geoffrey at arm's length yet still learn his whole story, and a blush flushed her cheeks. With a giggle she looked away from her reflection. Algy had always so despised fancy and fashionable women. Now here was his widow daring to think like them!

Although Louisa loathed the idea of killing any creature for sport she loved riding, and had been persuaded by Geoffrey's insistence that the Kington hunt were as hopeless as they were fashionable. The excitement was already fizzing away in her breast as she skipped down to breakfast, leaving her hat, whip and two pairs of gloves on the dressing table.

The dining room was deserted, but a range of chafing dishes hissed quietly in the silence. The Tonbridges were not so grand that they had staff on hand to serve at breakfast, so Louisa helped herself. She was glad to have privacy to make her choice. She had a healthy appetite, and the prospect of a day's hunting was whetting it still further.

Nothing had irritated Algernon more than women who fainted on picnic rides because of fashionably small appetites and tightly boned corsets. Louisa had learned to fill up, and put common sense before fashion. Except when it came to ball suppers, she thought ruefully, remembering the night before and making a mental note to tell the maid not to lace her quite so tightly for dinner this evening.

Louisa chose and ate a good warming breakfast of egg, bacon and kidneys. She was just wondering whether to try some of the bottled fruit compote when the mahogany door of the dining room glided open with a prosperous silence.

'Mrs Hesketh!' Geoffrey said as a matter of course, then stopped with a gasp of appreciation.

Flustered that her plan had apparently got off to such a good start, Louisa forgot all about keeping him at arm's length and felt herself melting inside. Those eyes of his, that dark thick hair, the playful smile as he stood framed in the doorway...

'Good morning, Mr Redvers,' Louisa said in the stiffly formal manner that decorum required. In England, her mother had often said, a lady had to act as though her every word and action was made in front of witnesses. Witnesses that could make or mar a reputation for ever.

'I had no idea that you really were such a sport, Mrs Hesketh!' He crossed the room to the breakfast board, still smiling at her. Louisa took in the cut of his coat, the jolly yellow checked waistcoat, thigh-skimming breeches and boots polished to a mirror-like shine.

Everything was obviously brand-new, but for once Louisa did not hear her ayah's disapproving sniff of "Trade!" as she looked at him. All Louisa saw was a handsome, successful man who was out to enjoy a good day's hunting.

Foxes, I hope, Louisa thought, although without much conviction as he chose from the chafing dishes then put down his breakfast plate at the cover beside her.

'I am sure that I will not have to ask whether you are a creeper or a pusher,' he murmured, helping himself to military pickle from one of the condiment sets arranged on the table.

Louisa did not have the first idea what he was talking about. In this sort of situation offence was the decent option, so Louisa took it.

'I trust you are not being forward, Mr Redvers.'

He put down the pickle spoon and turned a particularly guileless smile on her.

'*Me?* Oh, how could you suspect me of anything but the very highest motives, Mrs Hesketh?'

Louisa swallowed hard. He was a respectable distance away from her, but the fresh new scent of his outfit and the squeak of his immaculate new boots on the parquet floor made him seem too close for comfort. She thought of the way his money and influence had glittered in the eyes of Farmer Andrews the evening before as his daughter had been swept around the floor by this handsome enigma, and hardened her heart.

'Quite easily, Mr Redvers. Or are you using the name Allington today?'

It was a remark he had not expected, and his easy expression stiffened.

'I have told you,' he said evenly, that impenetrable gaze pinning her down, 'I do not use the name Allington. I like my privacy, and expect it to be honoured.'

His voice had a hard edge to it, which matched the icy glitter in his eyes.

'You like your privacy so much that one might almost think that you had something to hide, Mr Redvers,' Louisa countered quietly as Victoria Andrews and her father entered the room. Geoffrey stood up to greet them, but Louisa's manners were momentarily forgotten. She could not smile a welcome once she had seen how Victoria was dressed.

The farmer's daughter was wearing a dashing little outfit in Harris tweed with leather features at the cuffs and collar. Ideal for walking or watching, but most definitely not for riding. Geoffrey's surprise on arriving at the dining room flooded back to haunt Louisa. An invitation to the hunt must have had a subtle, hidden meaning for the guests—one that Louisa, as a newcomer, had missed.

As more people straggled into the dining room, Louisa's horror grew. She was the only lady dressed for hunting.

The borrowed lady's maid had obviously been too professional by half. A lady did as she liked, and it was not a servant's place to comment.

'Oh, dear…I did not realise that none of the other ladies would be riding. If you would all excuse me, I had better go back up to my room and change—'

'Stay where you are.' Geoffrey's voice was low but surprisingly authoritative.

'I cannot possibly ride out with a field of gentlemen, Mr Redvers!' Louisa retorted in alarm.

'Nonsense. It will be *fun*,' Geoffrey said briskly, in a way that could not be questioned—a real flash of the old efficiency coming out. 'I have already convinced myself that you are not going to be a creeper, Mrs Hesketh, and hold us all up at the gates. Make sure that you do not disappoint me.'

The other gentlemen might also be living more in fear of a creeper than of her reputation as a lady. Victoria Andrews and Mrs Brigstone, the bank manager's wife, were both looking at Louisa with such open envy that Louisa sensed that her reputation might actually be enhanced rather than ruined by a dash of moral courage. She remembered the prints of Skittles, a famous mistress, hanging in her father's study back at Karasha. Skittles had hardly been moral, but everyone had admired her courage. She had shown real dash on the hunting field, the gentlemen said with awe and the ladies said with appreciation.

'I am certainly not a creeper,' Louisa announced, learning fast. 'I am a pusher, Mr Redvers. Born and bred.'

'I knew you would be,' Geoffrey murmured with a certain satisfaction in his voice. He moved away from his seat to greet Edna Tonbridge, but as their hostess swept in she was far more interested in buttonholing Louisa.

'Oh, Louisa—I am *so* sorry! We each thought that none of the other ladies would be interested in hunting today, and now it seems that we all were—none would voice an opinion, and with you retiring early last night, before we had discussed the matter together—'

'Please do not mention it, Edna.' Louisa waved away the fluttering distraction of her hostess.

'Oh, if only there was enough time for *all* of us ladies to go up and change…' Mrs Tonbridge wailed, looking at the unhappy expressions of her other female guests. Her little coterie of gossip could then meander around the fields instead of being parked in a pony and trap out in the middle of nowhere, becoming colder by the minute.

'I must be the one to go and change, of course,' Louisa said, more eager to fit in with her hostess's plans than to make a point.

'Oh, no, Louisa! You must go out and enjoy yourself. It is just *such* a pity that we shall all be so far away from the action!'

And a blessing, Louisa thought to herself as she sent a maid to fetch her hat, whip and gloves from her suite. It would be a tricky business, managing to keep up beside Mr Geoffrey Redvers without causing comment—getting his confidence without scorn.

A message had gone down through the ranks in record time and as Louisa left the house a strawberry roan mare complete with side-saddle was being led up to the mounting block for her. It looked more than half asleep. Louisa wondered how on earth she was going to make a show on it, then remembered that in England a show was not what was required. As long as she could keep up and was not left miles behind the rest of the field—that would be the main thing. Anything more spectacular would probably be considered Very Bad Form.

When she had been helped to mount the little mare, Louisa tucked her spare pair of gloves into the small gap between the front of the saddle and its cloth.

There was nothing like putting on a fresh pair of dry gloves halfway through a riding day.

The morning was fine and bright, with the slightest hint of frost in the hollows. The last leaves of autumn were spinning through the air like coins, dark flakes against a high blue sky. It was a day that made all the worrying about how to do the right thing worthwhile. Louisa was going to have a good time. She had made up her mind.

The guests were to hack the two miles to the meet, which was in the next village. Louisa had pleaded an early night the evening before to stop Charles Darblay-Barre monopolising her time on the dance floor to an improper extent. Even so, she did not discourage the gentleman when he came to ride alongside her that morning. At least it meant that she was a respectable distance away from his friend, Geoffrey Redvers.

'You still have as much spirit as I remember, then, Louisa.'

Not enough to openly rebuff you, Louisa thought, and kept her gaze fixed firmly between the horse's ears.

'I can look after myself—you should know that by now, Charles!' Louisa said with quiet confidence.

'Hear that, Geoffrey?' Charles called across to his friend. 'Here is one young woman who will not have her head turned by fancy flattery and high living!'

'Perhaps that is just as well. For every dozen social butterflies there ought to be an honest toiler, if not a drawer of water,' Geoffrey said through gritted teeth as he attempted to control his horse. It did not like the marker posts that a ploughman had set out at the edge of a stubble field running along beside the lane. ' "Be good, sweet maid, and let who can be clever" !'

'Well!' Louisa said under her breath. 'There was no call for that comment. I will show *him*!'

Louisa found the hunt exhilarating. She had to concede that in one thing at least Geoffrey Redvers was right: the Kington hounds were astonishingly unsuccessful. They never had any trouble in picking up a scent—and that was the problem. Just as the field was getting into the rhythm of a good gallop, the pack of hounds would riot after a flock of sheep, or a badger, or another fox. With such a choice of scents they could never decide which to choose, and spent a lot of time milling around and speaking until the countryside rang.

Louisa did not mind these occasional mêlées as the runs were good and very exciting. Algy had always said that it was best to keep out to one side of a hunting field. The ditherers within the party always went for the easy option, blocking up gateways, while most of the rest of the field straggled about the well-worn ways. It only needed one to fall or falter there to create a tiresome tangle.

Louisa kept to the offside of the field, taking the line of the brave and the bold. Here, there were few others to get in her way. Minding her manners as an outsider, and a woman at that, she took care not to be right at the front. This was not as easy as she might have imagined. At every fence there would be only one member of the field ahead on her chosen line. It was always the same man—Geoffrey Redvers. He looked back over his shoulder regularly, and on approaching a fence would check his horse and turn aside, waving her through first. Conscious of his reputation as much as her own, Louisa made sure that she took each jump as well as she could, to show him that she could do it.

Until the moment when a truly enormous hedge reared up before them. To make matters worse it was a bullfinch—a hedge with a thin spreading top to be jumped *through*, rather than over. Louisa was not about to jib—not with Geoffrey Redvers waiting at the take-off side to see whether she would put her horse into the jump or let it run out.

Louisa was not about to take the easy option. She spurred her mare on faster, hoping that speed might give her enough impetus to make up for any shortcomings in her technique. The mare took off well and soared through the top of the fence. Instantly, Louisa was filled with total exhilaration at becoming part of the cold, crisp morning with its bright sky and winter-clean countryside—and then the mare crumpled on landing, bringing her rudely down to earth again.

'Mrs Hesketh!'

Louisa might have heard something like panic in Geoffrey's voice had she not been too busy slithering down into the ditch on the landing side of the hedge. The ground reverberated with another drumroll of hoofbeats as he spurred his own horse to jump over the obstacle, then slid to a halt beside Louisa's mount. Her mare had already scrambled to its feet, unharmed but breathing heavily. Louisa watched from the safety

of the ditch, expecting some extravagant display of
scorn as Geoffrey galloped off into the distance.

He did not ride away. As the rest of the field
crashed and hopped over the hedge at its lower point
some yards away, Geoffrey turned his horse, catching
up the loose reins of Louisa's borrowed mare, and
rode back to where she stood, ankle-deep in mud.
Louisa was surprised to see anxiety flickering across
his face as he rode up to meet her, but as soon as he
met her gaze he laughed.

'I thought it was impossible for a lady to fall out
of a side-saddle, Mrs Hesketh!'

'I did *not* fall. I jumped off when I felt the mare
slipping.' Louisa watched the rest of the field tittup
off into the distance, then tried to look back through
the bottom of the hedge behind her. 'Are there any
more to come?'

'Not by the route that you and I took.' Geoffrey
surveyed the back markers straggling through the
field gate and see-sawing over an eighteen-inch-high
gap in the hedge. He leapt down lightly from his
horse, which, like Louisa's, was blowing hard and
had no energy left now for seeing ghosts.

'I would ask if you are all right, Mrs Hesketh, but
I can see that you are very obviously quite recovered!'
He was smiling appreciatively as he advanced to offer
her a hand out of the ditch.

So much for my smart new rig, Louisa thought
crossly, looking down at the mud and twig accesso-
ries smeared all over her apron and breeches.

'I am more concerned about my borrowed horse.'
Louisa accepted his hand, but let it go as soon as was

practical. Although not before she had felt the warmth
and steady strength of his fingers through his gloves.

'You had better hurry and catch up with the field,
Mr Redvers,' Louisa went on. 'I believe there is to
be a second horse waiting for me at the luncheon
stop.'

'You are carrying on?' he said incredulously,
frowning. 'You might have been killed!'

'I am not the first, nor shall I be the last, person to
take a tumble whilst out hunting, Mr Redvers. Where
would the world be if everyone who received a set-
back gave up at the first opportunity?'

'That is a very daunting suggestion.' He sounded
surprised, but his eyes were thoughtful. Louisa knew
that she should have made good use of the impression
she had made on him by bustling off to check on her
horse, but she found that she could not.

For as she looked at him it was as though life had
stopped for a moment. There was no need for sense-
less social chit-chat. Louisa had fallen, he had stopped
to offer assistance. There should have been nothing
more to it than that, but there was. A great deal more,
but all unspoken.

Louisa could hardly believe it, but both the iron
reserve of her host and the shallow charm of the sociable Geoffrey Redvers had been stripped away.
Here was a considerate, thoughtful man, without any
need to make an impression on anyone. Words were
unnecessary—in any case, they could not have put
her feelings of an almost pleasant surprise into words.
Louisa would have let the silence stretch on, its expectant chill broken only by the cawing of rooks on

a distant stubble field and the faint music of the hunt circling away to their left. Geoffrey Redvers had other ideas.

'Now then, Mrs Hesketh, I suggest that we check over your horse and then get you to the halt by whatever means are most appropriate!'

Sounding very brisk and efficient, he swung away from her and back to the little strawberry roan mare. Both horses were peacefully cropping the grass now, but Geoffrey's horse was streaked with sweat from all the excitement. Wordlessly Louisa caught its reins and started to walk it about to cool it down. It was the least she could do. Geoffrey was paying such careful attention to her borrowed horse, running his hands down each leg and checking every hoof in turn.

'Didn't you know that if you catch a loose horse you will be stuck with it all day, Mrs Hesketh?' he joked with an admonishing shake of his head.

'This is not a loose horse. It is yours,' Louisa stated firmly. 'And I know now that you are far too much of a gentleman to leave me like that, Mr Redvers. Besides, how should you escape when I have your horse?'

'I should not be able to make a getaway on yours, that is for sure.'

'No, I do not think that riding side-saddle would be quite your style, Mr Redvers. Either in the country or the town.'

He pursed his lips, standing up to frown at her.

'I mean that the mare might have pulled a muscle. Look at the way she is resting that leg.'

Louisa studied the mare, whose cooling muscles were now stiffening up.

'Then I will walk her straight on to the stopping place. I saw a gathering of grooms and fresh horses on a ridge overlooking the field we crossed a moment ago,' Louisa said, taking the reins of her horse from him and looking back towards the open gate she had avoided in preference to the hedge that had been her downfall.

'I am surprised that a woman of your spirit isn't demanding that I should play the gentleman by swapping saddles and giving you my horse, Mrs Hesketh!' He twinkled at her lightly. Louisa had to look away. Things were not going to plan at all, and she had no idea how to gain his confidence now.

'There is no sense in *both* of us getting cold.' Louisa handed him the reins of his own horse then pulled out the spare pair of gloves from their hiding place beneath the mare's saddle.

Instead of mounting up as she had imagined, Geoffrey simply fell into step beside her as she started back towards where the second horsemen were waiting. Louisa was immediately uneasy.

'Should you not be going on to follow the field, Mr Redvers? What on earth will people say about me if we arrive at the stop together like this?'

'What on earth would people say about *me* if I let a lady walk half a mile on her own?' he countered cheerfully. 'And, after all, I only expect very modest payment for my company.'

'I think I should be the one who asks for payment,' Louisa replied, glad that her horse was blocking a full view of her companion. 'I think I should insist on a full explanation of your suspicious double life before I agree to go one step further, Mr Redvers.'

At this point she stopped walking. Grateful for the interruption, her horse dropped its head and began to graze again. Geoffrey Redvers carried on walking.

'I have already told you, Mrs Hesketh,' he said evenly over his shoulder. 'I like to keep my business life and contacts and my private life completely separate.'

Louisa stared after him. 'Yes, but which is the *real* you?'

He stopped and looked back at her with a mischievous smile. 'Ah…that is for me to know, and for you to find out!'

That made the matter clear, as far as Louisa was concerned. The fun-loving Mr Redvers was the genuine article, but such a fast life must carry a heavy toll. He must return to Holly House to recharge his batteries by living the life of a monkish hermit, she thought. That is why he never has the energy or inclination for anything like fun at Stanton Malreward.

'Very well, Mr Redvers!' she called, marching off in pursuit as quickly as her horse could manage. 'Although I shall expect a great deal more from you when next we meet at Holly House,' she finished in a low voice as she drew level with him again.

'Ah,' he said meaningfully. 'I should thank you for that, Mrs Hesketh. Keeping my little bolt-hole a secret. These folk are all very fine on their own territory, but I do not fancy entertaining them on *mine*, if you know what I mean.'

'Of course. And you have no need to worry that I shall be encroaching on your hospitality for much longer, Mr Allington...I mean Redvers.'

'Call me Geoffrey. It will make things a great deal easier. May I call you Louisa?'

'No, you may not!' Louisa replied archly. He had missed his chance for that intimacy back at Stanton Malreward.

'Then...you are determined to keep me at arm's length, Mrs Hesketh?'

'As long as there are grooms about to gossip, yes.' Louisa looked up at the loose gathering of staff on the high ridge of ground above them.

'There are no grooms at Holly House.'

'That is another reason why I shall be very glad to move into my own home. *Geoffrey*,' she added in a touch of devilment. Let him keep to the proprieties of formal names for once, while a lady was the one to take liberties.

'Do you know when Roseberry Hall will be finished, Louisa?' Ignoring convention, he disregarded her sharp little intake of breath, too.

'My great-aunt's suite needed very little work, as it turned out, and the kitchens are in working order. I shall be moving in next week.'

'Oh.'

That was all he said, but Louisa read far more into that single word than he had intended.

'You need not think that I am as easily swayed as your friend Miss Andrews, Geoffrey,' Louisa began sternly. 'I can guess how relieved you will be to get rid of me and have the whole of that depressing bach-

elor burrow to yourself, without let or hindrance. I
might believe that Sam and Maggie Higgins would
be sorry to see me go—they have been only too glad
of the chance of a few decent conversations since I
have been in residence—but as for you…at least there
is no danger of your sordid double life being revealed,
with me out of the way.'

'Who said anything about it being sordid?' he
snapped suddenly, and Louisa started. Looking across
at him quickly, she saw that his brows had met in a
solid line of fury, and the finely carved profile was as
set and threatening as any expression of the owner of
Holly House at his most morose.

'Oh, come along, now. No man with a clear conscience wants to keep his private and public lives
separate so fanatically.'

'I work very hard, Mrs Hesketh.' It was Geoffrey's
turn to use tight-lipped formality now. 'No one could
blame me for wishing to set it all aside once in a
while.'

'No?' Louisa risked tempting the tiger once more.
'I am only a beginner in these matters, but it seems
to me that people work in the city, and retire to the
country for their play. I never recall you being particularly carefree at Stanton Malreward, Geoffrey!'

'Perhaps that is because of the company that I am
forced to keep there.' He lengthened his stride, easily
leaving her standing as he approached the groom who
was setting up refreshments at the tailboard of a cart.

'Well, *really*!' Louisa exploded inwardly. She was
only just managing to keep her fury concealed from
the grooms, who were pretending not to notice that

their notorious house guest looked to be angling for Widow Hesketh.

Louisa had been excited about moving into Roseberry Hall, but now there would be an extra impulsion to leave Holly House. She was not about to stay where she was so clearly not wanted.

The rest of the hunting day was magnificent. While Louisa had been out on Edna Tonbridge's mare, her hosts had shifted heaven and earth to find her a really good side-saddle horse for her afternoon sport. Louisa's borrowed second horse was a real treat to ride: bold without being foolhardy, careful without being dull. She kept towards the front of the field all day, relieved that her skill as a rider was much greater than the hunt's fox-catching skills. They drew several times, but caught nothing. The foxes were always too quick, or too lucky, or a combination of both.

'There is no need to ask if you have been enjoying yourself today, Mrs Hesketh!' Charles Darblay-Barre said as Louisa wished the huntsman goodnight.

'I have had a wonderful time.' Louisa smiled with feeling, forgetting about the mud splashes and thorn scratches. To a man, the whole field was now even more dishevelled than she was. That was the sign of a really good time.

'Much as I hate to interrupt, I think we should be starting back.' Geoffrey looked up at clouds piling up to the north. 'The horses will get cold and start to stiffen if we sit around chatting.'

'I think I am stiffening up already,' Louisa confided to Charles as she rode back towards King's Folly.

'The result of that fall you took must be catching up on you. I am hardly surprised.' Geoffrey, who was riding on her offside, looked almost pleased to have found a flaw in her day.

'It will be more to do with sitting in one position all day, I think,' Louisa said smartly. 'Offside saddles cannot be as popular here as they are in India. I like to change halfway through the day.'

'Queer business, side-saddling,' Charles mused, trying not to look in the direction of Louisa's mud-draped apron. 'Don't you miss your other leg?'

'I do,' Geoffrey volunteered. 'In fact, I miss both of them from this position.'

'I was talking to Mr Darblay-Barre,' Louisa said, tapping her riding whip meaningfully against the girth of her horse's saddle.

Geoffrey's reply was swift and waspish.

'You have mud on your nose, Mrs Hesketh.'

It killed any conversation she might then have had with Charles stone-dead. Geoffrey smiled across at his friend triumphantly, as though that had been his intention.

'A gentleman would never mention such a thing.' Louisa pulled her veil down from the brim of her hat to try and conceal her face, then wished that she had not. It only brought attention to the fault and made Geoffrey laugh, which was more unbearable still. 'It is a telling fact that you have now done so *three* times in total, Geoffrey. Perhaps you have never exerted yourself enough to get dirty?' she added acidly, although she knew that it was not true. Geoffrey had been at the forefront of the field all day, which took skill and courage as well as hard work.

'Leading over fences tends to keep you cleaner,' Geoffrey observed with an impish grin.

'Ah, but Mrs Hesketh was never far behind.' Charles came to her defence, which was just as well. Louisa was too busy looking at Geoffrey's jacket, which was still looking smart, and the white breeches which only showed the slightest peppering of mud splashes over his knees and thighs.

'Never mind, Mrs Hesketh. Your state of *déshabillé* is due to your fall, I think,' he added in a regrettably loud voice as they turned into the drive of King's Folly.

Louisa's cheeks burned with shame. Her ears burned, too. In this cold, clear air Geoffrey's voice would have easily carried across the lawns to the house, where Mr and Mrs Tonbridge stood on the steps, waiting to greet their guests.

The shame of it. Not only had she misunderstood and made an exhibition of herself by going out in the first place, but the Tonbridges and their lady guests were bound to have a collective fit when they heard about her fall. She had no doubt that Geoffrey would soon tell them about it. That would give everyone a good laugh. The man was a menace to decent women, and ought to be given a taste of his own medicine.

And in that moment Louisa decided that she was the one to do it.

Chapter Six

Louisa soon found an opportunity to get her own
back on Geoffrey Redvers. As they reached the house
he jumped down lightly from his horse, his hardly
soiled breeches infuriatingly bright in the growing
dusk. Under Edna Tonbridge's supervision he immediately went around to help Louisa down from her
horse. To her delight Louisa saw that all the other
guests were watching their return out of the window.
This would be a fine time to put Mr Geoffrey Redvers
in his place.

'Oh, Geoffrey, dear,' Louisa said with a simper. 'I
am far too cold to wait for the boot boy—would you
help me so that I may go straight into the house?'

'Of course, Louisa!' Geoffrey risked using her
name under the eye of his hostess, where he knew he
would not be corrected. 'Here—take my jacket...'

Surprised and pleased at her sudden compliance,
the dashing Geoffrey pulled off his hunting jacket and
swirled it around Louisa's shoulders. Louisa was immediately enveloped by the warmth of him and the

musky scent of horses and hard work that lingered in the material.

At his command Louisa went to sit on the steps—but in following him she missed her footing on the edge of the flower border hemming King's Folly and nearly fell.

'Careful, Louisa! I have told you before that we need a light out here, Sidney!' Mrs Tonbridge scolded her husband, but Geoffrey stopped her. For once he was showing more interest in Louisa.

'She is tired, poor little thing. It has been a long day for her.'

If any other man had been so patronising, Louisa would have had to fight a scowl. As it was, she was too keen to have her revenge. Easy charm was the danger of Mr Geoffrey Redvers. He made even the most sickly sentiments sound fresh and new, as though they had been minted just for her. Or for any one of a hundred other women, Louisa reminded herself darkly.

'Clean boots?' he asked, taking up position with his back to her as Louisa sat on the steps.

'Oh, yes. I mean…I have been too tired to go anywhere to get them dirty, haven't I?' Louisa gave him a dazzling smile as he bent forward and looked back at her over his shoulder. She almost faltered when he returned her smile with interest, his dark hair falling over his eyes and giving him an exotic, gypsyish look.

Then Louisa remembered how insufferable he would be when it came to retelling the story of her fall to the other guests, and hardened her heart. Lifting her right foot so that Geoffrey could pull off her boot, she leaned back against the steps.

'Relax your foot,' he said with a smile. 'You are scrunching up your toes!'

Louisa fancied that she could feel the warmth of his fingers through the leather of her boots as he play-fully bounced her ankle up and down. Then she swal-lowed hard and said, 'Actually, I think I need a bit more purchase, Geoffrey. May I...?'

'Of course.'

There was that wicked, slow smile again, but Louisa was determined.

She lifted her left leg and planted the sole of her boot squarely on the seat of his breeches. Geoffrey pulled off her right boot as she pushed hard against him with the left—which just happened to be the foot that she had scuffled in the soil of the Tonbridges' muddy flowerbed.

Her boot slipped off easily this time and Geoffrey stood up—with the perfect imprint of Louisa's left boot on the seat of his breeches.

'Oh, how *very* funny!' Geoffrey groaned as Edna Tonbridge's squeaks of dismay told him of the disas-ter.

'It was an accident...' Louisa tried to look con-vincing but the laughter rolling out from the watchers in the drawing room was making her laugh, too. Geoffrey pulled off her other boot, then acknowl-edged the laughter of the crowd with a good-natured wave. Afterwards, he strolled up to stand as close to Louisa as he could get without actually stepping on her stockinged feet.

'I can see that I am going to have to watch you, Mrs Louisa Hesketh,' he murmured, looking down at her with a strange look in his gypsy-dark eyes. 'Very, *very* carefully!'

Louisa felt her insides turn to jelly. That penetrating stare was making her feel as though she was the only woman in the world. To have his jacket hanging around her shoulders already felt as if he was totally surrounding her. He was so close to her now that she could see the faint lines on his forehead which, back home at Stanton Malreward, usually furrowed his brow with concern. Here at King's Folly he looked twenty years younger and totally carefree.

And absolutely wonderful, Louisa admitted to herself.

And yet…

'I…must go and get ready for dinner,' Louisa said faintly, glad for any chance of escape. It was only when she had reached the safety of her suite that she realised she was still wearing his jacket around her shoulders.

The bath in Louisa's suite was deep, long and equipped with a little headrest that gave a lady the chance of a good soak without getting her hair wet. Louisa took advantage of it as soon as she could. A willow pattern jar full of rose-geranium-scented bath salts was an unimagined luxury after the utilitarian soap and water regime of Holly House. Louisa stepped into the foaming bath water and immediately felt the aches and pains of the day begin to slip away.

She spent a lovely long time in the bath, then lavished plenty of moisturizing cream onto her skin. When she was powdered and perfumed, the maid dressed her in a simple black evening gown spangled with jet, dressed her hair up and set it with matching combs. The maid had suggested diamonds, but Louisa was not too sure about that. Servants always liked to see their charges sparkling like Christmas trees, but Louisa was less ostentatious. She chose instead a triple string of pearls, and was quite pleased with the result. She dismissed the maid, then settled down in her dressing room with a magazine to wait for the sound of the dinner gong.

Only a few minutes after the maid had gone, there was a knock at the door. Louisa was too tired to get up, so she called out a welcome. It would only be the maid with some message or other, and she could let herself in.

Louisa was engrossed in an exciting piece by Kipling and miles away in thoughts of India. It was only when some time had passed without the noisy entrance that servants always made to avoid taking their charges unawares that Louisa rose from her seat to go and investigate. Perhaps the maid had not heard her, and was still waiting outside.

And that was when she came face to face with Geoffrey Redvers, creeping stealthily across her room towards the bed.

To his credit, Geoffrey jumped almost as violently as Louisa did. He now stood guiltily in the centre of her room, gesturing faintly towards where his hunting jacket lay folded neatly on the settee at the foot of her bed.

'I came for that…' he explained unnecessarily, torn between feigning embarrassment and openly admiring Louisa's gown as he regained his composure.

'But what on earth are you doing entering my room? Without invitation?' Louisa found herself adding incredulously.

'I did announce myself.' Nettled by the accusation, Geoffrey had now lost all pretence of embarrassment. 'I knocked, and said, It's me. When you did not run screaming to barricade yourself into the room I assumed that you would not mind me coming straight in. When you were nowhere to be seen I assumed you were busy in the dressing room and simply—'

'You have made a great many assumptions for one visit.' Louisa bridled, knowing now that it was her own exhaustion that had led to all this. If she had got up to answer that knock at her door properly she would have heard his voice and *definitely* not opened it—she liked to think.

'Anyway…now that I am here…' he was bright and breezy again now, despite the force with which Louisa pushed his jacket into his hands '…how about if I were to escort you down to dinner, Mrs Hesketh?'

He gave her a covert smile, as though he had lost the 'Louisa' again in order to get back into her good books.

'Miss Andrews is sure to miss her constant companion, is she not?' Louisa enquired with sweet venom.

'Oh, Charles is going to be taking her into dinner this evening,' Geoffrey said with the air of a practised philanderer. 'I thought it was about time that he had a crack at her. He seems to prefer women young enough to be his daughter.'

He put his hands, and the hunting jacket, behind his back and cleared his throat, for all the world like a Victorian patriarch. Louisa knew what that meant.

'I do believe that you are *jealous* of Charles, Mr Redvers!'

'I most certainly am not!'

'You are. You are jealous because Charles got to Miss Andrews first this evening. *Now* I suppose you are on your high horse because you are worried that she will find more in a man of maturity and experience than in someone who thinks the height of good manners is to tell all and sundry that a lady is tired when she is not!'

Geoffrey did not speak for some moments. When he did it was slowly and with some effort.

'Then you did not stumble because you were tired?'

'No.'

'I thought you would rather the Tonbridges thought that you were tired, so that you could get away for a rest from them before dinner.'

'I do have a tongue in my head, you know. I can make my own excuses when I need to,' Louisa said, but not unkindly. In his own way Geoffrey had been doing his best, after all.

'How are your breeches?' she asked, artlessly trying to change the subject. It was better to see him laugh than covered with all this concern.

'You would be better off asking the boot boy about

them. After all, he is the one who is going to have to stay up half the night scrubbing them clean.'

Louisa had not thought of that.

'Then…I shall go down and apologise before dinner, Mr Redvers,' Louisa said, suitably chastened.

He watched her, another slow smile crinkling the corners of his eyes in the way that was beginning to have a most unusual effect on Louisa.

'If we go right now, we shall have plenty of time for your remorse before dinner,' he began, then stopped himself with a sudden look of alarm. 'Oh…how stupid of me! I am sorry, Mrs Hesketh.'

His voice had dropped to a low whisper. Now he was backing towards the door, one hand spread wide in an attitude of appeasement.

'What is the matter? What has changed, Mr Redvers?' Louisa said, her voice dropping to a whisper as she followed him out onto the landing.

'I forgot myself for a moment. And your predicament.'

Louisa stared at him in bewilderment. Until that moment she had never considered herself to be in a predicament, but now she had two. How to bring the smile back to Geoffrey's face, and whatever it was that he obviously thought was troubling her.

'I have been very wrong to have been so jolly around you, Mrs Hesketh. I should have been more circumspect. More feeling towards your…circumstances.'

He was looking at her gown again, but this time not with the lazy, lascivious pleasure he usually reserved for Miss Andrews.

'Oh, you mean the black jet and pearls?' Louisa realised with relief that she could soon reassure him on that count. 'A coincidence, I assure you. It was nearly three years ago that—well, I am no longer in official mourning, Mr Redvers. I should hardly have gone out hunting today if I were, should I?'

'No. Of course not.' His relief brought none to Louisa.

'You think that this black gown is too severe?' She looked at him dubiously.

'Not at all! A misunderstanding on my part. Nothing more.' He looked genuinely pleased with himself now in a way that Louisa did not like.

'I suppose you left off mourning your late wife a long time ago, Geoffrey?'

'Good God, yes!' He gasped as though she had asked if he would shrug off a heavy coat on a hot day.

Louisa was not impressed. 'That is strange, considering the air of gloom and despondency hanging all about Holly House,' she mused. 'When I arrived at Holly House I considered that any bereavement must have been very recent.'

That brought him up short. 'I thought we had agreed that Stanton Malreward and King's Folly are to be treated as two different universes.'

'*You* agreed that yourself, as far as I recall.' Louisa looped the train of her gown over her wrist and prepared to go down the stairs. The movement silenced him, but he immediately offered his arm. After a moment's hesitation, Louisa accepted it, lightly resting her slender, pale hand on his wrist. Through the fabric of her evening glove she could feel the angular bone. Despite his easy throwing off of grief, Stephen Geoffrey Redvers Allington was evidently still not eating well enough.

'Would you care for a drink in the drawing room while we wait for dinner?' he enquired.

'I would rather get my apologies over and done with first,' Louisa said firmly, looking about for a door or corridor to the servants' wing. Geoffrey looked perplexed, but Louisa was determined.

'You were right, Geoffrey. It was unforgivable of me to make extra work for the servants. If you would escort me while I make amends…'

'This is rather irregular, isn't it?' He stopped, but he did not release Louisa's arm.

'That is as may be. But it would put my mind at rest and do something toward softening that poor boot boy's tasks, perhaps.'

Geoffrey inclined his head in agreement, then led her towards the kitchen. The boot boy was far too lowly to be presented to them in person, so Geoffrey negotiated with the butler. Louisa had a half crown in her evening bag which she had intended for the boy. Instead of giving it to him directly and making her apology in secret, everything had to go through the butler.

He was a tall, thin streak of a man in undertaker's black and spotless white gloves. Louisa could hardly bear to look at him as she muttered something about a practical joke, and how she was sorry that Mr Redvers' breeches had been made dirty unnecessarily. Then she had to hand the half crown to Geoffrey, who

gave it to the butler with a grave warning that there
were to be absolutely no deductions made, and that
he would be checking with the boy in the morning to
see that the full amount had been handed over.

'An empty threat,' he confided to Louisa as they
walked back towards the drawing room, 'but it might
just stop the old kite taking commission for handling
it.'

'I hope this means that we are even now, Mr
Redvers. I am sorry everyone laughed.'

'And you think that paying off the staff will stop
me having my revenge upon *you* in some devious and
terrible way?' Geoffrey started to chuckle as he saw
Charles Darblay-Barre leading Victoria Andrews towards the drawing room from another direction.
'Think again, Mrs Hesketh. Retribution may not have
been swift, but it will be devastating when it comes.
Rest assured of that!'

Louisa wondered what he could mean. She was beginning to wish that she had never played that stupid
joke on him now. Making her apology at third hand
to the butler had been bad enough. Now the joke was
going to rebound on her again in some dreadful way.

Her tension mounted as the dinner gong drew them
all to the dining room. Would Geoffrey's revenge
take the form of some stupid practical joke during
dinner? Louisa's nervousness was clear as she took
her place at the dinner table. She was almost relieved
to find herself seated between Mr Tonbridge and Mr
Brigstone, but that feeling soon passed. The men had
little conversation other than golf and racing—two
subjects about which Louisa knew little. She listened

and tried to learn, but it was difficult to make a contribution.

The bank manager's wife seemed to have become so used to being ignored over dinner that she never spoke, and rarely lifted a glance from her plate. A slight little woman dressed in shades of sludge, she was like a moth drawn along by the social aspirations of her husband. There was little to entertain Louisa at her end of the table.

Geoffrey, meanwhile, had the other end of the table in raptures. He was telling them about his day out with the hunt. And my misfortune, I suppose, Louisa thought glumly. Perhaps this was what his revenge would be—making her a laughing stock in front of all these guests. Then she reconsidered. Geoffrey liked to laugh, it was true, but his humour never seemed to be cruel. Louisa was never conscious of the guests looking in her direction as though she were the subject of their gossip.

Despite this, when Louisa retired to the drawing room with the other ladies she found herself the centre of attention. She recounted her experiences of the day's hunting with plenty of details about points and draws and riots, but without once mentioning Geoffrey Redvers. As no one used that particularly irritating simper in their voice which meant his name was about to enter the conversation, Louisa decided that Geoffrey could not have been eager to boast about escorting her to the second horse point.

This should have been a relief. Instead, Louisa began to wonder *why* Geoffrey had not wanted to make their brief association known. He had already made his thoughts on her stay at his home quite clear. He plainly could not stand her, and would be only too glad to lose her from his household.

No wonder he had kept their previous acquaintance a secret. He obviously wanted to keep Louisa at a distance, now and for ever. Strangely, Louisa felt a tiny pang at this realisation, and shivered.

Geoffrey's revenge could not have surfaced during dinner. Louisa sighed with relief as Mrs Tonbridge led the conversation onto less strenuous pursuits. She took coffee with the ladies and listened to the talk of dress patterns and the wilfulness of servants in polite silence. It all seemed a world away from the merry making-do at Stanton Malreward or the mucking in at Karasha.

When she had sat quietly for some time without making any further contribution to the conversation, Edna Tonbridge became quite concerned. 'The hunting was not too much for you, was it, dear? Geoffrey said that you seemed to get on rather well.'

Louisa was immediately curious. 'Is that all he said?' she asked, raising an eyebrow in surprise.

Mrs Tonbridge started to laugh. 'Ah—now I know why you have been so quiet! Our Geoffrey has finally got you under his spell. No wonder you are looking so beautiful this evening, Louisa! That light in your eyes has more to it than the reflected glory of your gown. Let me warn you, though, my dear—Geoffrey is a wonderful guest, but when it comes to the ladies that is all he ever is—a visitor rather than a lodger, if you take my meaning.' She leaned forward and patted Louisa's hand comfortingly. 'If I may be indiscreet and borrow a phrase from Mr Tonbridge, when it comes to the ladies, Geoffrey loves them, then leaves them!'

It was a fair warning, and one which Louisa took to heart. That could well be the way that Geoffrey Redvers would take his revenge—by trampling all over her feelings. Loving, then leaving. Louisa decided that she would have to be watchful and wary.

Eventually, the gentlemen straggled into the drawing room, still laughing at something that one of them had said. I suppose it must have been their dear Geoffrey, Louisa guessed as he came smiling into the room.

'We have been trying to decide who is to start off the entertainments this evening, ladies,' Mr Tonbridge announced through a haze of both high and expansive spirits. 'Geoffrey got the short straw. He is going to sing for us!' the host went on. 'The only problem is that he has wrenched his wrist on the hunting field and will not be able to accompany himself on the piano. We are therefore looking for a fair volunteer. Miss Andrews?'

Mr Tonbridge leaned towards the gentleman farmer's daughter, who shrank back with a demure giggle.

Louisa had been brought up in a place where real talent was so sparse that no one could afford false modesty, let alone the real sort. Every person did their piece when asked to contribute. It was all part of the Corinthian spirit, her father had repeated over the years as she had painfully learned to stifle her shy-

ness. If anyone held back, it was seen as denying their
fellows pleasure rather than as politeness.

So when she was asked in her turn by Mr
Tonbridge if she would play Louisa did her best to
hide her reluctance and agreed immediately, not realising that she should have simpered in the approved
fashion and given in only after entreaties and an excess of flattery from the gentlemen.

There was a tiny but audible gasp as she took her
place at the piano. Fortunately Louisa saw only envy
in the eyes of the ladies, but there was something
rather more sinister in the smiles of the gentlemen.
Real amusement, rather than straightforward pleasure
at the thought of some entertainment.

That was when the cost of what she had done began
to register with Louisa. If ever there was a time when
Geoffrey could exact revenge, then this was it. Louisa
was a competent drawing-room pianist, but not much
more than that.

Geoffrey Redvers will probably turn out to be a
student of La Scala and choose a piece black with
notes on purpose to show me up, Louisa thought
bleakly. She bristled with the imagined injustice of it
all, but there was nothing she could do.

Oh, well, she thought. I have put my head into this
musical noose of my own accord. I had better make
the best of it.

She rippled through several runs of notes, delight-
ing in the responsiveness of the keys beneath her fingers. The piano had a beautiful tone, and the sound
brought genuine smiles of pleasure to everyone's lips
as it danced around the room.

Geoffrey had been leafing through the Tonbridges'
small collection of sheet music but was evidently not
impressed by what he saw there. I don't suppose he
can find anything complicated enough for his revenge,
Louisa thought bitterly.

Then at last he leaned over her until he was close
enough to mutter almost directly into her ear.

'Are you able to extemporise, Mrs Hesketh?' he
hissed in enquiry, his brow furrowed as he tried to
decide which flowering of the Tonbridges' regrettable
taste would cause the least offence.

'Not to the extent of ''The Blue Danube'',' Louisa
murmured, trying to glance at the sheaf of music he
was shuffling with increasing desperation. Around
them the crowd was growing restless.

'Put up ''The Lost Chord''—I will try and find it
while you decide what delights you are going to lavish upon us.' Louisa gave him the smile of a co-
conspirator as he grimaced at the narrow alternatives
open to them.

'Very well.' He returned her smile, but at once
Louisa saw that something was very wrong. There
was a desperation in his eyes now that could not simply be explained by the dried tearstains on Mrs
Tonbridge's copy of 'The Children's Home'.

'You have to help me, Louisa! *I cannot read music
and I do not know any songs!*' he hissed desperately.

Louisa looked at him pointedly, expecting this to
be some attempt to get his own back for her earlier
treatment of him, but immediately realised that this
was no joke. He was deadly serious. She could see it

in the pale, tense expression on his face. He was willing her to do something.

Louisa was alarmed. This was serious. The gentlemen in the audience had started clearing their throats
and Edna Tonbridge was trying her best to stem a
trickle of conversation between the ladies. She
thought fast.

'Nonsense, Geoffrey! You cannot tell me that you
do not at least know the words and tune to ''Come
into the Garden, Maud''?' she whispered encourag-
ingly. 'Everyone knows that one.'

His alarm turned to naked horror.

'*What?* I could not possibly sing that! Not after
what Miss Marie Lloyd did to it!'

'Ah, but *you* will be singing it properly, won't
you?' Louisa said firmly, running through the first few
notes. 'What key would you like it in?'

He looked evasive. 'What do you suggest?'

Louisa struck a chord then placed her fingertips
lightly onto the keys in readiness.

'I suggest that you straighten up, take a deep breath
and start singing.'

Louisa brought her hands down onto the piano keys
again in an emphatic call to order, then launched into
the first few bars of the tune.

A ripple of delighted recognition ran through the
assembly, and with relief Louisa discovered that
Geoffrey had a good, light baritone voice which was
the equal of many drawing-room singers that she had
accompanied. He knew all the words, which was a
great advance on many so-called singers, and by a

combination of lucky chance and quick thinking on Louisa's part they managed to finish together.

Their audience loved it. To Louisa's delight they clapped appreciatively, but she felt a certain sympathy for her partner as several calls for an encore rose from the group. Quickly she rose from the piano stool and took his hand in the pretence of making mock bows to the assembly.

'What else do you know by heart, Geoffrey?'

'"The Ancient Mariner"?' he muttered glumly.

The audience would hardly be splitting their sides over that one, even if Louisa had been able to fit a tune to it.

'We will have to try something. Nobody else looks ready to leap up and do a turn. It is up to you again, Geoffrey.'

Louisa went back to the piano stool and pursed her lips in thought. She had not managed to get to the theatre in England yet, and did not know any modern songs—only popular ones that had survived the long journey to India. It was a puzzle.

'How about this?' In desperation she ran through a few bars of 'The Houses in Between' and was delighted to see relief flood into his face.

'I could not possibly sing that here, though. Could I?'

'It looks as though you will have to.' Louisa smiled, but this time it was an understanding gesture. 'No one else is looking eager to take the stage. You are the favourite, Geoffrey. You are the one they all want to hear!'

She turned to address the small company. They had

drawn up their chairs in a rough semicircle around the piano, and were now threatening to drown her accompaniment with their chatter.

'And now, ladies and gentlemen—' she announced, waiting for something like silence, 'For your delectation and delight, Mr Geoffrey Redvers will now reveal a talent for musical comedy that has remained a secret—until now. Maestro?'

She looked up at Geoffrey from beneath her lashes and treated him to a broad smile. It was meant as encouragement, but the look he gave her in return almost made her heart stop. It was a mix of admiration and delight, something like the look that Algy used to give her when she had been uncomplaining in the face of one of his wilder plant-hunting schemes. Yet there was also something else...

Louisa turned back to the piano keyboard quickly and launched into the well-remembered tune. With one song well received and a familiar one ahead, Geoffrey had relaxed and now started to enjoy himself. This showed in his performance, which the audience thought delightful. They laughed in all the right places, and clapped as vigorously as a genteel audience was allowed to do at the end.

There were many requests for more songs from the couple, but Louisa was not about to risk a slip. They had done well so far, she said, and it was always better to go out on a high note. Everyone laughed again at this little joke, much to her relief. Geoffrey was only too willing to stop singing. He pleaded a dry throat, and was immediately plied with champagne by his hosts.

Louisa accepted a glass too, and then a second. Champagne had been a very rare treat in India. Now Louisa was finding that she rather liked it. It slipped down so easily, and went very well with the tiny savouries of salmon and cheese that Mrs Tonbridge handed around so frequently. Louisa wanted to study everything, to gather as many ideas as she could to put into practice when she finally moved into Roseberry Hall.

'I must thank you, Mrs Hesketh.' A low voice broke into her thoughts of her new home, transporting her immediately back to the moment when Geoffrey had first smiled at her.

She turned to find him standing just behind her, holding out a glass of champagne. Louisa thought for a moment before accepting. Perhaps this was a peace offering, to make up for being short with her, for wanting her out of his house and out of his life. If so, she would have to accept. It was only common courtesy.

'Thank you,' Louisa said, graciously taking the glass from him, and accepting a tiny sip with a smile.

'I have no talent for music, you see,' Geoffrey went on evenly. 'An oversight in my education.'

'Nonsense. You have a very good voice, Geoffrey.'

'Any praise that I may have accepted was due in no small part to your accompaniment, Mrs Hesketh.'

He was smiling at her with that heart-stopping look again.

'Why don't you go on calling me Louisa?' Louisa heard someone say, then realised it was her own voice. For a few seconds they looked at each other, each waiting for the other to speak. Then an un-looked-for voice shattered the moment.

'Tell me, Geoffrey—' Edna Tonbridge interrupted them loudly '—are the Hackney Marshes worth a visit up to town? Sidney tells me next to nothing about the place. I should like to see the sights.'

'Oh, really, Edna!' Sidney Tonbridge said with an air of desperation, raising his eyebrows in mock horror. '"The Houses in Between" is a comic song!'

The laughter that followed swept Geoffrey away from Louisa and back into his circle of adoring friends. She watched as they engulfed him with their attention. It was impossible not to remember what it was like to have his luminous interest turned full on her, and now she found herself missing it.

'Actually, ladies and gentlemen,' Louisa heard Geoffrey say lazily to his adoring audience, 'I rather thought that my lovely accompanist and I might spend some time discussing what we might delight you with next. This will, of course, call for total concentration on our part...so if I might make use of your conservatory, Edna?'

There was a little gasp of delighted amusement as Geoffrey Redvers strolled away from the group that had encircled him and approached Louisa. She was mortified. The thought of his company had been bewitching, but not like this. Not so publicly.

'Oh...no, I do not think so, Mr Redvers,' Louisa said quickly, very conscious of the look that Victoria Andrews was giving her from the other side of the room.

'Oh, but *I* do, Mrs Hesketh!'

Geoffrey took her gloved hand, laying it against his arm and leading her towards the French doors. With the exception of Victoria Andrews and her father, the whole company smiled indulgently as they passed. Victoria Andrews and her father turned as they drew near and pointedly applied themselves to the buffet supper.

Louisa was greatly relieved that Geoffrey left the French doors open after they had walked out into the conservatory. At least that amount of propriety would be maintained.

The air in the conservatory was heavy and redolent with the scent of citrus plants. These were kept in fruit and flower all year round by the system of heating pipes, both extensive and expensive, which snaked around the conservatory walls.

'I wonder what Sam Higgins would make of all this?' Louisa leaned over to smell the waxy white perfection of a lemon blossom. Common decency meant that she had to be careful of being alone with any man, and Geoffrey Redvers in particular.

'Not as much as he would make of a gentleman's total lack of musical knowledge and skill,' Geoffrey said in a low voice, taking a seat on the edge of the ornamental pool in the centre of the conservatory. The goldfish rose and twisted in the oily water, expecting to be showered with food, but Geoffrey had not brought any snacks for them from the buffet table. The tiny candles set in their floating flower-shaped containers bobbed precariously as the fish flickered back and forth beneath them. Watching the fish and the lights idly, Geoffrey took a sip of champagne before continuing.

'Thank you again for helping me out earlier on.'

'It was nothing.' Louisa shrugged, trying to concentrate on the plants that thrust at her from all sides as she strolled around the paved path of the conservatory. It was like being back in the jungle. The jungle held predatory beasts which needed to be treated with great care, too. And respect, she added with a smile.

The smile faded as she caught sight of Geoffrey again. He was looking at her with undisguised relish. Suddenly the sensuous feel of her glittering black gown and the tightly sculpted look produced by her new corsets did not feel quite so exciting. Louisa now felt vulnerable, almost exposed beneath his scrutiny.

'I had to make my own way in the world from a very early age,' he said slowly, in a low voice that would not carry back into the drawing room. 'There was not time to learn anything but the basic social skills. Skill at music was an extravagance that I could not afford in terms of either time or money.'

'You acquitted yourself very well just now,' Louisa began, but he was evidently getting tired of flattery. He rose to his feet and walked over to where she was standing. There was no room to pass on the narrow conservatory path, and Louisa was in effect trapped in a corner.

'I always do,' he murmured, and the next moment Louisa found herself scooped up into his arms, being kissed as she had never been kissed before.

It felt like speeding down rapids, swinging out over

a precipice, a fast gallop over good country—everything terrifying, forbidden and exciting that Louisa had ever experienced, and much more besides. So exciting, in fact, that she had to put a stop to it.

Right now.

As soon as she could get her hand free to slap this Stephen Geoffrey Redvers Allington as he deserved... As soon as she could remember how to move...

The blow, when she finally managed to deliver it, stopped him immediately.

'Mr Redvers!' Louisa gasped as soon as she could catch her breath. 'How *dare* you?'

'Quite easily,' he said simply, a broad smile flashing in the light of the little candles floating in the pond. 'Almost as easily as you, by the feel of it.'

'Do you enjoy ruining a lady's reputation?' Louisa's face was burning, and not only with embarrassment. The truth had seldom hurt as much as it was stinging now.

'No,' he said, picking up the glass of champagne he had lodged beside the pool. He turned back towards the French doors. 'Oh, but how I do so *love* getting my own back on them!'

Louisa gasped. She had been tricked. That wretched, wretched man had bided his time, waited until she had no chance of escape and then pounced.

'You *cad!*' Louisa spat with all the fury that had been building up inside her.

'Not quite. At least *my* practical jokes are not carried out in the full view of all and sundry,' he finished, with a last glance at her over his shoulder before going back in to join the party.

Louisa squeezed her eyes tight shut. Still the image of his face shimmered in front of her. Still the feel of his lips, cool, firm and insistent upon her own, pressed against her like a physical presence. And almost over-whelming everything was the knowledge that she had been given almost as good as she had dealt out to him. She could not really make any complaint about her treatment. The warmth that was flooding through her veins left her in no doubt about that.

Geoffrey kept his distance for the rest of the eve-ning. When Edna Tonbridge started to cross-examine Louisa about their next entertainment, Geoffrey called across the room that they had both decided to claim fatigue.

Louisa busied herself with the light, inconsequen-tial chatter of her hostess, seasoned with comments by Charles Darblay-Barre and Mr and Mrs Brigstone. It was easy to ignore Geoffrey by simply choosing not to look in his direction.

Shutting out the light, teasing rise and fall of his voice was not so simple. It was difficult to stop her mind straying back to what had happened in the con-servatory, too. The only way Louisa managed to stop being overwhelmed by shame was by immersing her-self in the company of others.

The task grew ever more impossible as one by one the guests retired. Louisa went up to her room while there were still enough guests to dilute Geoffrey's presence. In the silent darkness of her room, watching the firelight throw a few last shadows across the ceiling above her bed, thoughts came only too easily. Sleep was a great deal more elusive.

It must be the effects of too much champagne, Louisa thought, crossly trying to deny the real reason for her sleeplessness. The fact that she had spent so much time that evening in close formation with Geoffrey Redvers could have nothing to do with it, of course.

The way that he had finally got his own back on her was having rather more of an effect. Louisa tried to convince herself that what she was feeling should be shame at the way she had been used. She lay staring into the darkness until a distant clock struck three, then could stand it no longer. Grabbing the Chinese silk wrap she kept for visiting, Louisa pulled on her new slippers, picked up and lit her bedside candle and stole out of her room.

The house was in darkness, and still with silence. It was so quiet that Louisa could hear the muffled call of an owl out in the gardens. She crept downstairs, desperate not to disturb anyone but in urgent need of a good book to read. The Tonbridges' library had been a delight when she had explored it the previous day. Delight was just what Louisa needed to take her mind off the events of that last evening. Something to read would help while away the hours until morning.

The library door was ajar, Louisa saw with relief. There would be no need to worry about the clank and clatter of opening it. She began to insinuate her way silently into the room, then stopped.

At the far side of the room, lit by the flickering

glow of a single candle and still in full evening dress, Geoffrey Redvers was busily tearing a book to pieces.

Although frozen for a second as wild thoughts of what had passed between them and what might yet be to come flashed through her mind, Louisa was unable to stop her voice bursting out into the silence.

'Geoffrey! What on *earth* are you doing?'

He jumped so violently that the candle saucer bounced and would have fallen had he not been quick enough to catch it.

'Louisa!' he gasped, moving quickly around the table to hide what he had been doing. 'I…I wanted to check on something that I saw earlier today…'

'Check on something? At this time of night? Come now—no honest person would be creeping around at this hour fully dressed!'

Louisa pulled her wrap tightly around herself as though it were protective armour. 'I heard tearing paper—have you been defacing Mr and Mrs Tonbridge's books?'

'No,' he snapped, clearly infuriated by her persistence.

'Then what *are* you doing, Geoffrey Redvers?' Louisa continued with unblinking insistence.

'Nothing that need concern you, Mrs Hesketh.' He was standing very straight and tall, like a soldier under interrogation. At least he has not tried to appeal to my better nature, Louisa thought, but not necessarily with much relief.

'And the paper tearing?' she persisted.

'An accident.'

Louisa saw him register the fact that confrontation

was obviously not going to stop her questions, so he tried a smile.

'Look—Louisa…that was an accident. It won't take me a minute to mix up a bit of paste and repair it. No one need know.' He finished with another smile, but his voice had a firm insistence about it that left Louisa in no doubt of what he really meant. 'It is the silliest thing…really it is. There is no need for anyone else to know about it.'

He was trying to be light-hearted about the matter, but Louisa heard the unspoken words: You will not be telling anyone, will you?

She regarded him, unblinking, for a long time. As she watched, his fingers danced back and forth along the edge of the table behind him, betraying an irritation that certainly was not visible in his face. Now that he had recovered from his initial shock at being disturbed, his expression had resumed the even, enigmatic charm of the dedicated philanderer.

'I came down to find myself a book to read,' Louisa said, then cursed herself silently. She did not need to explain her actions. *He* was the one who was supposed to be doing all the explaining!

'That will make a change from going equipped with an umbrella and a candle in the middle of the night!'

At least he had not mentioned the incident in the conservatory earlier that evening. Louisa would have died then and there if he had.

'I thought we had agreed to forget…' Louisa groped for the right way to put it and dropped her

voice to a hiss '…anything that might have been going on at Stanton Malreward!'

'I think that could probably be arranged,' he said
slowly as Louisa began a cautious circuit of the room,
hoping that there would be enough interesting books
on the side of the library furthest from him for her to
find something. '*If*, of course, you could manage to
forget anything that you may or may not have seen
here tonight…'

It was blackmail. Pure and simple. Louisa turned
to see his expression. What sort of a man was so
racked with guilt that he would use a lady's fear for
her good name as a lever to silence like this?

He was watching her intimately, like a cat watching
a mouse. Louisa returned his stare, determined not to
be cowed into submission. Finally she could stand it
no longer.

'I thought that you were going in search of paste
and paper?' Louisa said acidly as he continued to
watch her.

'Of course.' He gave a slight bow, but before he
moved Louisa looked away quickly to study the
books ranged on the shelves about the walls.

She might have managed to avoid his stare but
there was no mistaking the strange rustling sound she
heard before he left the room swiftly. It was the sound
of a newspaper being rolled up. Louisa looked around
just in time to see him disappear through the door—
carrying a rolled up newspaper, as she had suspected.

He must have been reading one of the bound volumes of old papers, and taken the damaged edition

off to mend elsewhere. Out of my sight, Louisa thought suspiciously.

Guided more by the thought of finding an interesting volume than by spying on Geoffrey, Louisa moved over to where he had been standing. The shelves were tightly packed with bound volumes of many different magazines and newspapers and Louisa ran a glance over them. Only one volume was missing, and this lay on the table where Geoffrey had been studying it. Louisa was more interested in finding a set of *Punch* magazines, which she always enjoyed, but as she drew near to the table saw that the open volume was a complete year of *The Bombay Times and Herald* for 1904. Out of curiosity, nothing more, she glanced at the open volume. The first edition was missing, the silk cord that would have threaded it into the volume lying empty. As Louisa moved past the table, a tiny fragment of paper fluttered out from somewhere and landed on the dark wood of the floor.

Instinctively, Louisa stooped and picked it up—and was alarmed to see that it was a scrap of newspaper. It must have been left behind when Geoffrey removed the edition from its folder.

Louisa's first instinct was to go after him with the missing scrap. Not even *he* would be able to make an invisible repair with a scrap missing.

Then she saw the two words printed on the scrap and stopped.

It was the name 'Stephen Allington'.

Chapter Seven

There could only be one explanation. The edition—
or *editions*, Louisa thought as she checked the date
on the first newspaper in the volume—of the newspaper that Geoffrey had taken away with him included something about Stephen Allington that he did
not want revealed.

That was why he had been poring over this collection of newspapers so intently. The fact that he had
jumped so violently when Louisa had interrupted him
only confirmed his guilt in her eyes. He must have
noticed the bound set of volumes at some time during
his stay and had guessed that they could incriminate
him. Charles might have made the mistake of calling
him Stephen Allington more than once. If his other
identity was ever revealed, and some other guest or
even his hosts had ever seen it in the newspaper and
remembered, his secret would be out.

Louisa quickly memorised the dates of the missing
newspapers, dropped the scrap of paper face down on
the table and blindly snatched up a book from the
nearest shelf. Tucking it under her arm, she shielded

her candle flame with her cupped palm and set off
hurriedly back to her bedroom.

She had a letter to write.

There would be no point in confronting Geoffrey
Redvers about her suspicions. He is bound to lie, she
thought bitterly. Such an accomplished charmer
would have a ready excuse for any tight corner. No,
Louisa decided, she would keep her own counsel and
make her own enquiries.

Notepaper, envelopes, pen and ink were provided
in the dressing table in her room, so it took Louisa
only a few moments to dash off a letter to the woman
who had been her next-door neighbour in Karasha. A
notorious gossip, Angela Histon would be able to find
out details of a shadowy past if anyone could. As a
bargaining counter, Louisa offered news of the
Tonbridges' party, their beautiful house and the delightful entertainments to which their guests had been
treated—although she left out any mention of her fall
whilst out hunting, or her suspect's shameless behaviour in the conservatory. It was one thing to be the
bearer of news, but quite another to be the subject of
it.

Buried amongst the news in her letter was an idle
request about Stephen Allington. Louisa mentioned
that he was her next-door neighbour in Stanton
Malreward, and that someone had remembered reading about him in the newspaper at the beginning of
'04—a thin excuse, but Louisa knew it would be
enough to put Angela on the trail. Once she had wind
of a good story Angela Histon had the tenacity of a
bloodhound.

Putting a letter with an Indian address into the post basket would be asking for trouble. Geoffrey would be unsettled already, and such a move might make him suspicious enough to intercept the letter.

Louisa pushed the blotting paper she had used into the bottom of her slumbering bedroom fire and put the letter into her handbag. Then she got back into bed. Sleep really would be impossible now. There was so much to think about.

She picked up the book that she had snatched from the library and looked at the title—*A History of the Buffs*. That looked boring enough to send anyone to sleep. Louisa could only hope that she would wake up at her usual time. She wanted to be up bright and early next morning to go and hunt for a post box to ensure it would be collected first thing on Monday. The sooner the letter to Angela Histon was on its way, the sooner Louisa would be able to discover the truth about this mysterious Mr Allington.

Despite all the disruption, Louisa did manage to wake up at seven o'clock as usual. She got up straight away and rang for the lady's maid. To stay in bed would have been to risk dropping off to sleep again. Louisa had never been one for lingering in bed when she was awake and a late start would annoy her all day. Besides, she had a special mission this morning.

Within two hours Louisa was walking back to King's Folly from the village, her letter to India safely delivered into the local post office. As she strolled along the curving drive towards the house, she had plenty of time to admire the surroundings. Although most of the trees had lost their leaves, there was still the beauty of their bare branches to admire. The rich, shimmering bark of cherry trees, the deep, spiralling fissures on the trunks of sweet chestnut trees and the tiny, tight catkins of the hazels meant that there was plenty to look at despite the dying of the year. There could be no spring without winter, and no winter without Christmas, Louisa comforted herself. The builder had assured her that Roseberry Hall would indeed have enough rooms ready to host a Christmas party, and she was already fizzing with excitement at the thought. Berries standing out as red as rubies against the stiff green satin of holly leaves in the winter wood fuelled her ambitions still further. A Christmas party for the friends she hoped to make in Stanton Malreward…and Stephen Allington?

Her thoughts plummeted back to the present as her glance caught sight of a familiar figure standing at one of the windows of King's Folly. Stephen Allington, or Geoffrey Redvers—whatever he liked to call himself—was standing four square in the window of one of the downstairs rooms. The breakfast room, Louisa decided after a quick calculation. It was just her luck that the late night, early morning and brisk walk had given her a needle-sharp appetite.

Instead of looking away, she returned Geoffrey's challenging stare as she continued up the steps of King's Folly and in through the front door.

'I wanted to thank you once again for coming to my rescue last night…Louisa,' he said as she walked into the breakfast room.

'Oh? And to which occasion do you refer, Mr

Redvers?' Louisa smiled at him sweetly, but the watchful expression in her eyes should have left him in no doubt that sweetness was not the only thing she had in mind. 'When I accompanied you at the piano? When you took advantage of me in the conservatory? Or when I was the unwitting accomplice to the go-ings-on in the library?'

He inhaled sharply, then gave an uncomfortable laugh. 'All three. I *know* that I can count on your discretion, Mrs Hesketh.'

There was an uncomfortable reminder in his tone of the threat of emotional blackmail hanging over her. Louisa watched him in mutinous silence. Dressed in a sober Sunday suit, he drew out his pocket watch to check the time—with an air of relief, Louisa thought.

'Well, the church service begins at eleven o'clock. I think I shall retire to the library again until it is time to leave.'

He pushed his watch back into his pocket, but did not seem in any hurry to actually go out of the room. Louisa turned to the breakfast table, biting back a comment about tearing up a few more volumes. After a few moments of uncomfortable hovering silence, Geoffrey spoke again.

'Well, then—that is about it. I shall doubtless see you about the place at some time, Louisa.'

'Doubtless.' Louisa no longer had the urge to re-buke him for the informality of using her Christian name. She did eventually look up, but by then it was too late. Geoffrey had left the room, leaving the door swinging closed in his wake.

* * *

Louisa was surprised to discover that not all the party attended church that morning. Mr Tonbridge and Mr Brigstone disappeared in the direction of the local golf links, while Mrs Tonbridge stayed at home to discuss fashion magazines with the bank manager's wife. Farmer Andrews drove his daughter and Louisa to church in his car, while the rest of the party walked. When they reached the church, several bicycles leaning against the wall of the churchyard seized Louisa's interest.

'Do you bicycle, Louisa?' Charles Darblay-Barre enquired as he offered her his arm for the walk up to the church.

'No, but I should like to try,' Louisa said, dutifully accepting his arm.

'You will have to employ Geoffrey to teach you. Need a lot of steadying, bicycles. Tricky things,' her escort murmured ruminatively, then brightened. 'I know—the headquarters of Darblay-Barre in London have recently invested in some bicycles for their junior clerks—and before you think we must be going soft in our collective old age it helps them to travel from home to work far more quickly than by public transport. They cannot then have the excuse that the cart horse dropped dead or the motor bus ran out of petrol! Why don't you pay a visit up to the warehouses, Louisa? I am sure that a bicycling lesson could be arranged!'

'It would have to be an occasion when Geoffrey was well out of the way,' Louisa said thoughtfully. 'I can just imagine what he thinks about lady bicyclists.

He would probably rather see a woman get the vote
than get on a bicycle.'

'Oh, I don't know about that,' Charles said airily.
'I think you underestimate our Geoffrey, my dear. All
he needs is a little more understanding in some areas.'

Louisa frowned in disapproval as Victoria Andrews
let out a gale of shrill laughter at one of Geoffrey's
comments as they all entered the church.

'*And* a little less encouragement in others!' Louisa
added firmly.

She needed no persuasion to arrange another trip
to London. Instead of travelling back to Stanton
Malreward on Monday morning as she had intended,
she used Roseberry Hall's newly installed telephone
equipment to send a message to the village that she
would be delayed. Then she accompanied Charles
Darblay-Barre up to the London warehouses of
Darblay-Barre Tea Traders. Geoffrey had a meeting
with his bank, which was on the other side of town,
so she was confident that her first bicycling lesson
would go unobserved.

The rich aroma of teas from across the world fra-
granced the wharf and added to Louisa's growing excitement. Charles showed her into the offices of
Darblay-Barre and introduced her to the warehouse
foreman, who was a small, precise man called Mr
Livesey. It was then that Louisa began to have doubts.
She had travelled all this way to a busy place of work
simply to satisfy her curiosity about bicycle riding.
Everything about Mr Livesey spoke of efficiency,
from his neatly clipped moustache to his immacu-

lately pressed working clothes. Several times during Charles's introduction, Mr Livesey's eyes flicked towards the window that looked out over the warehouse and its workers. He was keeping a discreet eye on the small army of graders, tasters and clerks who busied about in near silence, as though the high-roofed warehouse was almost a place of worship.

Louisa cringed as Charles explained why she was visiting. Mr Livesey never flinched. He accepted the request as though it were the most natural thing in the world for an otherwise respectable widow to go riding a bicycle around the yard of his warehouse.

'Wait, Charles…' Louisa said as they prepared to leave the office. 'Might I be shown around the warehouse first? I should love to see what goes on here!'

And it would soothe my conscience about disturbing Mr Livesey and his workers, Louisa thought to herself.

Both men were surprised and delighted that Louisa should show such an interest, and quickly took her to the tasting room. Here, chests of tea from Africa, India and China were sampled and blended together to make teas for any and every occasion. Fragrances of jasmine and lemon were added to make delicate drinks to appeal to the ladies. The ingredients and proportions of each new blend were meticulously recorded in a ledger.

This careful record-keeping served two purposes, Mr Livesey explained. The first reason was that the same mixtures had to be produced reliably every time, so that a customer who bought Darblay-Barre's 'Rose-scented China' could be sure of getting the same taste and quality with each packet they bought. The second reason for keeping detailed records was equally important. A column on the right-hand side of each ledger page recorded the quantity of each blend of tea that had been sold. Geoffrey kept a close eye on these figures, Charles told Louisa with pride. Any blend that did not sell in respectable amounts was quickly removed from the list to make room for one that might do better.

Then came the best part of the visit. Louisa watched as the Darblay-Barre tea-taster filled a row of tiny teapots with boiling water, allowed the tea in each to brew for a few minutes, then poured out a single cup from each pot. When there was a row of more than a dozen white china cups filled with hot tea in various shades from pale gold to deepest black, he started tasting each in turn. Every cup was numbered, and after quaffing a goodly mouthful and savouring it fully, the taster noted down his remarks.

'The tasters usually spit each sample out,' Charles confided to her gleefully. 'I am very glad to see that they have not done so today, in the presence of a lady!'

The tea-taster took a sip of water before continuing to the next sample. Louisa found the whole process very interesting. She would have loved to follow him down the line, trying each sample in turn. Only one thing stopped her from asking for a try. She could not possibly have considered spitting out each mouthful, and the thought of bouncing about on a bicycle immediately after drinking so much tea was not a happy one.

'Do you have a blend flavoured with citron?' she asked eventually, eager to try at least one type of the famous Darblay-Barre tea. 'It was always my favourite in India, but I have not tasted it since I left.'

'Doesn't Geoffrey keep any at home?' Charles enquired. Louisa looked at him quickly.

'At home?' she queried, trying to keep her face from betraying her surprise, but she had felt herself go pale.

'At Stanton Malreward,' Charles added with a slow smile.

Louisa did not know what to do. Fortunately Charles had turned away from her to ask Mr Livesey to fetch a sample of citron tea. Her confusion completely stopped her from thinking of anything sensible to say, but Charles calmed her jangled nerves with a quiet chuckle.

'It is quite all right, Louisa,' he said softly, out of the tea-taster's hearing. 'I know everything.'

'Then I am surprised that Geoffrey—or whatever he chooses to call himself—has not invited you to stay at Holly House, Charles. You two are obviously such close friends.'

'That is precisely why I turned down his invitation, Louisa. Geoffrey will be kept quite busy enough entertaining one house guest. My presence in the house would only be an imposition.'

That made Louisa feel ten times worse. Not only was she imposing on Geoffrey's hospitality, she was keeping his business partner away, too.

'I shall not be staying at Holly House for very much longer, Charles. You will be able to visit as and when you like without worrying about shredding poor Geoffrey's nerves and good manners too far,' she announced.

'Learn to ride a bicycle, and you will be able to ride over and visit Holly House whenever you like!' Charles said affably.

'Whenever *Geoffrey* likes, you mean. That might be rather infrequently,' Louisa replied as Mr Livesey returned with two neat packages wrapped up in thick green paper, and a small sample teapot. He handed the packages to Louisa before filling the teapot with boiling water. The packets of tea and the brewing blend in the teapot released a light, fruity fragrance into the tasting room which made Louisa's mouth water.

The tea was a delight. She savoured every sip from the small china sampling cup and smiled.

'Thank you very much for letting me visit your warehouse,' she said to Charles and Mr Livesey with real feeling.

'You may not be thanking us when you have had a taste of bicycling!' Charles laughed, leading her out of the office and over to a small door at the rear of the warehouse.

The door opened into a smoothly concreted alleyway between the sheer walls of two warehouses. Standing against the far wall was a brand-new bicycle. Louisa hurried forward, then remembered Charles's words about needing a lot of steadying.

'I think I shall have a little private practice on my own,' she said meaningfully, and was very glad when

Charles took up a position in a far corner of the empty alleyway.

The bicycle had an awkward crossbar, but Louisa was not a woman to be put off easily. As Charles politely averted his eyes she gathered up the thick skirt of her tweed costume and managed to get astride the machine.

Getting her balance was rather more difficult. She started off by supporting herself with one hand on the wall. Then, after a lot of practice and a considerable leap of faith, she managed to wobble away from the wall in an unsteady line. At first she had to put down either one foot or the other every few feet, but gradually her confidence grew. Before long she was gliding along between the high grey walls of the warehouse with something approaching confidence.

It was almost as exciting as horse-riding. Greatly daring, Louisa tried pedalling a little harder. Helped by a slight down-slope, she began to gather speed, whizzing along without a care in the world—until Geoffrey Redvers stepped out of a doorway straight in front of her.

Louisa's hands clamped convulsively on the brakes and she slithered to a halt in a confusion of spinning wheels and petticoats.

'*Good God alive!*' Geoffrey yelled, rushing to pick her up. 'You might have been killed!'

'Oh, hardly, Geoffrey!' Charles remonstrated gently, hurrying to see if Louisa had come to any harm. Her decision to dress in a thick skirt and boots had paid off, and apart from a few bumps and severely bruised pride she was unhurt.

'I am sure it is great fun. When one is used to it,' Louisa said, leaning the handlebars of the bicycle towards him. 'Perhaps you should try it, Geoffrey.'

He stepped back, aghast. 'Good Lord! I would never indulge in anything half so undignified!'

He looked genuinely shocked, prompting Charles to laugh out loud.

'Louisa is right, Geoffrey. You should try—fresh air and exercise is far better for a young man than spending hours crouched over ledgers!'

'I thought that you were miles away. At a meeting,' Louisa said crossly. It was exactly like Geoffrey Redvers to miss all the expert cycling she had managed yet arrive in time to tip her up.

'The meeting finished early,' he countered. 'I thought that you would have returned to Holly House by now, Louisa.'

'I was considering investing in one of these,' Louisa said, reasoning that he would understand an investment slant rather than idle chit-chat.

'Then I am surprised that you have not employed Willis and son of Dunston to advise you about it,' he said with a crooked smile at Charles. 'I thought you would not have made a move without consulting them.'

'I *am* capable of making my own decisions, you know!' Louisa bridled, but Geoffrey seemed oblivious to her annoyance.

'It is getting rather late—if you intend returning to Stanton Malreward today, Louisa, I think you should come with me now. The docks are not a pleasant place for a lady to linger, and the cab driver men-

tioned to me earlier that the station is already busy,'
he said firmly.

Although Louisa could hardly bear to impose on
him, she could not refuse his offer of company for
the trip. She was still unused to the hustle and bustle
of London, and the prospect of making her way across
town alone had already started to worry her.

As soon as Geoffrey had informed Charles of the
outcome of his meeting and passed on some paperwork, he escorted Louisa to a cab rank and from there
to the station.

The cab driver had been right. For some reason,
the train back to Gloucester was packed. Geoffrey
found Louisa a seat in a first-class carriage, then in-
structed her to wait for him at the other end. Louisa
was quite relieved that she would not have to relive
her embarrassing bicycling accident over and over
again during the journey to Gloucester. He would
have been bound to bring the matter up at least twice.

The company in her carriage was pleasant, if reserved, and the hours of the journey slid away quite
easily. By the time the train wheezed into Gloucester
station, it had grown quite dark.

Louisa had a short wait on the platform, and spent
the time studying the first-class carriages to see where
Geoffrey was. Several well-dressed ladies emerged
from one carriage, closely followed by her host.
Louisa wondered whether he had been playing the
part of the large-hearted socialite during the journey,
or the close-lipped country landowner.

The latter, she decided, as the ladies paid no attention to him whatsoever and went their separate ways without a backward glance.

'Williams will be waiting outside in the car.' He caught Louisa's elbow and steered her towards the exit. She barely had time to retrieve her ticket from inside her glove before she was being shepherded past the ticket inspector and out to the station approach.

'I trust you enjoyed your weekend away, Mrs Hesketh?' he said as Williams retrieved their hand luggage and loaded it into the car. The rest would follow on by carrier's cart.

'It was most enjoyable, thank you, Mr Redvers,' Louisa said carefully. 'With a few notable exceptions.'

'Nothing that need cast a shadow over your continuing stay at Holly House, I trust?'

'I feel that the time is fast approaching when I must move out. I cannot impose on your hospitality for much longer, Mr Redvers,' Louisa said, painfully aware that the chauffeur would be listening.

They travelled the few miles on to Holly House in silence. As they drew near to the house, Louisa was surprised and pleased to see that several rooms were lit, a soft golden glow shining from the windows on the ground floor. The place did not seem as intimidating now as the dark, lonely place it had been when Louisa first arrived.

'I gave orders that Grip should be tied up before our arrival, Mrs Hesketh. I know how you dislike his attentions,' Geoffrey said as the car slowed to a halt.

Louisa felt crushed again. Not only was her host unable to entertain his friend and business partner while she was living in his house, but now the poor man even had to ignore his dog.

'You really should not have bothered, Mr Redvers. It is my place as a guest to fit in with your ways,' Louisa said, wishing that she could be braver when it came to Grip the mastiff.

Sam Higgins burst out of the house to open the car door as soon as the vehicle stopped.

'Dinner will be served in an hour, Mr Redvers— madam. There has been a lot of post delivered while you were away, Mr Redvers,' he announced as he led the way into the house. Taking Louisa's coat, hat and gloves, he opened the door of the drawing room for her. 'I'll bring it all in to you with your tea, sir,' he said before disappearing towards the service corridor.

A bright fire was crackling in the grate and Louisa went over to warm her hands.

'It is nothing short of miraculous, the difference a good fire makes to this room,' her host said unexpectedly.

Louisa looked up at him in amazement. 'I would have thought that your first reaction would have been to douse the fire and save the coal, considering the poor little smoulder that I was greeted with on the first night that I arrived here!'

'Perhaps I have been economising on the wrong things,' he said, and his voice was low and thoughtful. He sounded almost sad. With a smile, Louisa tried to encourage him to say more, but Higgins had been too efficient. His knock at the door stopped Mr Redvers, as she must call him now, from unburdening himself any further. Instead he called Higgins into the room.

The servant brought a tray of tea and light refreshments, balancing a brimming post basket on top.

'Your tea, sir,' Higgins said as he put down the tray and lifted off the post basket. 'With all your post from the past four days—and a letter for you, Mrs Hesketh.'

Higgins poked the Holly House post basket at Louisa in a gesture that was a world away from the Tonbridges' icicle of a butler with his silver salver.

'A letter?' Louisa was intrigued. She picked up the letter addressed to her which was lying on the top of the pile. Its envelope was too clean and fresh to have travelled all the way from India, and she knew no one in England yet who might write to her. It would have been something very special indeed for Edna Tonbridge to write to her so soon after they had parted.

Higgins had forgotten the letter opener, but rather than send him off on a long search for it Louisa risked her fingernails and opened the letter herself.

It was from Mrs Willis, the wife of Henry Willis of Dunston and mother of young Henry, Louisa's financial advisor. Louisa's face broke into a smile of delight as she scanned the thick, deckle-edged notepaper.

'Oh, an invitation to dine tomorrow evening from Mrs Willis, Higgins! Would you tell Maggie to make sure that my grey silk gown will be ready, please?'

'And tell Williams to have the car ready, too,' Geoffrey added from behind his correspondence.

'Oh…I am not sure…' Louisa began. The car was

exciting, but an unknown quantity. She would feel safer in the pony and trap.

'Nonsense. We cannot have you turning up at a place like Brooklands in the trap.' Geoffrey lowered the letter he was studying a fraction, but glanced at her only briefly. 'After all, this is quite an occasion. The launch of Mrs Hesketh into Stanton Malreward society.'

He sounded quite serious, and for once Louisa agreed with him. An invitation to dine from one of the locals! Louisa could hardly believe her luck. In India, the rumours circulated that English society was notorious for its strict rules and regulations. A new-comer must always wait to be invited, and never push themselves forward by making the first move. It was said that some people waited for years, sometimes for ever, before being welcomed into a close-knit English community.

This early invitation was something of a coup and Louisa knew it. A lot would depend on the impression she made at this first soirée. She did not count her appointment with young Henry Willis as a social oc-casion as that would be strictly business, but to be invited to dinner in local society was a real advance.

'Yes.' She made up her mind suddenly and nodded to Higgins. 'Perhaps I shall cast caution to the wind after all! Tell Williams that he can look forward to a trip in the motor tomorrow evening.'

Higgins nodded and went off to deliver her mes-sages. Louisa could hardly wait for him to go before questioning her host.

'Did you receive an invitation too? What in

heaven's name will people say when we arrive together?'

'That will not be a problem. We shall not be arriving together.'

Louisa was aghast. 'You surely cannot be thinking of going in the pony and trap, Geoffrey?'

'I am not thinking of going at all. I am not invited. It seems as though the Willis family have their hooks in your money, and now intend reeling *you* in as well, Louisa.'

'What is that supposed to mean?'

With great care, Geoffrey folded the letter he was reading and laid it down on a nearby table before leaning forward to Louisa accusingly.

'You mean to say that there is nothing suspicious about the way that your business is taken on by young Willis, then you suddenly get an invitation to dine from his dear mama? Surely simple addition is not beyond you, Mrs Hesketh? One middle-class couple divided by a prodigal son plus one rich widow equals a secure future in any calculation.'

'That is a horribly cynical view!'

'But accurate, I think you will find.'

'The Willis family must have really upset you over something.' Louisa met his superior smile of amusement with scorn. 'And the feeling must be mutual, as they have not invited you to this bun fight of theirs.'

'If I know the Willises, buns are the very last thing you will find at their little soirée. It may interest you to know that I have worked very hard to fill the position of Stanton Malreward's curmudgeonly local hermit, Louisa. It is a task which has involved a lot of work, turning down every invitation I have ever received whilst living here. It has worked even better than I imagined. Now I never get invited anywhere by anyone, much less the Willis family. Does that satisfy you?'

He stood up, ready to leave the room, but Louisa had not finished with him.

'Perhaps you should start accepting invitations, Geoffrey.'

'And expose myself to all the falsity of life such as I see in London and the Home Counties? No, thank you,' he said with real feeling.

'Yet you enjoy all that socialising so much when you are there. And the fawning of all the ladies,' Louisa added craftily.

'All an act, I assure you. *This* is the real me,' he said with a crooked smile, but Louisa was neither convinced nor impressed.

'An act that you maintain very well.' Her voice was low and almost accusing.

'I have had a great deal of practice,' he murmured with equal firmness. 'Now, Louisa, if you would excuse me I have some letters to write before dinner. I shall leave you to your plans and preparations for the social event of the century.'

Louisa wished him goodbye, although that was the last thing she really meant. The nerve of the man! As though she had nothing better to do than primp and preen in front of a looking-glass.

Then a twinge of uncertainty suddenly unnerved her. Did his words mean that she would need a day to get ready? Resisting the temptation to run to the looking-glass to check her appearance, Louisa tried to calm herself by running through the things she had to do the following day. There was the task of checking the arrangements for the evening with Maggie, sorting out menus for the week's meals, an urgent acceptance to send to Mrs Willis and, most importantly and enjoyably of all, visiting Roseberry Hall.

After toiling doggedly through her chores the following morning, Louisa got a new lease of life when the time came to visit her new home. It was a mild, dry day so she decided to walk. The thought of a bicycle for the journey was not so pleasant this morning. Unless, of course, it was a bicycle with a very soft and comfortable saddle.

Approaching Roseberry Hall through the trees instead of up the formal drive lent even more excitement to her project, and took her mind off all her aches and pains.

The transformation that Roseberry Hall had undergone was almost incredible. Higgins had suggested a good journeyman gardener, who, together with some local boys, had trimmed back all the shrubs and tidied all the lawns. The drive had been freshly gravelled and rolled, and white-painted stones now edged the turning circle outside the front door. Those small details alone made Roseberry Hall look ten times better. Other than the urgent repair of leaks in the roof, work on the exterior of the house could wait until spring with its better weather and longer hours of daylight for working. Guests to the planned Christmas party would be arriving and leaving in darkness, so the appearance of the outside of the house was not as important as a welcoming and clean interior.

The smell of fresh paint and newly sawn wood excited Louisa still further. The entrance hall was wearing a cool undercoat of cream paint and it was now possible to see the detail on the carved coving that hemmed the high ceiling. Despite the clutter of lumpy sacks, tins and offcuts of wood, Louisa hugged herself at the thought that her guests would soon be enjoying these beautiful surroundings as much as she did.

The kitchen was almost finished. All that had to be done was to finally connect up the hot-water pipes to the boilers and add a last coat of paint to the walls and woodwork. Choosing the colour of this final coat was the province of the cook that Louisa would soon have to find. The room that was chill and silent at the moment would soon be busy with the clatter of cookery and the chatter of staff.

Louisa could hardly wait.

Her guests would have a warm welcome and the kitchens were ready to cater for them, so Louisa then went to check that they would have somewhere to relax. Curtains and carpet had arrived from London the day before and Louisa could not resist strolling across to admire them at close quarters. Even the sound of her shoes in the deserted room was exciting: the click of her heels on the polished wood of the floor, then the change as she stepped on to the muffling luxuriance of the Indian wool and cotton mix carpet. The carpet was warm with autumn tints of rich red and russet, while the curtains of figured damask picked up the colours and echoed them in heavy,

floor-length folds. Each was tied back with a cord of
rich old gold, while generous swags of matching material draped from the pelmets.

The only thing the room needed was furniture.
Louisa decided to travel to Cheltenham the following
day to do some more shopping. She would need new
furniture for her own bedroom and suite, too. The new
bathroom was already installed, and while Great-Aunt
Vernon's furniture was perfectly serviceable, 'perfectly serviceable' was not exactly what Louisa had
in mind for herself. Louisa wanted to be spoiled. She
wanted to indulge herself with light colours and new
things instead of dark, heavy Victorian furnishings.

It would soon be a home as well as a house, and
Louisa was eager to see it happen.

Dinner at the Willis home was everything that
Louisa had hoped it would be. There were dozens of
people at their fashionable villa in Cheltenham. She
made quite an entrance, arriving in her best grey silk
gown courtesy of Williams and the Redvers motor,
and everyone was very friendly. They were all interested to hear about her new house, and many offered
suggestions of reliable retailers for her next shopping
expedition.

Louisa was quick to take them up on their suggestions. She went back to Cheltenham the following day
in a spending mood. As she was discussing bedlinen
with an obsequious shop assistant, Mrs Dolly Digby,
one of the guests at the Willises' party, stopped to
talk and invited her to lunch. Louisa basked in increasing delight. Things were going wonderfully.

Even more wonderfully when Mrs Digby invited her to a tea party 'at home' the following day. This would give Louisa an opening when the time came to issue the invitations for her intended Christmas party. Her delight increased when she discovered that Mr and Mrs Digby had two eligible—although not very young—daughters. One eligible gentleman to balance up the numbers was easy: Charles Darblay-Barre.

Louisa lingered over the prospect of a second eligible gentleman. It should be Geoffrey Redvers, but that posed several problems. If he was as distant to the locals as he claimed, he was unlikely to want to attend. Then there was that suspicious business in the library at King's Folly. And that kiss in the conservatory...

Louisa shook herself abruptly. She had made up her mind. Geoffrey Redvers was far too dangerous to invite to her party, but to omit him would seem the height of bad manners. She would invite him all the same, but simply have to hope that he would display his hermit-like qualities and refuse the offer.

Together with the Tonbridges, the Willis family and several contacts she had made at their soirées, that brought Louisa's potential guest list to twenty-two. More than enough for a first attempt, she decided. There would be plenty more opportunities for grand gatherings when Roseberry Hall was completely finished.

She drew up the official guest list that evening, ready to send to the stationers the following day. The white paste-board invitations with the black curlicues and engraved italic script were coming a little bit closer to reality.

Geoffrey came in as she was blotting the covering letter.

'I am surprised that a lady such as yourself should consider writing letters from a gentleman's address.' He raised one eyebrow in quizzical amusement.

'But I have not used your address. I have used my own. Roseberry Hall.'

'Then you had better make sure that the postman does not send the replies straight down into a bucket of lime-wash, Louisa!'

He was laughing at her, but Louisa did not take any notice. Here in Holly House he was so totally different from the man who had seized her, and kissed her, and shamed her, that she did not care.

'Things are advancing at a considerable rate,' Louisa said with pride. 'In fact, I intend moving in before the end of the week.'

'So soon?' He looked thoughtful. 'I would have thought Roseberry Hall would have needed a great deal more time spent upon it. Once builders are in residence, calendars tend to get torn up.'

'Ah, but I took the precaution of telling them that I would withhold a premium for every day that the work took in excess of their original estimate. *And* I have ensured that the surveyor you suggested makes regular checks to confirm that the builders are not skimping on the work or cutting corners.'

'My word. You are a regular martinet, are you not?'

Louisa frowned. 'Goodness—I hope not. What the

men get up to is no concern of mine, as long as the work is finished on time and in good order. If it is, then they will be paid on time, with a little extra for their trouble—but they do not know that yet, so I would be grateful if you would not mention it outside of this room, Mr Redvers,' she added quickly.

'Geoffrey,' he reminded her.

'Geoffrey,' she conceded.

Louisa's reservations at this intimacy were tempered by the thought that she now wanted to gain his confidence. With luck, he would then feel able to refuse her party invitation. The thought of a guest who attended only through duty amid a flock of others who were there to enjoy themselves mightily was not a happy one.

'Very well, then, Geoffrey—you can be the first to know that I shall be holding a party at Roseberry Hall on the twenty-third of December.'

'With a guest list crammed with all your fine new friends, I suppose?'

Louisa took her time sealing the envelope, pressing down the creases very carefully. If she said yes, he might really refuse to come when she issued his invitation because it would be bringing London too close to home. When he was standing as close to her as he was at the moment, the thought of him refusing her invitation was difficult to enjoy.

In the end, Louisa made a murmuring noncommittal noise which could have meant anything. This double life of his must prove more of a problem than she imagined.

'I met old Henry Willis in Gloucester today,'

Geoffrey said airily. 'He is delighted at the swathes his son is cutting through the paperwork at his office. There is no job that the young chap will not take on around the office, apparently. It sounds as though he has got a finger in every pie, to me. And you know what they say about too many cooks…'

'Well, I have found the service that I have received from Willis and Son to be admirable,' Louisa countered, her eyes flashing amber in the soft gas light. 'Young Henry Willis is so eager to please. He has got a great many new ideas, and is always contacting me with some new scheme hot off the presses.'

'Investment is not always the place for new ideas, Louisa. The tried and trusted is generally the safer bet. Carriages over bicycles!' he added archly.

Louisa had a quick reply to that.

'Ah, but young Henry Willis always stresses that he has my very best interests at heart. He can never do enough for me.'

'I dare say,' Geoffrey drawled, picking up a newspaper from the sofa table. 'Just take care that you do not get carried away by a confident manner and promises of wealth and success. The scheme has not yet been invented that does not include *some* element of risk. If an investment sounds too good to be true, then the chances are that it *is* too good to be true!'

'Not the schemes that Henry Willis recommends. Take the one that he suggested to me only yesterday, after dinner.' Louisa looked at her host from under her lashes, accentuating the fact that she was willing to go out and socialise in the little world around Stanton Malreward, even if he was not. 'A young man of Mr Willis's acquaintance has recently been appointed manager of one of the coal mines in the Forest of Dean. He is full of good ideas, but needs capital to fuel his enterprise.'

'Would his name be Brotherton, by any chance?'

'Why, yes!' Louisa was delighted that Geoffrey's expression had softened from what she called his 'Holly House look' into interest. 'Do you know him?'

'Indeed I do. As almost every businessman and bank manager must, for miles around.' Geoffrey did not sound impressed. He was dismissive, almost amused, and Louisa resented his attitude.

'Everyone has to start somewhere,' Louisa said shortly. 'Even the famous Geoffrey Redvers. Where would you be today if everyone you had approached for a start in your business life had turned you down?'

'I know all about hard-luck stories,' Geoffrey countered. 'But I am afraid that there is only one rule in business investment. Sad though it is, it is based on solid fact. If a bank is not sufficiently impressed with the ideas that a potential customer is putting forward, then there is something wrong with that customer's idea. The potential customer should then either change themselves or change their ideas. That is the only way to succeed. Anyone who invests in lame-dog schemes that have not been able to obtain funding elsewhere deserves everything that they get. Or perhaps that should be they deserve to lose everything they gamble—because that is what it is. A gamble. And an unsecured one, at that.'

'Goodness! You really have taken against Mr Brotherton!' Louisa arched the fine line of her brows at him. 'Surely the fact that he comes highly recommended to me by young Henry Willis should count for something?'

'Not if they were at school together, or belong to the same gentleman's club, or are second cousins twice removed, it does not. Be careful, Louisa. Nepotism and intrigue are powerful antidotes to good business sense.'

Louisa turned away from him. The investment outlined for her by young Henry Willis had seemed so attractive over Darjeeling tea and macaroons in the comfort of his office. Now Geoffrey's stark black and white assessment had worried her.

Despite her concerns, Louisa was not about to give him the satisfaction of seeing how much his words had unsettled her. She decided that this was a matter to be sorted out directly between her and young Henry Willis.

Chapter Eight

Louisa arranged a meeting at the office of Willis and Son the next day. Yes, young Henry told her without embarrassment, he and Brotherton were good friends. They had been since school days. Young Henry could not bear to see his friend's ideas languishing for want of a few hundred pounds, and was determined to help him all he could.

Louisa thought that this honesty must count for something, and decided to give young Henry Willis the benefit of the doubt. A small investment in Mr Brotherton might be a wise move after all. She did, however, make one small concession to caution. As Geoffrey Redvers had opened her eyes to possible dangers, she had decided a change in the rate of her investment. In this small, secret compromise to Geoffrey's warning, Louisa decided that to put all her nest eggs in one basket might be a little risky. Five hundred pounds had been mentioned as the sum that this Mr Brotherton would need to finance the first part of his scheme: test-drilling a new site in a valley where the coal reserves had not yet been exploited.

Armed with good test results, Louisa reasoned, Mr Brotherton would be in a stronger position to approach professional bankers for a loan to finance the rest of his schemes.

Young Henry Willis was not happy. He tried to persuade Louisa to maintain all her investment with Brotherton, even to the extent of sending out for more tea and slices of cherry cake. Louisa remained immovable. She wanted the bulk of her money moved back to the dull but dependable stocks that her great-aunt had lived on. Only a total of five hundred was to be invested speculatively. Most of this was to be invested in Mr Brotherton's mining venture, while the rest would go into Darblay-Barre tea importers.

Let us see if investing in our mysterious Mr Redvers yields good results, Louisa thought with satisfaction. It would be amusing if the Darblay-Barre shares went down while Mr Brotherton prospered. Although not very amusing for my finances, Louisa thought with a wry smile.

The next few days flew by in a flurry of preparations. Louisa engaged a cook, Mrs Briggs, who immediately had the kitchens painted a bright primrose-yellow—'better for seeking out the dust, madam!' Louisa was told darkly.

Then the new cook spent a week closeted with cauldrons, steam and spirits like a storybook witch, making Christmas puddings, cakes and mincemeat until the smell of fresh paint lingering through Roseberry Hall was almost masked by the musk of spices.

The invitations arrived, were wondered at, then despatched in good time for the great day.

The first acceptances were waiting on the little yew wood side table when Louisa finally went to take possession of her new house on the twelfth of December. This prompted another shopping trip to town, to buy some little glass balls and frosted stars for the Christmas tree that was to be the centre-piece of the tessellated entrance hall.

The house was warm and welcoming now, but there was a large empty space in the hall left ready for a Christmas tree. Louisa never walked through the hall without stopping to look at the space and wonder.

Back in Karasha, the bungalow had never been decorated before Christmas Eve. It felt as though that would be the proper time to bring in the tree, but Louisa was tempted by the novelty of being her own mistress at last. She waited until she could bear it no longer, then sent the journeyman gardener and his boys out to cut down a tree from Badger's Spinney. It was brought into the house just before the party, which gave Louisa plenty of time to enjoy decorating it. There was holly and ivy in the woods around Roseberry Hall too, but with an eye to tradition Louisa decided that the evergreens could be brought in on Christmas Eve, and no earlier.

Over the next few days the remaining replies to her invitations arrived. Only one person declined, and that was Geoffrey Redvers.

Louisa was not surprised. In fact she was rather relieved. Even so, she was disturbed to find that his refusal had affected her. As the sociable Geoffrey

Redvers he certainly would have been a liability, but here on his home ground, Louisa felt, he would have been the restrained and dour version. He might even have been more interested in her new house than in the romantic possibilities of the lady guests. In this subdued manifestation he would have been the perfect guest, quiet yet attentive. He might possibly have lavished some of that restrained attention on her, as the hostess.

Louisa began to realise that it was this thought rather than the problem of being left with an extra lady guest on his refusal that was fuelling her concerns. With a shiver she tried to remember how alarmed she had been when he had frightened her out into the night at Holly House. It was difficult to imagine being frightened of him now. Especially after what had happened in the conservatory at King's Folly…and the time when she had almost run him over on the Darblay-Barre company bicycle. Louisa giggled, quick to put aside those more disturbing thoughts.

Although her mind should have been filled with menus and table decorations, one corner of it still kept straying back to toy with the thought of Geoffrey Redvers. Surely it was not fair that he would ignite a party at the Tonbridges', yet could not be bothered to do the same for her party. This irked her for a long time, but the longer it rankled away at the back of her mind, the more she wondered whether there might be a good reason behind his refusal.

While he had almost convinced her that there was nothing sinister behind his dual personalities, Louisa began to look at it from his point of view. If he appeared at the party, the two halves of his life, town and country, would be meeting in one place. The fear of exposure would not make it an enjoyable occasion for him, or for her guests. Perhaps Geoffrey Redvers did have a good point in declining her invitation.

That might have been the case—but it did not stop Louisa wondering.

At long last the day of the party finally arrived. Louisa spent most of the day checking and re-checking the arrangements, the food and the table decorations. The hours crawled by, but as soon as Charles arrived to 'try out the catering in advance', as he called it, time began to evaporate. Very soon Roseberry Hall was ringing with the sound of chatter and laughter, and the expensive perfumes of the lady guests were mingling with the rich resinous scent of the glittering Christmas tree.

Louisa was having so much fun that she barely had time to think. Charles was enjoying himself mightily with the Digby sisters, and young Henry Willis was joining in the fun with a will. When Louisa did allow herself a few moments at the edge of the throng to reflect, it was to smile contentedly. Things were going very well. At the beginning of the evening, she had been so nervous that she had not been able to hold either a glass or a plate because her hands had been trembling so much. Now that the party had been going for nearly two hours, she had relaxed sufficiently to accept a glass of champagne from Elliot, her new butler. No one was looking lost or lonely, everyone was smiling and the hum of contented conversation was interspersed with occasional laughter.

Louisa was almost going to congratulate herself when Elliot insinuated his way through the throng. Louisa's heart plummeted. Something must have gone wrong. It must be an emergency in the kitchen—

'If I may have a word, Mrs Hesketh?'

Louisa excused herself from the silky flattery of young Henry Willis and followed Elliot out into the hall.

'Mr Redvers has arrived, madam. From Holly House,' the butler added, as though any other Mr Redvers might come calling.

Louisa's heart bounced back up, and without realising it she smiled.

'Very good, Elliot.' Louisa dismissed him kindly, then set off towards the small room that she would have liked to call the library—if there had been time to collect any books together yet. 'Bring us some refreshments, would you, Elliot?' she called over her shoulder.

The butler cleared his throat.

'Actually, madam, Mr Redvers is…' he cleared his throat again, in what passed for agitation in butlers '…*in the kitchen*!' His voice dropped with the horror of it.

Louisa's eyes widened. This was serious. There really *had* been a disaster in the kitchen—although not of the type that she had most dreaded. It was serious, all the same. What sort of state would the place be in?

Louisa dashed down to the kitchens, fearing the worst.

She need not have worried. All the washing-up had been spirited away to the scullery, and nothing but spare trays of party food was visible on the kitchen tables.

Geoffrey Redvers was standing at the far side of the room, uncomfortable in a heavy dark coat and hat. In the days since she had moved out of Holly House, Louisa had only seen brief glimpses of him as he'd walked with Grip in the grounds of his house or was driven down the lane in his car. He was even taller than she recalled, but his looks were exactly as she always remembered them.

'Mr Redvers?' Coolly formal in front of the staff, Louisa walked up to him, hand outstretched.

'Mrs Hesketh.' He replied in kind, shaking her hand gravely. He was clearly uncomfortable at the sight of Mrs Briggs stirring hot punch at the range and Elliot hovering in the kitchen corridor beyond.

'Why don't you come in to the party, Mr Redvers? Everyone would be delighted to see you.'

'Indeed. That is exactly why this sort of party is not my idea of entertainment, Mrs Hesketh. I merely came to give my good wishes for the evening,' he said sharply.

Louisa looked at him questioningly. It was a very strange thing to do—travel to a party that you had no intention of attending to say that you would not be coming. Especially as he had already declined by letter.

'At least agree to stay for some punch, Mr Redvers?'

He was wavering, and Louisa knew it. Everyone was having such a good time at the party that she could not bear to think of anyone being sent away unsatisfied—least of all Geoffrey Redvers. He had been very good to her in the past, giving her a place to stay when she'd had nowhere.

And he was, after all, *very* good-looking.

Mrs Briggs came to the rescue. Flourishing a tea towel, she opened an oven door and freed a gale of savoury scent which rushed into the room. It was irresistible, and Louisa played on the fact.

'Would you prefer some hot cheese pastries?' she asked.

His indecision broadened into a smile which Louisa was quick to encourage. 'As Mr Redvers does not care for company, we will take our refreshments in the library as suggested, Elliot. Everyone else is in the drawing room, Mr Redvers,' Louisa added as she led the way through the kitchen and down the service corridor.

That was when the trouble began. As Louisa and Geoffrey crossed the hall, young Henry Willis burst out of the drawing room, opening the door on the happy murmur of conversation within.

'Louisa! Come on—I am quite lost without you to talk to—' He stopped, and his voice abruptly became sullen. 'Oh...hello, Redvers. Fancy seeing you here,' he finished suspiciously.

'I came to see whether you had managed to lose

all Mrs Hesketh's money yet,' Geoffrey said laconically.

Louisa laughed, expecting that it had been intended as a joke, but neither of the men looked in the mood to be amused. Geoffrey had stopped dead to freeze Willis with a stare. For his part, young Henry Willis was looking decidedly uneasy.

'Keep the party going, Henry,' Louisa said evenly, desperate to salvage the situation. 'Mr Redvers has merely called in as he was passing.' She started off towards the library again, hoping that young Henry Willis would at least do as she said. It would be impossible to expect Geoffrey to obey orders. He was a law unto himself.

A stiff silence crackled behind her, but she refused to look back. Opening the library door, she walked straight in, and only turned when she had reached the far side of the circular table in the centre of the room.

'I do not expect my guests to be insulted when they are here to enjoy themselves,' she said furiously as Geoffrey stalked into the room and closed the door firmly behind him.

'You will notice that he never denied the charge.' Geoffrey threw his hat onto the table and dug his hand into the pocket of his coat. 'This is the real reason why I came,' he muttered, drawing a small parcel from his pocket and holding it out to Louisa.

She stared at it dumbly for several moments.

'Oh…Geoffrey…' Words struggled out with difficulty. He had brought her a Christmas present, and all she had done so far was rebuke him. 'I—I do not know what to say…'

' "Thank you" usually suffices.'

'Oh…yes, of course.' Louisa coloured as she remembered her manners. 'Thank you, Geoffrey. I was
a little taken aback as I had not expected anything at
all, of course.'

'And I do *not* expect anything in return,' he said
firmly, prompting another small panic from Louisa.

'Oh…but there is something for you! Not so much
a Christmas present, more a token of my thanks for
your kindness in letting me stay in your house,'
Louisa said, flustered. 'It is out in the coach house.
Unfortunately Sami will not have had time to wrap
it—'

'Open your own present,' he commanded, and
Louisa obeyed.

It was a slim volume of Thomas Hardy's poetry.
Louisa's eyes opened wide at the quality of the paper
and the sweet smell of the fine binding.

'A contribution towards your new library,' he said
quietly, looking around the empty shelves lining the
library walls from floor to ceiling. The rich dark wood
had been polished to a deep glow that came alive in
the soft gas light.

'Thank you,' Louisa said softly. Looking up at him,
she suddenly caught her breath. 'I—I am quite lost
for words…'

'Then do not try to say anything.'

He crossed the distance between them in two
strides, caught her up in his arms and silenced her
with a kiss. It was so sudden that at first Louisa was
too shocked to do anything. Then her senses were
filled with the warmth, fragrance and masculinity of

him, and she felt the warm lassitude start to run like
honey through her veins again. This is shocking, she
told herself. Almost against her will her taut muscles
relaxed against the reassuring strength of his body.

He has caught me up a second time… The thought
drifted through her mind. This is *unforgivable*…

Some moments later he drew away, but reluctantly.
'I am sorry, Louisa. It is simply that after that brief
liaison in the conservatory at the Tonbridges' I have
been not been able to think of anything but you.'

'Well!' Louisa managed to catch her breath but her
senses were still reeling. 'You have certainly never
given any indication of it! You were so quiet on the
journey back to Holly House—and over the days I
spent there until I moved in here—and there has been
so little sign of you since then…'

'It has been unforgivable of me,' he breathed, but
he did not let her go. There was a certain look in his
eyes that was playing upon Louisa's nerves like a
limpid summer breeze. She had been out doe-hacking
with Algernon plenty of times before their marriage,
and she knew exactly what that sort of look meant.
The next few moments would surely need all her
moral courage at a time when she felt totally drained
and unable to resist.

'Yes. Unforgivable…my thoughts entirely, Mr
Redvers,' Louisa said in a voice that was supposed to
be sharp with reproach but was actually husky with
some emotion that she dared not name. His hands
whispered over the silk of her bodice as he released
her, slowly, and took a step back.

'You puzzle me,' he said with an ironic smile. 'I

would have expected another smart slap from you for taking such a liberty. If I had known the reception such an action might receive, I would have tried my luck sooner!'

It was a rare flash of the self-confident Geoffrey trying to shine through. If any other man had ever dared to say such a thing to her—if any other man had dared to *do* such a thing—Louisa would have been stung into action. Instead she simply watched him with her amber eyes full of questions. His voice had been soft, with none of the humour with which Geoffrey always filled his words. She was learning enough about this Stephen Geoffrey Redvers Allington now to know that the devil-may-care attitude of his other, sociable self was simply a front.

If she now read him correctly, the real man—the thinking, feeling being behind the fine words—was mortified. He had overstepped the bounds of decent behaviour.

Louisa did not know whether or not to trust her intuition. It might be an elaborate trap to lure her into lowering her guard. If it was, and she told him to forget the incident, it would give him unspoken licence to take up where he had left off on some future occasion.

On the other hand, if his feelings were genuine and she made a fuss, it would solve nothing and prevent them ever becoming close again.

With some alarm Louisa realised that she did not want to put him off—not entirely. With a faint feeling of resentment she realised that she had slipped, quite innocently, under his spell. He might have bewitched

all those society women with the shallow charm of
the sociable Mr Geoffrey Redvers, but it was something else entirely that had beguiled Louisa. Beneath
the illusion of the efficient businessman who treated
women as bloodlessly as he might deal with business
clients—so far, but no further—there was a thinking,
feeling man.

'I think perhaps you should go now, Mr Redvers,'
Louisa said in a low voice.

Although the words were a formal dismissal, her
expression was soft and her eyes dark pools in the
lamplight.

'Unless, of course, you wish to come and join the
party?' she added. 'You would be more than welcome.'

'No...' He backed away with a rueful smile, the
mask of assurance dropping momentarily. 'No. To act
as I would wish to this evening would cause confusion in the other guests, don't you think?' The fine
dark line of his brows lifted with wry amusement.

Both realised that this was an easy way out of a
difficult situation with dignity.

'Of course.' Louisa inclined her head graciously. 'I
shall have Sami deliver your present to Holly House
in the morning.'

'Thank you.' He was equally cool, but his eyes
now had a brightness that Louisa had not noticed before. He strolled slowly towards the door.

If Louisa had been uncharitable she might have
thought he was giving her enough time to call him
back, but she was not feeling uncharitable. She was
too busy revelling in the warm glow that was still

circulating through her body. She could watch him go, almost certain now that he would return. And not as the sweet-talking but shallow Geoffrey Redvers who inhabited the drawing rooms of his fashionable friends. If Louisa was to allow him into her life it would be as the reserved host who had let her share his home.

The thought was comforting in a way that Louisa had not experienced for a long time—not since Algy, she remembered with a pang.

Opening the door of the library, Geoffrey turned to smile at Louisa once more. 'I think it best that I do not stay for refreshments. I should not want to delay you in returning to your party, Mrs Hesketh,' he said softly.

Louisa smiled, and followed him to the door. He was slow to remove his hand from the door handle as he held it open for her, and as he withdrew his arm it brushed lightly against her gown. Louisa stopped, and for a second they were trapped in a look that needed no explanation. Then suddenly the squeak of Elliot's boots on the tiled floor of the service corridor made them spring apart.

'I shall not be needing refreshments in the library now, Elliot. Give them to Sami to take into the drawing room, then show Mr Redvers to the door, would you? And please make sure that the consignment in the stable block is sent over to Holly House first thing in the morning.'

'Of course, madam.' The picture of restrained good manners, Elliot bowed first to Louisa then to Geoffrey before gliding over to the front door.

Geoffrey raised his eyebrows in amusement. 'Not back out through the kitchens?'

'No, sir,' the butler intoned gravely. 'You will find your dog tied to the boot-scraper outside the front doors.'

Louisa had to smile at that. Elliot's efficiency even extended to Grip. He had not wanted the dog cluttering up the back kitchen stairs, even if it did belong to a wealthy neighbour.

Not for the first time, Louisa thanked goodness that she had been lucky enough to find good staff. And good neighbours, she added silently to herself.

Geoffrey returned her smile knowingly as he left.

The party continued until well past midnight. Everyone congratulated Louisa time and again on her new house, her staff and her excellent entertainment. Louisa smiled and thanked them all generously, but it was not only their compliments that had put an extra glow in her complexion and a lively sparkle into her eyes.

Louisa was in love, but she was desperately trying not to admit it to herself.

Louisa did not see Geoffrey the following day. She told herself that this was not really surprising. It was Christmas Eve after all, and he must have preparations of his own to make for the great day.

On Christmas morning she was surprised and rather shocked to see that he did not attend the parish church service in Dunston. As Sami drove her home, Louisa looked long and hard at the place where her carriage had originally come to rest in the ditch those few short weeks ago. That all seemed like a dream now. Louisa began to wonder whether she had dreamed the whole episode of their kiss in the library on the night of the party. They were obviously still as remote from each other as ever.

One thing was certain. No matter how stealthily the feeling that she was in love with him tried to creep up on her, Louisa could do nothing. She dared not risk visiting Holly House, not even with Christmas wishes on Christmas Day. A lady must always wait for the gentleman to make the first, and every, move.

St Stephen's day came and went, as quietly as Christmas had done. The first delivery of thank-you letters soon arrived, and Louisa tried to put aside her own concerns by working through them one by one. The task took nearly a whole morning. There were good wishes to send out for the coming new year, too. And still, more enjoyably, there were invitations to be accepted.

As Louisa reached the final letter in the bottom of the post basket, she stopped in surprise. Picking the letter up, she examined it closely. The handwriting belonged to old Henry Willis, the senior partner of Willis and Son, financial advisors.

She had already dealt with a long and flowery letter written by his son. This second letter had probably been written at the insistence of Mrs Willis, Louisa guessed, after the interest she had paid to Louisa's background and situation on the evening of the party. Young Henry's letter had already thanked her for the splendid time that he and his parents had enjoyed at her party. Louisa wondered what on earth the father was doing sending a duplicate thank-you note. Perhaps he does not trust his son to do the job properly, she thought with a smile, remembering Geoffrey's dire warnings against Willis in general and his son in particular.

Always a martyr to curiosity, Louisa tore the letter open hurriedly. The contents of the letter were even more puzzling than she had imagined. Mr Willis senior was summoning her urgently to his office. The matter was so grave that, should she not be able to attend during office hours, she should go straight to see Mr Willis at his house, Brooklands, without delay.

The morning room seemed to have suddenly gone very cold. Louisa reread the letter, terrified that she knew exactly what had happened. Geoffrey must have been right all along. She had been foolish to let young Henry Willis handle her money, and now the investment in his friend Brotherton had gone wrong. She thought of the sum: three hundred and fifty pounds. That amount would have covered quite a few bills for several years. To have lost all that money would be appalling. Thank goodness she had seen sense enough to limit her investment in this Mr Brotherton and his mine.

She put down the letter and stared out through the window across the frosty parkland of Roseberry Hall. Losing all that money was too horrible to contemplate, but it was a stark lesson. She had been too proud and wilful to take Geoffrey's advice, and now she must suffer for it.

At least it is only money, Louisa thought, trying to

put a brave face on things. And not as much money as it might have been. I was foolish, but at least I still have my house, my health, and my happiness.

By four o'clock that afternoon Louisa was left with only her health, and it felt as though that was failing fast. When she had arrived at his office, Mr Willis senior had immediately broken off an important meeting. Louisa had quickly realised then that things were even worse than she had feared.

Young Henry Willis had not obeyed her instructions to restrict her speculative investments to five hundred pounds. He had not even divided the risk. He had invested all of her money—every penny—in his friend Brotherton. This Brotherton had repaid his friend's misguided trust by alienating all the workers in the existing mine that he had bought.

The miners of the forest might know little about book learning and balance sheets, but they knew everything there was to know about mining coal. Brotherton's grand ideas about sinking new shafts had found plenty of new coal deposits within days, but the test digging had cost a fortune as the new seam was in the side of a steep valley. The position of the seam would make the extraction of coal far too expensive. Manpower and money had been wasted for weeks and investments like Louisa's had been absorbed like rainwater through porous rock.

It was all gone. Louisa was, to all intents and purposes, ruined.

Louisa and many others who had trusted young Henry Willis with their money had seen it all disappear. The culprit had tried to cover up his mistake by issuing false reports to shareholders and investors, hoping that some scheme would miraculously appear and rescue him, but the end was inevitable. Checking idly through some files, old Mr Willis had come to a discrepancy. When he'd followed it through, more and more tangles in the web of deceit had come to light and young Henry had been forced to confess. It had been left to his father to take over the cases and try to limit the damage.

It was impossible in the case of Louisa's investment. All her money had gone. As if that was not bad enough, the next post that day brought the final bills for the work on Roseberry Hall. Without the hope of any dividends or interest payments that should have been due the same week, Louisa did not have enough ready cash to settle them. She had confidently expected that her investment income would amply cover her expenses.

She had been wrong.

Louisa had felt too stunned to accept old Mr Willis's apologetic invitation to dine. Instead she had thanked him with a glacial control, and swept from his office as though she were off to plan vengeance.

In reality she had no idea what to do. Her life in England was over, before it had properly started.

Louisa travelled back to Stanton Malreward in a state of shock. Only when the carriage stopped so that Sami could get down and open the gates of Roseberry Hall did she manage to rouse herself.

'Wait, Sami. I shall walk from here,' she said absently, stepping down from the carriage before he had a chance to offer his hand in assistance.

Louisa needed time to think, away from the clattering rumble of the carriage. Her legs would barely support her, let alone make the journey all the way up to the house. All she could do at first was to stand dumbly at the gates, looking across the green grassy grounds towards the house for which she had no immediate means of paying.

Yet she could not even afford paralysis. Sami, the groom, must not suspect that anything was wrong. If he did, the news that something was up would spread like wildfire through the servants' hall.

Forcing herself to act normally, Louisa strolled into the shelter of the big beech trees that hemmed the boundary between Roseberry land and the grounds of Holly House. She stumbled along, barely seeing where she was going. She had harboured so many plans...so many ideas for Roseberry Hall. Now she would not even be here to see the primroses flowering in the spring.

She had seen similar things happen back in India. Once tradesmen realised that they would not be getting paid, credit would evaporate. Local tradesmen—and here in England that would mean the butcher, the fishmonger, the chandlers and all—would be quick to scent trouble and credit would be refused. All Louisa's staff would have to go, and then it would be her house, and then—

Louisa screamed as a huge shape launched itself at her. Catching her foot in a mossy beech bole, she

tripped, to be engulfed by Grip with a joyful, slob-
bering greeting.

'Louisa!' Geoffrey pulled the dog away and lifted
her gently to her feet. 'Oh, what a calamity! Grip saw
you before I did—he would never normally jump over
the dividing wall like that. Oh, my goodness! Has he
hurt you?'

Tears had been welling in Louisa's eyes for a long
time and with the fright that Grip had given her she
could no longer hold them back. Now they began to
trickle soundlessly down her cheeks as the shock of
her ruin and now this ambush undermined her resolve.

'I—I...' she began, but Geoffrey had already taken
command of the situation. Pulling an immaculately
pressed white handkerchief from his pocket, he flourished it at her and took a firm grip on her elbow.

'You shall come back to Holly House with me.
Higgins can tell your staff that you will be staying
for tea—and I shall hear *no arguments*,' he said firmly
as Louisa opened her mouth to protest.

He steered her towards the lane, then returned to
send Grip back home, over the wall.

While he was away Louisa managed to dry her
tears and find her voice.

'Oh...Geoffrey...I am in the most *dreadful* trouble...' she began, but had to stop as tears threatened
to choke her again.

'Nothing that cannot be put right, I am sure,' he
said with an even tone of authority. As they reached
the lane his supporting hand released her in case any-

one should see, but not before giving her elbow a reassuring squeeze.

He walked quickly, but reduced his normally long stride so that Louisa could keep up with him easily. They did not speak on the short walk to Holly House. The great unspoken agreement of the Empire was that no emotion could possibly be displayed in the open air. One look at Louisa's face had told Geoffrey that any word, any gesture on his part might be disastrous. For her part, Louisa was relieved at the uncomfortable, expectant silence that hung heavily between them. She knew that she could not risk speaking without breaking down again. If only she could hold on until they reached the privacy of the house…

As they neared the final bend in the drive towards Holly House, Geoffrey took her arm again. 'Lean on me,' he ordered in a low voice that Louisa no longer had the will to disobey.

As they rounded the shrubbery he called out to Higgins in a loud voice. Higgins came running, his usual smile disappearing the moment he saw Louisa's expression.

'Grip has frightened Mrs Hesketh, Sam,' Geoffrey announced, hurrying her into the house. 'Get over to Roseberry Hall and tell them that the lady will be staying here until she has recovered, will you? And tell Maggie to bring some hot sweet tea and anything else she might have for a case of shock.'

Higgins bounded off to obey, and Geoffrey led Louisa into the drawing room. When the heavy door closed with a reassuring thud, Louisa turned to him in an agony of released emotion.

'Oh, Mr Redvers! What in the world am I going to do?'

'You must begin by calling me Geoffrey again, if things are as bad as all that,' he said, crossing to a small sofa table where a drinks tray stood. Pouring out a large measure of brandy into a cut-glass tumbler, he pushed it into her hands.

Louisa's hands were shaking so much that she could not hold the glass, and he had to take it back and put it down on the table for her.

'Geoffrey...I have lost *everything*...'

'Willis?' he murmured through taut lips.

Louisa nodded, twisting his handkerchief into a knot of damp confusion.

'Oh, if *only* I had listened to you right at the beginning, Geoffrey! Then I would still have Roseberry Hall, and the staff would not be put under the threat of all this strain, and—'

'Shh.'

Geoffrey took her in his arms and looked down deep into her eyes. Louisa melted against him, exhausted with worry and the feeling that this sudden closeness was the most natural thing in the world. He drew her closer still and kissed the top of her head with a touch so light that Louisa barely felt it. He was holding her as though she were as delicate as fine bone china: gently, yet with a sure firmness of touch that could not be denied.

'Everything will be all right,' he murmured into the soft luxuriance of her hair.

Louisa was totally reassured, but not about the business of Roseberry Hall. She laid her cheek against the warm, safe expanse of his broad chest and drank in the intoxicating fragrance of him. She knew that it was only a matter of time before he lifted her face for a kiss, and that she would have to deny him; but until then she wanted to savour every single second of this special, nurturing closeness. The strong, steady rhythm of his heart lulled her into such a sense of security that when he next spoke she had to make a real effort to drag herself back to the problems of the present.

'You will see, Louisa. Matters will straighten themselves out.'

'Yes, but how?'

'You have not lost every last penny, have you? Only any money that you might have had invested with Willis and Son.'

'That is true,' she conceded, puzzled but rather relieved that he should have turned his attention to pursuing her problems rather than pressing his attentions. 'The only trouble is that the little property and investments I have are all in India. It is bound to take a long time to realise them. Until then I shall have nothing!'

'Now do not start worrying unnecessarily,' he said evenly, releasing her as a quiet knock came at the door.

Louisa jumped guiltily, but Geoffrey smiled in reassurance. Maggie brought in a tray of tea and cakes, and she searched Louisa's expression with a sidelong glance as she set the tray down on the table. Geoffrey did not continue until Maggie had gone out and closed the door behind her. After a moment, he went to the door and looked out, checking to see that Maggie had indeed disappeared back down the service corridor.

'Have you any bills that are seriously overdue at the moment?' he said when he had closed the door again with a click.

'No! I have always been very careful to pay bills as soon as they come in. Until today…' Louisa showed signs of breaking down again, but he interrupted quickly.

'Then you will have to learn to start delaying payment whenever you can.'

'Oh, but I could not *possibly* do that!'

Geoffrey smiled at her, the corners of his eyes crinkling in genuine amusement despite the gravity of the situation. 'I am afraid that it is a common business practice—to delay settling bills until the last possible moment. You will have to learn to do it too, Louisa. At least until you can realise some of your assets in India.'

Louisa frowned, still tugging at the handkerchief absently. She was gazing towards the tea tray as Geoffrey filled a bone-china cup with citron-scented tea, but she was not actually seeing anything.

'If I sold Roseberry Hall, I expect I would be able to cover all the debts I have incurred in rebuilding it, and still have enough left over to travel back to India,' she said quietly as he handed her the cup and saucer then offered the sugar bowl and tongs. Despite sweet tea being the usual remedy for shock, Louisa could not bring herself to add any sugar to it and shook her head. When Geoffrey had poured himself a cup, he took a seat at a respectable distance away from her on the settee.

'I thought you were enjoying life here in England, Louisa?'

'I am—I mean, I was.' Louisa stirred her tea slowly, staring into the depths as though the answer to all her problems might be hiding there. 'The problem is that I doubt my assets in India would cover my costs *and* enable me to go on living in Roseberry Hall for very long. The running costs will be high: I had been relying on investment income to cover everything. Now I have nothing invested...'

Geoffrey put his cup down hurriedly and slipped his arm around her shoulders to comfort her. With his free hand he flourished another handkerchief, but Louisa waved it away. With a supreme effort she managed to regain control of her emotions.

'Is your house in India occupied at the moment?' Geoffrey said gently when she had recovered a little.

'No—it was shut up until such time that I decided whether or not I would be staying in England. I wanted to put off making a decision about selling it until I was sure that my new life was going to be everything I had hoped for.'

'Then you should send orders for it to be opened up without delay and rented out. That would bring you in a little money. Without wishing to pry, would that provide enough to keep you in Roseberry Hall?'

Louisa shook her head slowly. 'I do not know. I hardly think so.'

'It would take some time to release your funds, too, I suppose.' He sighed heavily, but checked himself when he realised that Louisa's expression was trembling again.

She tried to salvage something from the situation.

'I do have a small pension...'

At the thought of the life she had lost Louisa's composure began to dissolve again.

'There you are—you have more money than you thought!' Geoffrey gave her a companionable squeeze. 'It might possibly be enough to rent you a small house. A similar property to the one that I believe you were thinking of renting in Cheltenham, to escape from the embarrassment of living here with me.'

That surprised Louisa out of her self-pity.

'You knew that I had considered leaving here before?'

'Talk gets around. In the circles I used to frequent,' he said idly.

Louisa suddenly became very aware of his hand lying lightly on her shoulder. She looked at it nervously, and as though guessing her expression he drew his hand casually back into his lap.

'I will do everything in my power to help you, Louisa,' he said gravely. 'If you wish, you could leave Roseberry Hall right now and move back in here directly, all found. Don't worry—' he hurried to calm her '—it would all be quite decently arranged, if that is what you would be worried about.'

He put out his hand towards her face, but before Louisa could shrink back as convention demanded he was gently stroking away the trace of her worried frown with one finger. The touch was one of brotherly concern rather than anything more sinister. Although she should have been relieved, Louisa began to feel a creeping certainty that her feelings for Geoffrey might run deeper and more turbulently than his response to her.

'I should be away in London for most of the time, Louisa, and at weekends I am sure you will be off socialising at house parties and the like—'

'But what about *you*? Your social life is far busier than mine could ever be…'

He shrugged lightly. 'To tell you the truth, I am getting a little tired of playing the role of ''extra man''. You were right, Louisa. It will do me good to settle down, to get some experience of the responsibilities of country living. In the very near future I intend to be spending a great deal more of my time here in Stanton Malreward.'

'I am not so sure that hostesses like Mrs Tonbridge will take too kindly to *that*,' Louisa muttered, drawing away from him. On the other hand, Miss Victoria Andrews would probably be quite delighted at the prospect. Louisa thought back to the way that Geoffrey had always behaved in *her* presence. There was never any of the touching concern that he was showing towards Louisa now. Only the looks of a suitor and the voice of a lover had been good enough for Miss Victoria Andrews. With this news that Geoffrey now intended to settle down, that could mean only one thing. Miss Andrews was about to move from the role of innocent love interest to that of wife.

Louisa closed her eyes, and tried desperately to think of her financial situation.

Geoffrey must have sensed the change in her. He did not try to retain a hold on her, but let her slip from his hands. Lost in despair, Louisa looked up into his face and saw that his expression had none of the gay deceiver about it now. Instead it should have been as reassuring as kind words.

Slowly Louisa began to realise that was all he must be offering. Any silly dreams she might have had that his kisses had meant anything had been exactly that. Nothing but silly dreams.

Geoffrey might be offering his help and support, but at that moment a romance with Louisa could not have been further from his mind.

Chapter Nine

The realisation was dawning on Louisa that Geoffrey's embrace and brotherly kisses were probably no more than that. He had rushed to rescue her from Grip, and from then on simple Christian concern had guided his actions. She had been upset—he had merely offered her a shoulder to cry on. Literally.

The unguarded comment he had made about settling down must mean that there would definitely be some personal advancement for Miss Andrews, and soon. He had been all over the girl at every party Louisa had attended. Now he must have decided to make the arrangement permanent. Spending more time at Holly House must be part of the plan. Geoffrey could hardly expect to marry a farmer's daughter if he knew nothing about land and stewardship.

'Are you sure that I will not be in the way if I stay here?' Louisa bit her lip uncertainly. She did not want to ruin either his prospects or her own reputation. 'The arrangement will be bound to cause comment after I have moved out from here once already. This time I shall pay you rent, of course, with a proper arrangement drawn up…'

'Nonsense!' He was quick to wave away her concerns with an indulgent smile. 'We are both adult enough not to need that type of thing, Louisa. And besides…' he stood back and looked at her kindly '…with a full social circle such as yours, it will surely not be long before some eligible gentleman snaps you up. Will it?'

That confirmed her worst fears. Geoffrey might be interested in her welfare, but little more than that.

There is only one gentleman that I would be interested in, Louisa thought sadly, but it is too late. I could never bring myself to return any advances that Geoffrey may have made, and now he is spoken for.

She managed to find a smile from somewhere and tried to put that disappointment behind her.

'Oh, I think I am quite beyond all that!' she said, and it felt as if it was true. The only man she wanted was Geoffrey Redvers, yet he was unattainable. Quite apart from his good looks and natural charm, he was so level-headed when he chose to be. She watched him now, drawing himself up to his full height as he sat beside her and clearing his throat ready to get down to business.

'Right. The first thing that anyone in a spot of bother should do is to lower their outgoings while maximising their income. The second option is not open to you, of course—'

'Why not?' Louisa interrupted quickly.

His eyes twinkled with a flash of amusement.

'Well, unless you fancy taking a job behind the bar

at The Crown or scaring crows in the fields, there is not a great deal of employment here in the depths of the country! Particularly for a lady such as yourself, Louisa.'

'Oh.' Suitably deflated, Louisa began to slide towards despair again.

'Cheer up! That still leaves us the first avenue open for use. I shall go and shake up old Willis. His son has probably squandered any cash he had left on wine, women and song by now, but that is not *your* fault. It should not be your problem, either.'

Louisa brightened at that.

'Do you think you may be actually able to get my money back after all, Geoffrey?'

He looked doubtful. 'I do not know about that. I might be able to bring some pressure to bear on old Willis to do the decent thing, but I imagine the sum that you had invested with them is a terrific amount of money for a small country practice to replace if it has indeed all been squandered. And I know for a fact that it would be no good at all to try and appeal to young Henry's good nature. He does not have one. And if his father cannot or will not produce the cash, then it looks like a matter for the courts.'

Louisa took in a sharp breath. Courts would mean newspaper stories. To appear in an English newspaper would be a dreadful thing.

Her mind flashed back suddenly to Geoffrey's suspicious actions in the Tonbridges' library. Perhaps it had been something like this, some financial disaster, that had made him desperate to remove editions from that volume of newspapers. Desperate matters must have called for desperate measures.

'I would rather not become involved with the courts,' she said faintly. 'All the publicity…'

'I quite understand,' he said, and it was with a depth of feeling that Louisa could now appreciate. They smiled at each other, if not with the look of co-conspirators, then with an understanding that went beyond words.

'Come along. Let us have some more tea, Louisa. That is the sovereign remedy for shock, and disaster, and just about anything else that life has to offer!'

He rang for more tea, and when Higgins arrived Louisa was persuaded to remove her hat, coat and gloves. She was reluctant at first, wondering what Higgins would think if she were to appear to be making herself too much at home again, but Geoffrey insisted.

'We have some complicated financial matters to sort out, Higgins,' he said affably. 'So if you could bring pens and plenty of paper from the study, and make sure that we are not disturbed…?'

Higgins agreed. Louisa was relieved to see that it was without a single trace of either amusement or curiosity.

They worked over the figures time and time again, but the conclusion was always the same. Louisa had plenty of capital to cover the building costs, but she would have to raise money through Roseberry Hall to do it. Her small annuity would not be enough to fund a remortgage. Selling Roseberry Hall was the only way to clear her debts.

'I am sorry.' Geoffrey shook his head, staring at the columns of figures before him as though he was trying to push them into profit by an act of will. 'It looks as though Roseberry Hall will definitely have to go.'

Louisa did not cry. At least, not in front of Geoffrey. There followed long, sleepless hours at night when the apparent hopelessness of her situation did try to overwhelm her, but she fought all the despair as hard as she could. She found that trying to think and work her way through the situation helped, at least in a small way. Now that it was obvious Roseberry Hall could not be saved, she let Geoffrey introduce her to a trustworthy agent for the sale. Mr Matravers was delighted with the commission, and saw no problem about selling the house and getting a good price for it, too.

Louisa should have been pleased, but the death of all her dreams was far too painful. She let the agent deal with everything, arranging to be well away from Roseberry Hall when he brought clients to view the property.

Although it was still winter, it turned out to be a good time of the year to be selling. Few properties were on the market as people who could pick and choose when they wanted to sell their houses were waiting until springtime, when their gardens would look their best. Roseberry Hall did not rely on the beauty of its grounds alone. It was a well-built house that had been renovated to a very high standard. Added bonuses to this were its secluded grounds and the pretty countryside around Stanton Malreward.

Roseberry Hall was in a good position to attract buyers. It was a choice property, with the plans for its continued restoration already drawn up and paid for.

Even the newly turned flowerbeds beneath each ground-floor window added to its attractions. Higgins had sent over two thousand wallflower plants, each with a large ball of soil to withstand the move, and Louisa's gardener and his boys had worked like slaves to get them all planted as quickly as possible.

Within a few months the wallflowers would flounce colourful petticoats against the soft grey stone of Roseberry Hall. Louisa could imagine the scene, with all those flowers glowing and fragrant in the warm spring sunshine. With beautiful grounds to set it off and all the decorations inside so clean, fresh and new, Roseberry Hall simply begged to be bought.

Louisa could not bear it.

To her surprise and secret disappointment, the agent was proved right when he said that it would sell in no time at all. Within a month of receiving the dreadful news from the firm of Willis and Son, half a dozen clients had been shown around the house. At least three of those were so eager to purchase Roseberry Hall that it was likely that a private arrangement could be made well before the date set for the auction. It all depended on who could come up with the necessary funds first, the agent told Louisa with great satisfaction over tea in his office one afternoon in the middle of a February freeze.

Louisa knew that he was only doing his job, and doing it very well, but the sale still meant the loss of the home that she had barely had time to enjoy.

Louisa had liked Roseberry Hall at first sight, and now she loved it.

The asking price of Roseberry Hall was intended to provide enough money to settle all Louisa's bills and still leave a small profit. This would be more than enough to buy her another, much smaller property and provide for its running costs. A smaller home would be more economical to run, and there were plenty of respectable, suitable houses in and around the village of Stanton Malreward. It should have been easy for Louisa to find herself a nice little house, but it proved to be very difficult.

Louisa already loved the area, but she knew that she could not bear to go on living anywhere near Stanton Malreward and seeing someone else enjoying life at Roseberry Hall.

Neither would she be able to bear leaving the village. That would mean leaving behind Geoffrey Redvers, and Louisa realised now that she would not be able to do that either.

Over the past weeks, when she had been at her lowest ebb, he had been there. He had dealt with the agent and the builders when Louisa had felt unable to face anyone. He had always been on hand with moral support and Maggie Higgins' excellent cooking when things were too awful to endure.

After some thought, Louisa had decided to turn down his offer of a suite at Holly House. She'd decided instead to stay in Roseberry Hall until the very last moment, to enjoy what she could of the dream she had built. The only time she left the house was when prospective buyers came to view it. She knew that they would stalk around the house as though they owned it already, bringing tape measures and their own ideas.

And then, towards the end of February, came both the best and the worst of news. The thing that Louisa was most dreading, but which was supposed to free her from all the weeks of worry.

The agent wrote to tell her that the sale of Roseberry Hall was to be completed on the twenty-first of March. The first day of spring, Louisa thought sadly. It should have been a happy time but the approaching date would now fill her with dread.

Louisa had agreed with Geoffrey that Roseberry Hall should be sold as quickly as possible, as long as the sale price was as high as could be reasonably expected. Mr Matravers, the agent, must be delighted with himself for fulfilling the request so quickly and so well, Louisa thought. With a heavy sigh she made a note in her diary to send a card and small present around to his office to thank him for his efficiency. It was a simple task but her pen crawled over every letter of the diary message.

The ironic thing about the whole matter was that Louisa now had some hope of seeing at least part of her investment rescued. Together with Charles Darblay-Barre and with the full weight of their prestigious company behind him, Geoffrey had exerted pressure on the firm of Willis and Son to do something about the money that had been lost.

At first old Mr Willis had been adamant that he was not going to bail out his son. However, letters on the impressive headed notepaper of the London solicitors retained by Darblay-Barre Tea Traders eventually had an effect. Reluctantly, Willis and Son had drawn up an agreement to repay Louisa's money at the rate of twenty-five pounds a month, with interest. It would be some time before she regained all her capital, but Louisa no longer cared.

The arrangement had come far too late to stop the sale of Roseberry Hall. If only the tradesmen had been willing to wait a few years for their money rather than a few months, Louisa thought with bitter amusement, I need never have put my beautiful house on the market at all.

When she called at the offices of Matravers, Matravers and Nephew to thank Mr Matravers, the agent was beside himself with delight. He could not wait to tell Louisa details of the transaction that she felt had ruined her life. Client confidentiality did not stop him dancing around the subject, telling Louisa little snippets here and there that might have tantalised anyone who had more interest in selling their house than in staying in it.

The buyer was a gentleman, Louisa was told with delight, who wished to settle in the area and needed a family house in anticipation of a happy event. Louisa tried to silence the enthusiastic agent by asking whether that was not a rather indiscreet thing to say to a lady, but Mr Matravers was not to be put off. With a broad smile he told Louisa that she could have no better purchaser of her house than a man of quality who would know how to appreciate and enjoy it. She was sure to like him.

On that point Louisa knew that the agent was

wrong. She would hate the buyer of Roseberry Hall with all her heart, and with every atom of her being.

The twenty-first of March dawned bright and brisk in a month that had been mild, almost warm. For Louisa the day would have been dark and dreadful whatever the weather.

It was the day that the transfer of Roseberry Hall was to be completed.

She had visited Holly House for dinner the previous evening, but had left early. She had not wanted to miss a minute of her last night at Roseberry Hall. In reality, as soon as she'd reached home time had begun to hang heavily. It had been pointless trying to read. She'd found that her mind would not settle to anything.

Walking around the grounds on the morning of the transfer only made her feel even more miserable. The daffodils were out in all their glory. Over years of neglect, great swathes of them had naturalised themselves along the woodland edges of the park, nodding in the lightest breeze. The great beech trees were pushing out the sharp points of buds, the tracery of their twigs a lacy fretwork against the clear blue spring sky. Everything promised a spectacular spring show, but Louisa would no longer be there to see it all come to its full beauty.

She had to get away.

Geoffrey had told her the previous evening that he had business to attend to in Gloucester that morning. Although he had not expected to be back home until late afternoon, Louisa walked over to Holly House

soon after lunch. Sitting around in Roseberry Hall
with everything packed up in boxes and trunks ready
to move to a rented villa in Cheltenham later that day
had been almost as depressing as walking around the
grounds. Louisa knew that she ought to be checking
each room of the house, making sure that the servants
had remembered everything ready for the new owner
to take possession, but it was impossible.

The trouble was that the house felt a part of her
now. Getting ready to lose it was like preparing for a
surgical operation. The thought of it made Louisa
shiver, and sadness was never far away. It was better
to get out and about, to do something positive rather
than moping around in the kitchens of the home that
was no longer her own, drinking endless cups of tea
and waiting for the inevitable.

The afternoon sun was high and surprisingly hot as
she walked over to Holly House. The birds had been
singing since before dawn, and showed no signs of
flagging. Every type of bird was joining in the chorus.
Even the village cockerels were adding their chal-
lenges to the swish of the roadmen's scythes as they
made the first cut of the grass verges along the lane.

Louisa took her time walking along the lane. She
knew that it would be far too early for Geoffrey to
be home, and that meant Grip would be loitering in
the shade of the shrubbery beside the front door, waiting for his master to return.

Walking past the drive to Holly House, Louisa
skirted the property and went around the back to find
Sam Higgins. Hearing the dry scratch of his weeding
hoe working through the vegetable garden, Louisa

called through the hedge to him. He put down his hoe, then went round to catch the dog so that Louisa could have safe passage to the front door of the house. Poor Grip had never learned from the scolding he had received for ambushing Louisa. He was always so pleased to see her that his welcomes were overwhelming, and he could not understand why she did not enjoy games of chase and mock biting.

Louisa was shown into the dining room by Maggie Higgins, and within minutes the girl had fetched a large jug of chilled lemonade and a sugar-frosted glass for Louisa. There were copies of *Country Life* and *Punch* on a low table over by one of the windows, so Louisa should have found plenty to occupy her. Instead, she could not settle to anything and felt unusually alone. It did not feel natural, to be here in Geoffrey's house without him. For the first time in her life Louisa was lonely. She missed him, and felt his absence as a real loss.

She changed restlessly between magazines, took a few sips of lemonade, then stood up to look out of the window. Higgins had disappeared back to his work in the kitchen garden long ago, and the only movement outside was Grip, who had settled back down to pant in the shade of the shrubbery. As Louisa watched him, the dog raised his head sharply. His ears cocked. After turning his head from side to side he suddenly scrambled to his feet and galloped off at a thunder down the drive.

Louisa knew what that meant. Checking her appearance in the looking-glass over the fireplace, she smoothed her hair and straightened the ruffle of lace at the neck of her blouse. The actions should have been measured and assured, but Louisa found that her fingers were trembling. This must be love. Nothing like this had ever happened to her before—not even with Algy. She had liked her husband, of course, and respected him, but now she realised that the feelings she had experienced for Algy had not included love. Not this deep, turbulent, bubbling emotion that filled her mind and body too.

It was hopeless, of course. She realised that, even though Geoffrey had never spoken about Victoria Andrews since the day that he had come to Louisa's rescue. From that moment, when she had realised that her feelings for him were not returned, Louisa had chosen to become a social outcast. She had refused all the invitations that she'd received from that day onwards. Pleading influenza or a previous engagement were good excuses, although not when used too often.

Louisa hardly cared whether people were becoming suspicious at her disappearance from the social scene. The thought of accidentally running into Geoffrey with Victoria on his arm far outweighed any worries about what other people were thinking.

She went to wait at the window, desperate for the first sight of Geoffrey's return. It would not do to seem too eager, of course, so she stood well back, tall and slender in her delicate cotton frock, the flame of her dark hair coiled on the top of her head. In case her hands should be at all damp with expectation, Louisa pulled on her short lace gloves to complete the picture of a sophisticated lady, waiting to receive.

It felt like an age before Louisa saw and felt the car rumble into view. Grip was galloping alongside, and that was the only thing that stopped Louisa going straight out to meet Geoffrey. Instead she waited until he had got out of the car and walked into the hall, then she went out to greet him.

He looked tired and hot from the journey, but his face lit up when he saw Louisa. Giving his hat to Higgins, he hurried forward to chivvy her back into the dining room.

'Louisa! Exactly the person that I wanted to see!'

She felt herself blushing, and tried to remember that he now rightfully belonged to Victoria Andrews.

'I arrived early—how lovely that you did, too!'

He smiled down at her in a mixture of anticipation and delight.

'Not only am I home early, Louisa, but I have brought with me more gifts than any Greek!'

'You must have been spoiling yourself,' Louisa said carefully, knowing that Miss Victoria Andrews was the more likely candidate for that.

'No, not at all. They are presents for *you*. I know how much this day means to you,' he finished softly.

'Oh...' Louisa drew back a little, her eyes suddenly bright with threatening tears. It was good that he had remembered, but the sadness of the day was suddenly rushing back to envelop her again.

'I have brought you several little things to cheer you up,' he said, drawing out a small square box from his pocket.

'Geoffrey! What on earth will the servants think, if they see you giving me gifts like this?' Louisa said, almost breathless with the thought. To be truthful, it was not only the servants who troubled her. Miss Victoria Andrews was sure to create a scene if she ever found out about this.

'No one *will* know, Louisa. Unless you are going to protest too loudly, of course!'

Louisa almost laughed, but the day was too sad for that.

'Hurry up and open it,' he commanded, to stop her simply turning the little box over in her hands. Louisa had not expected anything and said as much as she thanked him, but when the little box opened to reveal a pair of earrings, dancing with tiny diamonds, astonishment robbed her of all words. Her horror increased as Geoffrey produced a second, larger package for her. It contained a filigree necklace of more diamonds, which made a perfect match to the earrings.

What on earth could he be thinking of? To give diamonds to a woman when he was already spoken for by another? Louisa could not move, but in one swift movement Geoffrey lifted the necklace from its bed of white satin and slipped it around her neck. Before Louisa had time to protest he had fastened the clip.

'Very grand for this time of the day!' He laughed.

When Louisa said nothing, he put one tentative finger beneath her chin and lifted her head so that Louisa could see her reflection in the looking-glass above the fireplace.

The blaze of diamonds made her skin seem even paler than it was. Louisa stared at her reflection, half afraid to think what all this extravagance might mean.

Geoffrey was still standing behind her. He was look-ing eagerly for her reaction, searching her features with his eyes. After fastening the necklace his hands had dropped lightly to rest on her shoulders. Louisa did nothing, but then suddenly his hands tried to slip easily to her waist. Then she moved aside sharply.

She was on her guard at once. She had been right to be suspicious. Men did not behave in this manner unless they were up to something. Louisa had read enough novels to know that.

Geoffrey looked puzzled, but he still had one last card to play.

'Well…I can understand that jewellery is a matter of personal taste and that you might be too distracted today to enjoy it, but *here*, to guarantee your happi-ness and wipe away every last tear…' He reached into the inside breast pocket of his jacket and drew out a fold of papers secured in a brown paper wrapper. 'A third present—just for you, Louisa. This one is hardly as beautiful or romantic as the jewellery, but I like to think that it will be better received…'

Louisa turned to face him, her eyes even more questioning now. Handing her the sheaf of papers, Geoffrey stood back to revel in her reaction to this third mysterious present. As Louisa turned the offi-cial-looking package around in her hands he spoke again, through a broadening smile of delight at his cleverness and artful deceit.

'Some men may think that they cannot go wrong with a gift of chocolate, flowers or perfume, but for myself—I lay more faith in something like this.'

The wrapper fell away from beneath Louisa's fingers and she saw what he had handed to her.

It was the deeds to Roseberry Hall.

Louisa stared at the sheaf of papers for long moments before speaking. This could mean only one thing.

'*You* were the mysterious purchaser of Roseberry Hall? The gentleman that Mr Matravers was so delighted to have helped?' she said slowly at last, her words dropping like raindrops into the expectant silence.

'The very same.' Geoffrey gave a little mock bow.

Louisa was in no mood for mockery. All that worry about Roseberry Hall, who might buy it, how they would treat it…she had barely had one decent night's sleep for weeks. And all the time *he* had been secretly dealing behind her back—listening to her worrying on and on, while all the time he'd had it in his power to put her mind at rest—

'You bought *my* house,' Louisa said slowly, the impotent fury that had been building up inside her over the last weeks finally finding an outlet.

Geoffrey was quite oblivious to the change in her. He was so proud of what he had done that he allowed himself a small chuckle. 'Yes, Louisa. It is all yours again. I am returning it to its rightful owner!'

'You *beast*! You…you *fiend*!' Louisa whirled around and aimed a blow at his head but he caught her wrist and managed to deflect it, his eyes wide with alarm.

'Louisa! What on earth is the matter? I thought you would be delighted!'

Louisa wrestled her wrist free from his grip, galvanised with fury at what she saw as his deception.

'You…you *beast*! You listened to me worrying and never said a thing! *Not a single thing!* You let me go on thinking that Roseberry Hall was lost, and that I would never see inside it ever again, when all the time—'

He silenced her with a kiss. Firm and forceful, he kissed her until her body lost all its taut rage in a flood of that familiar warm lassitude. This is the way he seduces all women, Louisa thought, and the memory of his delight over Miss Victoria Andrews froze her with fury once more. Summoning up all her strength Louisa pushed him away forcibly.

'How *dare* you?' Her voice was a whisper of rage, and she crossed quickly to the bell-pull beside the fireplace.

'I am not a great one for apologies, Louisa. Let us simply say that I hope you will consider my little deception was worth it in the end.' He put out a hand and stopped her summoning Higgins.

Alarmed, Louisa immediately started for the door, but again Geoffrey was too quick for her. Taking her hand, he led her firmly over to the sofa drawn up before the large window that looked out over the lawn and woodland beyond.

'Sit down, Louisa. No—there will be no more kissing, I promise. At least not for the present.'

When her look of horror only increased at this, Geoffrey began to look uncomfortably efficient and businesslike.

'We have a great deal to talk about, Louisa.'

Louisa had no option but to follow him to the sofa, but she had no intention of sitting down beside him. She had a dark and terrible suspicion that she could guess what he would want to talk about.

In less than six months, Louisa had seen Holly House and its owner transformed from dark despair to a bright, expectant future. It was hardly believable. She had seen both the light and the dark side of Geoffrey Redvers' character, and now it seemed that he was about to combine the two. If he was going to marry at all, it would be to Miss Victoria Andrews. Everyone had been saying as much, from the gossipy letters of Edna Tonbridge to the half-heard whispers between Maggie and Sam Higgins.

In that case, there could only be one reason why Geoffrey was giving Louisa diamonds and trying to hand over the deeds of the house she loved.

The sunlight flooding into the drawing room could not lift the dark suspicions of what that reason was. When she would not sit down beside him, he stood, looking past her and towards the window.

'I am not proud of my past, Louisa,' Geoffrey began, speaking in a low, quick voice. 'Not proud at all. I came from nothing—a real street urchin. The only difference between me and the little monsters of Fagin's den was the desperate need that I have always felt to better myself—to escape.'

He had not yet looked at her directly, but was staring across to the woodland that hemmed the far side of the lawn. Beyond those trees lay Roseberry Hall. Hidden, but convenient, Louisa thought furiously, but said nothing. He would condemn himself soon enough with his own words.

Geoffrey paused, clearly very troubled. Then he looked down into her face. Taking her hands in his he made a visible effort to brace himself for a revelation. 'Louisa…there are dreadful things in my past. Things that you should know—'

'No!' Louisa ripped her hands out of his grasp and now stood before him defiantly. 'I am not interested in your past, or the sordid little future that you no doubt think that you have lined up for me!'

'Louisa…it is not like that at all,' he said softly, but all Louisa heard was the sweet, honeyed tones of a seasoned seducer practising all his art upon her. 'You did not want me to spell things out to you earlier, so I hope that you can appreciate…how things stand with a man in my position. I have considerations which make it impossible for you and I to ever marry…'

Louisa felt her throat constrict, but managed to squeeze one faint word past the obstruction.

'What?' she whispered, so softly that he inclined his head unbearably close to hers.

'I am sorry, Louisa. Over the past few weeks and months you have cast a spell over me the like of which I have never experienced before. I want—I *need* you close to me—but it would not be fair to offer you marriage—'

'What!' This time the word burst out loud and clear as Louisa put her hands up to her neck in fury. 'You make a great play of making me a gift of *my own house*, drape me with trinkets like an odalisque—'

here she tore off the necklace and threw it with all her might against the marble fireplace before storming past him towards the door '—and yet the object of it all is not marriage, but something else entirely?'

'Well...*no*...'

The sight of his amazement at her reaction only fuelled Louisa's fury still further. The sheer, bare-faced *nerve* of the man! She marched to the door, but he got there first, barring her way.

'Louisa—don't be silly. Let me explain. You are welcome to live in Roseberry Hall—that is what I bought it for. It is yours for life, as is only right and proper. You can come and go as you please there, unshackled by the tedium of a husband, yet still enjoying life here at Holly House too because you and I—'

Louisa slapped him so hard that the colour immediately leapt to his face in four angry stripes. Before she could draw back for a further attack Geoffrey snatched at her hand, but Louisa was too quick for him. Squirming out of his grasp, she wrenched open the drawing-room door and fled out into the hall. Higgins was hovering in the kitchen passage. A silver tray stood on the table beside him set with a bottle of champagne and two crystal glasses. Louisa rushed towards him, her first impulse to dash the tray and everything on it to the ground, but she stopped within inches of Higgins, who stood rooted to the spot.

'You can tell your master that I would rather *die* than accept his proposal!' she announced through clenched teeth, then turned on her heel and stormed out of the house.

* * *

It was a long, hot walk back to Roseberry Hall under the burnished afternoon sun. Louisa did not notice. She was so furious with the high and mighty Mr Geoffrey Redvers for even considering that she might act as his kept woman that she could not think of anything else. She had been wrong to imagine that the quiet, reserved man who had helped her on that first night in Stanton Malreward was the real Geoffrey Redvers. Very wrong. Both the country version and the dashing socialite used women for their own ends. Shamelessly.

Louisa stamped up the steps of Roseberry Hall, almost bundling straight past Daisy, the maid, who was waiting in the hall.

'If you please, ma'am. An urgent letter arrived in the afternoon post—'

'Not now, Daisy. If Mr Redvers should call, tell him that I am not at home. For *any* reason.'

Louisa knew that she could hardly exclude a man from what was technically now his own house, but she would have a good try. She threw her hat down on the hall table and strode towards the stairs, but the maid persisted. 'It was a special delivery, ma'am. It has come all the way from India.'

Louisa stopped. An arrow of memory shot straight through the fierce heat and her even fiercer fury. The letter must be a reply from Angela Histon. She might have been able to find out something of her tormentor's previous life out in India.

Now Louisa would find out exactly how shabbily Geoffrey had behaved in the past. It would not be business problems, she decided—no, after what she had gone through today, it was sure to be women who had brought him to ruin. If he had not ruined them first.

Spinning around, Louisa abandoned all thoughts of hiding in her room and headed instead for the library. Picking up the letter from the mail basket on the way, she asked Daisy to fetch her some cold lemonade then went into the small, private room to read her letter.

The room had long since been emptied ready for the removal men, and the bare floorboards echoed to the click of her walking boots. The only thing that remained to be packed away was a small writing case standing on the windowsill in case of any last-minute letters that needed to be written.

Louisa took out a small silver paper knife and slit open the letter. It was a long one, running to several sheets. Ten yards of gossip and half an inch of news, Louisa thought darkly, opening the folds and preparing herself for a long-drawn-out list of the ailments and treatments that Angela Histon revelled in.

She could not have been more wrong. Her ex-neighbour had only one topic in mind, and that was the man that England knew as Geoffrey Redvers, but who had lived in India as Stephen Allington.

Louisa stared at the letter, trying to understand the deceptively simple words that she was reading. When she came to the end, she read it through again. Daisy arrived with the lemonade. Louisa barely seemed to notice. Then, as the girl was leaving, Louisa dashed for the door. Daisy jumped in alarm at the sudden movement, but her alarm was to increase vividly with the next orders her mistress gave.

'Have Sami and the gardeners check the grounds immediately, Daisy! They must make sure that Mr Redvers is nowhere within them, and then lock and bolt the gates. Under no circumstances is Mr Redvers ever to come anywhere near this house or these grounds. *Ever again*, for as long as I am still living here. Do you understand?'

'Yes, ma'am.' Daisy bobbed a curtsey, but Louisa had not finished yet.

'Send a boy into town to tell Mr Matravers, the estate agent, that Roseberry Hall is to go onto the market again. I shall be renting the house in Cheltenham as arranged, and all correspondence should be sent there. With immediate effect.'

At least the rented villa in Cheltenham has plenty of neighbours, Louisa added silently. Decent people who would soon see off any ne'er-do-well who might come pestering a lady.

Louisa went up to her room, taking the letter with her. Time to think was the last thing that she needed, but matters had to be sorted out. As long as she was living in Roseberry Hall and Geoffrey Redvers owned it, there was a danger that he would come visiting. There would be danger in any case, she thought with a shiver, resisting the urge to reread Angela Histon's letter. There had been enough details in it to give her nightmares, let alone sinister thoughts during the day.

The reality of being in this house as his sitting tenant would be bad enough—but she would face that if and when it happened. The main thing was to get out of Roseberry Hall as quickly as possible.

To think that barely an hour earlier she would have

given the world for him to make a marriage proposal.
Now that she knew the full horror of what had happened to his first wife, Louisa gave a shiver of relief
that she had avoided that fate.

She went upstairs and sat down at the desk in her
room. Virtually everything else in the house had been
packed away for her eventual move, but her own
room was as yet untouched.

She picked up a pen to write to Edna Tonbridge,
ready to reveal everything to her about the sainted
Geoffrey. The man was such a real danger to women
that everyone should be warned as soon as possible.

After writing the address and date, Louisa paused.
If Stephen Geoffrey Redvers Allington had been
crafty enough to be acquitted of all blame for his
wife's death, as the missing newspaper articles had
evidently said, he would have no trouble in wriggling
out of an accusation at second hand. The Tonbridges
were his friends—as was half London, it seemed.

Society will be sure to believe him and disbelieve
me, Louisa realised bleakly. No. I will not risk making a fool of myself in that way.

Instead she wrote a sad little note to Edna
Tonbridge, explaining that she was leaving Roseberry
Hall and would provide a new address as soon as
possible. Until then, any correspondence should be
sent to The Crown at Stanton Malreward. Sami would
be going back to stay there until she was settled in
the new house. He could carry letters to her lodgings,
if necessary.

When her letter to Surrey was finished, Louisa
wrote glowing references for Daisy and Violet, the

maids, and Mrs Briggs, the cook. Sami would always have a position with her, but paying him would be a worry until she received the balance from the sale of Roseberry Hall.

That in itself posed a problem. The obvious solution to all her problems would be to transport herself and Sami back to India. She could live in the bungalow there as before. Money would not be a problem. Algy had left her reasonably well provided for, and there would be the balance from Roseberry Hall to invest.

Rather more wisely than the last time I invested money, Louisa thought ruefully.

As she rose from the writing desk, a movement outside caught her eye. Geoffrey was cantering his horse up the grassy verge alongside the drive.

The flutter that Louisa's heart always gave when she saw him was immediately quashed by the thought of the letter lying on her desk.

'*Murderer,*' she said aloud through clenched teeth, then went out to the head of the stairs to instruct Daisy that the visitor was to be turned away.

It did no good. Louisa hid behind the half-open door of her room to listen, but she was soon drawn out onto the landing. Geoffrey refused to accept the excuse, pushed past Daisy and into the hall of Roseberry Hall. There was nothing left for Louisa but to confront him.

'I gave strict instructions that I was not to be disturbed, Mr *Redvers*.' Louisa's voice rang out from the landing, putting a careful emphasis on his assumed name. He looked up, surprised.

'I did not think I would be able to flush you out into the open so easily, Mrs Hesketh.' He used the formality carefully, conscious of Daisy cowering in the background. Louisa looked him straight in his deep, dark eyes and wondered what enormities he had witnessed.

He will see no more *here*, she vowed, trying to stop herself shaking.

'You are no longer welcome here, Mr Redvers. Kindly get out of my house before I am forced to call for a constable.'

Until that moment he had been smiling. The tone of Louisa's voice froze his expression into tight-lipped annoyance. He turned this onto Daisy.

'Leave us,' he snapped, causing Daisy to dash straight for the kitchen passage.

'Daisy!' Louisa stopped her escape with a thunderous call. 'Stay exactly where you are!'

'What I have to say to you cannot possibly be said in front of a servant,' Geoffrey called out, reaching the foot of the stairs in two strides. Daisy squeaked, and Louisa fled back into the safety of her room, slamming the door behind her.

'Daisy! Fetch Sami! Tell him that there is a mad-man on the loose!'

Geoffrey was unimpressed, and she heard him start up the stairs. 'Oh, for heaven's sake, Louisa! Can't we talk this over like two rational human beings?'

Hearing the steady tread of his feet on the uncarpeted stairs, Louisa locked the door of her room noisily.

'You have already lost any hold on rationality by

bursting in here, Mr Redvers,' she called out through the door. 'As for me, well, you will forgive me if I do not feel very rational at the moment. What woman could—with a man barging his way into her home, threatening the staff and refusing to leave when told?'

'I haven't threatened anyone!'

'But I *have* asked you to leave, and you have refused. For the last time of asking, get out of my house, Mr Redvers!'

He had reached the landing and Louisa heard him draw very close to her door. By this time she was trembling so much that she could not trust her legs to carry her, and had to stay rooted to the spot. Looking around the room wildly, she wondered what she could use as a weapon when he burst into the room, as she was sure he would. The man was surely capable of anything.

There was a moment's silence from the other side of the door. Louisa used it to get as far as the bell-pull. Then she pulled and pulled at it, hearing the faint but reassuring ring far away down in the servants' quarters.

'Are you still there, Mr Redvers?' she ventured at last.

'Of course,' came the even, deceptively calm voice.

'Then, for the *very last* time of asking, *get out of my house!*' Louisa shouted, her voice shrill with fear and nervous exhaustion.

There was another interminable silence. Then he spoke again.

'Very well.' His voice was resigned, 'If there is to

be no reasoning with you, Louisa, then I *shall* leave. But before I go I shall leave you these...'

She heard the hollow sound of something being thrown down on the floor outside.

'Since, despite everything that has happened, you still refer to this place as your house, you will need them. Goodbye, Louisa. I shall not trouble you further.'

Louisa heard a clattering from downstairs in the hall as Sami arrived, but Geoffrey was as courteous in the face of his challenge as he would have been on any ordinary visit. Louisa heard him leave, and then the great front door of Roseberry Hall thundered shut behind him.

Only when Louisa had watched him ride the length of the drive and disappear into the woodland beyond did she risk opening her bedroom door.

On the floor outside her room lay the deeds of Roseberry Hall.

Chapter Ten

Louisa stared at the deeds for a long time. Finally, she picked them up, wrapped them in a fold of paper and wrote the Holly-House address on the wrapper. Sami delivered it straight away, and did not wait for a reply.

Louisa did not see Geoffrey again before she left Roseberry Hall. Within three hours she had finished her packing and was being installed in the small town house in Cheltenham. Domestic arrangements had been included in the rental price, so while the servants unpacked her things Louisa forced herself to explore her new home.

Although the terrace where she now lived was shady and saw little of the sun, it overlooked a pretty lawned area and was only a short walk from the parade with all its shops. Louisa was quick to write to Edna Tonbridge with her new address, but she was surprised to receive a reply almost by return. Edna had news.

It seemed that her darling Geoffrey Redvers had been like a bear with a sore head for days, and no

one could shake him out of it. Not even an invitation
to the party she was giving the following week could
entice him out of the suite he was now occupying in
London. Only money troubles could have turned him
into such a hermit, Edna hinted darkly. Louisa wondered what the life of a hermit could possibly be in
a luxury hotel. Not as terrible as he deserved, that
was for sure.

Louisa knew the real reason why he had closeted
himself away, and it gave her no pleasure. He must
have used a great deal of his ready cash to buy
Roseberry Hall. Now he had two neighbouring houses
with two neighbouring estates in the country, but
lived in a soulless hotel suite in town.

Louisa might have felt guilty if the words of
Angcla Histon's letter had not still been branded pain-
fully across almost every waking minute of her days.
It must be no more than he deserved.

Still, that was no reason for Louisa to cut herself
off from all social contacts. She replied to the invitation that Edna had included with her letter to say
that she would be delighted to come to the next party.
After all, Edna had said that there was no hope of
Geoffrey attending.

She had meant it as a warning, but Louisa took it
as a reassurance.

Louisa looked out her violet gown for the party.
There would be no posy of home-grown Parma vio-
lets for her shoulder this time. No hope of ever seeing
Sam and Maggie Higgins again, either, Louisa

thought sadly as she eased a small bunch of shop-bought sweet violets into her posy-holder.

She had been apprehensive when she'd first arrived at the Tonbridges' house, but as time ticked on and Geoffrey Redvers really did not appear Louisa began to relax. She almost began to enjoy herself, but at the back of her mind there was always one nagging thought. The party was enjoyable, but it lacked that certain sparkle that had ignited the previous gathering at King's Folly.

There was no doubt about it. The party, and almost everyone in it, was missing Geoffrey.

He is not here, and if anyone could be said to be to blame it is me, Louisa found herself thinking in an idle moment between dances. Then she pinned on a new smile and tried to reassure herself. If anyone is to blame, she told herself, then it is the man himself. Trying to hide his wicked past with a false identity. Deceiving all these good people into thinking that he is a gentleman.

At midnight, a ball supper was served. The evening had been quite mild, and with so much dancing the offerings of chilled fruit soup and sorbets were very welcome. Louisa liked the tiny hot cheese pastries, too, and wondered if Edna had used the Roseberry Hall recipe. She began to look around for her hostess, and was told that she had been called away into the hall.

Louisa strolled out to look for her, and was alarmed to see Charles Darblay-Barre standing in the lighted porch. Mrs Tonbridge was talking to him animatedly, her high, tinkling voice rattling around the spacious hallway.

'Ah, Louisa, my dear!' Charles followed his hostess into the hall, handing his hat and stick to the butler in passing. 'So sorry to have been delayed. Broken axle, you know. Knew I should have taken up bicycling, like you were game enough to do!'

'You are alone?' Louisa looked past him towards the front door, but the butler had already closed and locked it again.

'Not if you would agree to be my partner!' Charles said with a smile.

'I suppose it would be too much to hope that your work has not brought you into contact with Mr Redvers over the past few weeks, Mr Darblay-Barre?'

'Ah,' he said meaningfully. 'Well…Geoffrey has been rather absorbed of late.'

I am sure that he has, Louisa thought to herself bitterly. He must suspect that I know his guilty secret, and that is why he is keeping out of the social circuit. He thinks I will tell everyone and shame him.

Could she ever be capable of such a thing? Louisa knew she was not, but it pained her that Stephen Geoffrey Redvers Allington plainly imagined that she was.

'Geoffrey is a good man at heart,' Mr Darblay-Barre said. There had been a rather hopeful note in his voice, Louisa thought.

'Ah, but do you know him as well as you think you do, Charles?' she said as they sipped punch at the refreshment table.

'Better than most.' He was looking at her enquiringly. 'There is no pretence in him, Mrs Hesketh. What you see is what you get.'

'That is what I should be afraid of,' Louisa began, but at that moment the trio struck up the old familiar strains of 'The Blue Danube', and Charles claimed the dance from her.

'You do not seem at all curious about Geoffrey's whereabouts this evening, Louisa.'

Louisa's concerns about giving Charles Darblay-Barre a false impression suddenly came back to haunt her. They made her aware of a very uncomfortable truth. Stephen Geoffrey Redvers Allington was a dangerous man, but she could not stop her mind dwelling on him. Charles, on the other hand, was a perfectly nice gentleman but she did not want him as a suitor. Anything she might say to her present partner would damn her, one way or another.

'I think your friend is only pursued by women in search of a husband, Charles,' she said after considerable thought.

'Meaning that you are not?'

'That, sir, is an impertinence,' Louisa retorted sharply. The colour had rushed to her face, but not for the reason that her partner suspected.

'Of course. My apologies, Louisa.' Charles was suitably contrite. 'That was unforgivable.'

'No...no, Charles. The dance floor is a little crowded, and I am feeling the heat. It was wrong of me to be so sharp.'

He was immediately all concern.

'Of course. I was quite forgetting that you must

have been on your feet all evening, Louisa. If you would like to take a rest in the conservatory—'

'Thank you, Charles. It is kind of you to offer, but while I have the greatest respect for you as a gentleman I feel it would be unwise for me to accept such an offer,' Louisa said carefully, tempering the words with a smile.

He began to look uncomfortable, which was not what Louisa had intended at all.

'I did not mean to offend you,' she said with a worried frown.

'No—no, I quite understand, Louisa. I was simply offering to provide protection against—well, the less desirable members of the assembly...'

He looked across the dance floor to where young Henry Willis was dancing with Victoria Andrews. Whether the young man's laughter was fuelled by his companion or by the glass of champagne was difficult to tell. In either event, Louisa found it hard to hide her distaste. Not only of Willis, but that Victoria Andrews should feel able to attend a party without her fiancé. *And* behave in such a shameless way by dancing with a single man.

'I am very surprised that the Tonbridges should entertain such a bounder,' Charles said with feeling.

'It is true that if I were a man I should take great pleasure in knocking him down for what he has put me through,' Louisa said with equal fervour. 'As it is, his father is going to bail him out. I am supposed to be getting most of my principal sum returned eventually, so in theory I should not lose too much in the end. While I still have some faith left in old Mr

Willis, I do not trust his son one inch. I shall only believe in the return of my money when every last penny of it is safely installed in my bank account.'

'Very wise,' Charles smiled, 'although I believe you have your house back already?'

'Ah.' Louisa let the waltz take another turn before continuing. 'How did you learn of that?' she asked, although the answer was obvious.

'A friend.'

'And I have no need to ask which one.'

'It was an honest, genuine gesture on his part, Louisa.'

'Genuine, perhaps. In as much as he knew what he wanted, saw a way to obtain it—as he thought—and went straight ahead. Whatever the cost.'

'Things are not always as they seem, Louisa. Perhaps you should have given Geoffrey a chance to explain.'

'I like to think that I was quick enough to see what he had in mind for me,' Louisa said with a humourless laugh. 'Besides, I now know the reason why you have called him Stephen in unguarded moments. If you knew about his dual identity, presumably you know much more about him than you have been telling me—or anyone else, Charles.'

Now it was her partner's turn to hesitate.

'Ah…'

Louisa had been concentrating on her dancing, but now she turned all her scrutiny on her partner.

'It sounds as though you might have saved me from all this much sooner, Mr Charles Darblay-Barre.'

'That is because it has hardly been my place to say anything, Mrs Louisa Hesketh.'

'It is a shame that the person involved showed similar secrecy.'

Charles was not about to stand for that. 'Oh, now that is hardly fair, Louisa!' he retorted sharply. 'If you had let him explain everything when he wanted to, Geoffrey would have told you the whole story himself! I expect,' he added, painfully aware that he had said too much.

'Does that mean he tells *you* everything?' Louisa used the tone of a prosecuting counsel cross-questioning a particularly gullible witness.

'No…' Wrong-footed by her probing, Charles resorted to the best form of defence. 'No—now look here, Louisa! I came here to dance, not to face an interrogation about matters that should concern only you and Geoffrey. Now, may we kindly drop the subject and set about enjoying ourselves?'

Hiding her bad grace, Louisa meekly did as she was told. It was true. Parties were for enjoyment, not recriminations. Geoffrey was not here, so he should be the very last thing on her mind.

That was not the case. After the tantalising hint that Charles knew more than he was telling, Louisa could not stop wondering exactly what Geoffrey had told his friend. Did Charles know about the argument between them—which had all started after she had stopped him from revealing something, she remembered now—and the things that she had said?

Every one of those things came back to haunt her now. And the way that Geoffrey had ridden over to the house…perhaps to explain. She had not even given him a chance. Murder could hardly be explained away, but she should perhaps have given him the chance to put his own case…on reflection…

'Oh, come along and smile, Louisa! Things are not as bad as all that, surely? The music is jolly, the company grand—with the odd exception—and you are without doubt the most attractive woman here. I am clearly the envy of every man here—that has got me smiling. You are surely the envy of every woman here—that should make you smile, too. Come along!'

Charles Darblay-Barre had such a jolly way about him that Louisa could not help but smile, although it was a little weakly. As the music quickened towards its climax she lost herself in the swirling enjoyment of the dance, revelling in the sure-footedness of her partner as he whirled her around the floor—and straight out through the French doors into the Tonbridges' very own tropical jungle.

'My goodness, Charles!' Louisa exclaimed with a breathless giggle. 'Straight out into the conservatory! What on earth will the Tonbridges say?'

'They already know all that they need to know,' Charles whispered with a wink, squeezing her elbow as he released her. Louisa saw then that he was smiling at something—or someone—behind her, and turned.

Stephen Geoffrey Redvers Allington was standing in the shadows of the far corner of the conservatory. With a gasp Louisa froze, then looked for escape, but Charles was blocking her way.

'Geoffrey has something very important to say to

you, Louisa. I am here merely as your escort. For the moment, at least.'

He exchanged another look with Geoffrey.

With horror she saw her dancing partner step smartly back towards the French doors and close them firmly. Then someone inside the room drew the curtains tightly over all the windows and the conservatory was lit only by candles floating on the surface of the ornamental pool.

Tense with terror, Louisa stood rooted to the spot as the man she now knew to be a wife-murderer *and* a liar stepped forward. The fact that he looked neither triumphant nor murderous did not help her nerves at all.

'Mrs Hesketh. Louisa.' Geoffrey forced the words out with difficulty. 'I am so very pleased to see you.'

He did not look pleased. He looked sick.

'Why?' Louisa whispered, not merely questioning his appearance in the conservatory but the whole business of his life, his names, the scandal…

'Louisa, you left without letting me explain—I have been a fool to take this long to find the courage again but when you hear what I have to say you will realise how difficult it would have been for me to tell you my story when you confronted me about Roseberry Hall. I needed time—'

'To think up another plausible identity?' Louisa said, icy control now overcoming her initial fear. He had stopped within three feet of her, but showed no sign of coming any closer.

'Wait—let me say what I must without interruption. Edna and Sidney are aware of the bare bones of the situation here tonight, and Charles will act as chaperon for long enough for me to speak frankly.'

Louisa stared at him with concentration for some time. He returned her gaze without flinching, and it became obvious that Louisa was not going to be allowed to leave the conservatory of her own free will. She pursed her lips into a thin line of disapproval.

'Very well.' She transferred her concentration to her evening gloves, smoothing every tiny wrinkle with an artificial care that screamed suppressed fury.

'I *do* want to marry you, Louisa, but I did not feel that I could because of what has happened in my past. I came from nothing. After seeing poverty and hardship at close quarters I was fired with a determination to succeed at any price. If that included clawing my way up through the ranks of the Darblay-Barre tea company and moving to India to ingratiate my way into the owner's family, then that was what I did. I was so desperate to get away from my roots that I married my first wife solely for ambition, not love.'

He had been speaking quickly but now paused, waiting for Louisa's reaction. She said nothing. Continuing to concentrate on her gloves, she even refused to look up at him.

He gave a heavy sigh, then continued. 'For various reasons…Agnes and I did not get on. Matters came to a head at a large party we hosted. There were plenty of those. Agnes was a difficult woman to please at the best of times, and with the local commissioner and many other dignitaries attending our soirée she had been particularly eager that nothing should go wrong. Preparations had reached fever pitch over several weeks.'

Behind her, Louisa sensed Charles Darblay-Barre move uncomfortably. It was as though he would have liked to comment, but Geoffrey silenced him with a look over her shoulder.

'Unfortunately, on the night of the party everything that could go wrong did go wrong. The weather broke: the appalling conditions and an outbreak of sickness conspired to keep away the most favoured guests but spared the people that Agnes considered tiresome or "low". A disaster in the kitchen delayed dinner for nearly two hours, by which time Agnes and the staff were at each other's throats, in front of our guests as well as behind the scenes. One by one our guests made their excuses and escaped.'

'But as host there was no escape for you,' Louisa supplied quietly.

'No.'

A few moments earlier Louisa might have looked for some sign of squirming under her scrutiny, but now all she saw was the tightening of the small muscles at the corners of his mouth and across his brow.

'Go on,' she said softly. In the soft gloom of the conservatory one of the floating candles sputtered and hissed into the water.

'Agnes and I…had words. Once again it was all through the house and in front of the servants. In the end she followed me to my room after I had expressly wished to bring the matter to an end. That was when something inside me snapped. If she would not leave me alone of her own accord, then I would make sure that she was compelled to do so. I threw her bodily into her own room and locked the door on her. Then I turned my back and walked away.

'At that point she was screaming abuse, but that was nothing unusual.' He stopped and bit his lip before continuing.

'Go on,' Louisa probed. She had wanted honesty. To lance the wound was the least she could do.

'I left the house and took to my horse, intending to ride off my fury. Looking back at the house as I left the stables, I saw that something was not right...there was too much light coming from the back of the house. I dashed back, but it was too late. Agnes had knocked over an oil lamp and set the room alight. She was locked in her room, unable to escape. And I had done it. I killed her, Louisa. Murdered her as surely as if I had been in that room and doused her with kerosene—'

'No. No, you did not, Stephen. You know that is not true...' Charles Darblay-Barre was stepping forward as he spoke, but Louisa barely noticed. Her gaze was fastened solely on the man before her. She reached out her hand, the fingers brushing his shoulder as lightly as thistledown.

'That is exactly what Stephen told the coroner, Mrs Hesketh, who took it for the anguished remorse that it was, and still is,' Charles said quietly. 'Agnes was always the architect of her own disasters, including that one. She had been drinking heavily that night— there was no shortage of witnesses—and, accustomed to the domestic arrangements, it was only when Geoffrey raised the alarm that the servants would approach anywhere near her room. Agnes was not the sort of girl to be approached when she had been drowning her sorrows.'

It was a harsh thing to say, but Louisa remembered the instant dislike that she had taken to the self-satisfied young woman in the portrait at Holly House. Louisa looked to Charles for confirmation, hardly thinking now that this story could be a conspiracy between them, but desperate to learn the truth.

'I should know,' Charles said quietly. 'I was Agnes's father. I have never attached any blame to Stephen,' he went on in answer to the question that was in Louisa's eyes but could not reach her lips. 'He fought so very hard to save her, Louisa. Without a thought for his own safety.'

Louisa's eyes flickered towards Geoffrey, then back to his father-in-law.

'Thank you for your help, Charles, but I think,' she said slowly, 'that Stephen and I need to discuss this matter alone now.'

Charles watched them silently for some time. Eventually he nodded and withdrew back into the drawing room.

When the French doors had been closed and the curtains rearranged for a second time Louisa suddenly realised how quiet the conservatory had become. In the shadowy silence another floating candle fizzled out. The silence was painful and tense.

'If we stay here for much longer we will be plunged into darkness,' Louisa said for want of anything else.

'Do you really wish to talk?' His voice had regained the smallest hint of its usual soft timbre, and Louisa found that she really did want to hear everything that he wanted to say.

'I do.'

'If my past had been different I would have proposed to you like a shot, Louisa. Make no mistake about that. It is simply that—well, until I reached the age of twenty-five I was as self-serving as it is possible to get. If that was not bad enough, I then married for all the wrong reasons and none of the right ones. And after *that*—'

'You have explained the rest,' Louisa interrupted quickly, rather than let him dwell on the tragedy. 'And now I suppose that you are going to tell me that your career will be advancing in the direction of Miss Victoria Andrews?'

His face cleared of all expression, as though he was genuinely puzzled at what she had said.

'Of course not!' he said incredulously. '*You* are the only woman that I would ever consider marrying.'

Louisa was totally astonished, but anything she might have managed to say was quickly silenced by his next words.

'If such a thing were possible.'

It took some moments for Louisa to marshal a reply.

'I hope…it was not thoughts of marrying well that were behind that first evening here in the conservatory? The purchase of Roseberry Hall proved rather the opposite, I would have said. Rather more a case of setting a mackerel to catch a sprat at that stage,' she said, but any intended humour was stifled with sadness. 'Would it be indiscreet to ask—as you have made a point of telling me that you would marry me if you could but that you cannot—to ask why not?'

'It is another echo from my past.' Once again his voice was low with foreboding. 'Charles knows how things were between Agnes and myself, but he does not know all the reasons why. It was never a love match, as I have told you, but things went from bad to worse on our wedding night.'

Louisa blushed and cleared her throat meaningfully. 'Oh…then I am quite sure that you should not be telling me anything about *that*, Stephen.' She used only his proper name now, as fitting to a time of honesty.

'It is the only other reason why I have not asked you to marry me, Louisa. You deserve some sort of an explanation, yet I simply do not know where or how to begin. The truth is pretty shabby.'

'Is that your opinion, or that of someone you have confided in?'

Geoffrey stared at her with open horror.

'Do you think I would ever discuss such a thing? What respectable person would dream of even broaching such a delicate subject?'

'I really cannot have the first idea…perhaps that is what gentlemen's clubs are for?' Louisa said lamely.

She did possess one scrap of shameful knowledge about What Gentlemen Sometimes Did When In Town, but the sort of persons involved in that type of transaction would hardly come under the heading of 'respectable'.

'But…that reputation of yours! The Tonbridges

and everyone else have always warned me to take care. You are not supposed to be safe with women! Have none of your other conquests ever...complained?'

'There is a world of difference between making love to a woman in words and having an affair,' he said shortly.

Louisa could not think what to do or say next. It was tricky, and no mistake. She loved him, that was certain. Now that she understood something of his past she could understand his reticence in proposing. So far. If he had proposed five minutes earlier she would have accepted with only enough delay to be thought proper. He had revealed nothing in his past so far that could not be overcome—until now—and if he was too much of a gentleman to reveal any further details, then he would expect Louisa to be far too much of a lady to enquire further.

Eventually she reached out and took his hand in a slow, hesitant gesture.

'If you were to put aside all considerations of...what passed between you and your wife, would you truly wish to marry me?' she asked at last.

'Oh, of course!'

'Then...because I have grown very fond of you, Mr Stephen Geoffrey Redvers Allington, I shall accept your proposal of marriage. If you should choose to make one.'

He frowned. 'But you could not possibly marry me, Louisa.'

'Of course I could. As long as you answer any question I might ask you about your wife truthfully.'

Louisa had considered this very carefully. She liked to think now that she knew the man seated before her well enough to tell when he was lying. He might affect the easy charm of Geoffrey Redvers, but it would not fool her for a moment any more. She would know when Stephen Allington was telling the truth.

He studied her for a long time. When he spoke, it was with heavy resignation.

'Of course.'

Louisa took a deep breath. She had been looking into his eyes, but now she looked away towards the ornate grille covering the water tank beneath the floor of the conservatory.

'Did you ever strike her, Stephen?'

She heard him sigh with relief.

'No. Never. Although there were those who told me they would have done—no. It was not that.'

Louisa could not think of anything that would be as hideous as violence.

'Then at least you were not cruel toward her on purpose.'

Louisa had turned back to him with a smile, expecting to see him as happy as she was. Instead he looked uneasy. Louisa was instantly on her guard again and, sensing it, he tried to offer an explanation.

'I did not think that I was either cruel or unreasonable—but Agnes considered me to be.'

Louisa thought about this. She had accepted his explanation of the need to keep his business life and his solitary home life completely separate, and he did not have the air of shallow charm that Geoffrey affected when trying to impress. This was something

altogether different. The awful suspicion was beginning to take shape in Louisa's mind that the trouble
between Stephen Allington and his wife might well
have had something to do with the subject that was
not supposed ever to cross a lady's mind, much less
her lips.

'If we were to marry, Stephen…' Louisa began almost casually, trying to broach the subject without
actually mentioning it '…I wonder if I might be allowed to have again the suite of rooms I occupied
when I first stayed at Holly House?'

'Naturally, you would have a completely free
hand.'

'And—naturally—your suite would remain as it is
now, Stephen, although we should be separated by an
empty suite. It being so much of a fuss and bother to
move, of course.'

They looked at each other directly, each one knowing now where the trouble lay.

'Of course,' he said firmly, without any trace of the
evasion that had haunted him earlier.

That would at least mean a whole suite of rooms
between them, rather than a simple connecting door
with no lock.

'Very well,' Louisa stated, giving his hand a
squeeze. 'We will say no more about the subject.
Except that if you were to propose to me, Mr
Allington, I think that Edna and Sidney's company
inside the house would be very grateful to hear about
it!'

Wordlessly he stood up, drawing Louisa to her feet.
Then his hands slid around her waist, drawing her

close. Lifting her chin, he kissed her with all the light, lingering pleasure that Louisa had experienced before. She felt herself sinking further and further into his embrace, parting her lips as though in a smile. In response his touch became more insistent, pressing his body against her as his mouth covered hers, possessing her with a growing excitement that Louisa remembered.

Only too well.

'Mr Allington!' she reminded him sharply, pulling away with a giggle and trying to catch her breath. That was easier said than done. His kisses had ignited a fire deep within Louisa that she knew would have been better left unkindled. 'We are barely engaged yet!'

'Of course,' he said, but his hands were still gliding over her dress in a barely restrained rite of possession. 'We must go back and join the assembly. Although perhaps not without this…'

He drew a tiny leather-covered box from his waistcoat pocket, opened it then handed it to her, brushing another kiss over her brow as he did so.

A ring nestled inside the box, crackling with a fire of rubies and diamonds set in gold. Louisa gave a little gasp at the beauty of it.

'Your new necklace and earrings are still safely back at Holly House,' he breathed, taking the engagement ring from its velvet bed and sliding it onto the third finger of Louisa's left hand.

'What on earth will Mr Andrews and Victoria say?' Louisa murmured with delight.

'I am more concerned about what Edna Tonbridge

will say!' Stephen laughed, but Louisa could see that he was almost serious.

'She certainly warned me about you,' Louisa said, then gave him a look that was supposed to be admonishing. 'I don't suppose that this ring is part of another elaborate revenge upon me for putting that boot mark on your beautiful white breeches, is it?'

He leaned forward with a laugh, resting his head against hers with relief.

'Oh, my love! If you knew what it has taken to arrange all this, not to mention baring my soul then actually steeling myself to the task of actually asking you to marry me—you would not even *think* that!'

'All right.' Louisa chuckled, putting her hands to that dark, gypsy luxuriance of his hair. 'I will believe you. Now, if you are agreeable, Mr Allington, we shall go in to the drawing room and astonish everyone.'

Louisa and Stephen agreed that it might be more simple if he kept to the name Geoffrey in public. If anyone bothered to query the name published in the banns, they would explain that Redvers was his business name, and leave it at that. Few people would stretch the boundaries of polite conversation by questioning further.

The Tonbridges and their guests had been primed by Charles Darblay-Barre to expect a happy announcement, so the astonishment when Louisa and Geoffrey emerged from the conservatory was rather better disguised than the curiosity. Their Geoffrey was not the marrying kind; they had been certain of that. Now he had been snapped up by this widow from India. It was almost too good—or, in the case of Farmer Andrews, Victoria's father, too bad—to be true.

Geoffrey too was sensitive to the atmosphere, but gave his new fiancée a reassuring squeeze.

'I will soon sort them out,' he whispered confidently to Louisa. Sidney Tonbridge, their host, encouraged everyone to toast the happy couple with champagne while hiding any reservations he might have.

Unfortunately Geoffrey's reassurance had the opposite effect on the company. When he announced that the wedding would take place as soon as possible, a little gasp rippled around the guests and they looked at each other knowingly.

'*Geoffrey!*' Louisa whispered fiercely in panic.

'Oh…no, I am sorry—' he corrected himself hurriedly '—I would not like you all to get the wrong idea! The truth is that I have been a single man for too long, and, as Louisa is always telling me that I do not eat well enough, I thought that the sooner I could get my hands on her most excellent cook the better!'

A gale of genuine laughter burst from the audience at that. This double meaning was more like the old Geoffrey that they knew and loved.

Louisa looked up at him enquiringly, wondering whether this man that she had grown to know and love could ever leave the sociable act of Geoffrey Redvers behind.

'Don't worry, Louisa,' he said, as though reading

her mind. 'As soon as we can decently make our escape we will leave parties and chit-chat and all the other empty pleasantries far behind us!'

Stephen was as good as his word. His first wedding, to Agnes, had been planned like a military campaign, organised months in advance and with hundreds of members of the very richest cream of society, most of which Stephen had never seen before, and never saw again.

He vowed that his second wedding was to be different. Louisa was delighted. The Tonbridges and their friends were good company for the occasional party, but she did not want them wandering all over her home, trying to influence her taste and warning her of the horrors of marriage.

Their wedding was so quiet that Charles Darblay-Barre was the only society guest. The ceremony took place in the tiny Norman church at Stanton Malreward, and afterwards they had a huge, informal picnic on the lawns of Holly House to which all the staff and villagers were invited.

'I enjoyed that,' Stephen said with an air of surprise as the new and official Mr and Mrs Allington drove off to catch the Paris sleeper. 'Perhaps we could throw another party like it for King George's Coronation. Flaming June, a day off work for the King and Queen, food in the open air—it would be marvellous…'

'And I thought that you were intending to leave the mad social whirl behind you?' Louisa teased him gently.

'I hardly think that one party between now and next Christmas will set me back on the road to ruin. Not when I have you by my side.' He smiled, kissing her softly.

There had been no time for Louisa to think about the honeymoon beyond arranging her trousseau. A train journey—no matter how luxurious—hardly seemed the place to worry about such things either. However, things became rather more pressing when their bags were taken up to the honeymoon suite at a discreetly beautiful hotel in the centre of Paris.

Louisa looked around at all the gilding, the silk and satin upholstery that adorned their room, and wondered. Stephen tipped and thanked every last porter with speed, but he was not in quite such a hurry to join Louisa as she went to look out of the window. Only a few yards away ran the Champs Elysées with its busy yet stately bustle of grand motor cars and impressive carriages.

'Our suites back at Holly House have been arranged as you suggested,' Stephen began slowly, one hand slipping tentatively around her waist. 'But…well, this being our honeymoon and everything, I thought it only proper…'

His voice died away, perhaps hoping that Louisa would fill the void, but she had no urge to continue the conversation either.

'I shall not ever trouble you again,' he murmured at last.

'I cannot imagine you ever troubling me at all, Stephen,' she said softly.

'No—you don't understand, Louisa. I mean…'
'Shh.'

Louisa turned and touched one finger to his lips before reaching up to put her hands around his neck. His skin was smooth and cool beneath her fingers, with the velvety brush of a recent haircut at the nape of his neck. They kissed, despite being so close to the window.

'All will be well,' she murmured, and he believed her.

Louisa was conscious of an unusual noise as she woke. It was a puzzle—Roseberry was always so still and silent at night—and then she remembered. Of course. She was not at home. The sound was the ticking of Stephen's pocket watch. It was lying on the bedside table, close to her.

Louisa lay still, listening. The thickness of the closed curtains meant that it was as dark as midnight in the room, but the general silence that hung about the hotel must mean that the hour was much later than that. They had not dined until eight, then returned to their room shortly before eleven after taking a walk to the banks of the Seine by moonlight, and then…things had got a little confused. It was the effect of all the champagne, Louisa decided, realising that she now had a raging thirst.

Reaching for the glass and carafe that stood on her bedside table was going to be very difficult. Stephen's arm was draped around her, his hand cradling her shoulder. Any movements would have to be stealthy to avoid wakening him.

It took her an age to inch the bedclothes back, but

as she made the first tentative movements to slide out of bed he sat up.

'Louisa?'

'I am only getting myself a drink.'

She heard him sigh as he subsided back onto the pillow.

'I love you,' Louisa breathed as he moved to kiss the delicate skin beneath her ear.

'Still?' He smiled down at her.

'More every minute.' Louisa lifted her hand to his cheek, noticing that the white silk of her nightgown sleeve gave colour to his skin as she laid her arm against him. 'And, if you agree, I shall ask Sam and Maggie to move my things into the room adjoining yours as soon as we get back to Holly House. This is hardly the place to raise her name, but I think—' Louisa lowered her voice to a whisper '—that Agnes must have been far too gently brought up for her own good.'

'Then you found nothing...' Louisa felt his embarrassment warming the darkness between them '...to alarm or distress you about last evening?'

'On the contrary.' Louisa slid back down into his arms. 'I love you, Stephen.'

'And I adore you,' he murmured, bending down to nuzzle into the soft fragrance of her hair.

MILLS & BOON®

Historical Romance™

Coming next month

THE PROPERTY OF A GENTLEMAN
by Helen Dickson

A Regency delight!

Being practically bequeathed to the man who had been
responsible for ruining her reputation was hardly Eve's
idea of a romantic proposal. Eve wanted to say that she
wasn't even remotely tempted, if only Marcus wasn't so
devastatingly handsome!

AN IDEAL MATCH
by Anne Herries

A Regency delight!

Miss Jane Osmore wanted a perfect match for her ward,
Amanda, and, ignoring her own feelings, she thought Max
would be ideal. But Max had the idea that he should make
his *own* choice, and it wouldn't be Amanda!

On sale from 11th September 1998

Available from WH Smith, John Menzies and Volume One

MILLS & BOON®

Emma Darcy

The Collection

✳ ✳ ✳ ✳

This autumn Mills & Boon® brings you a powerful
collection of three full-length novels by an
outstanding romance author:

Always Love
To Tame a Wild Heart
The Seduction of Keira

Over 500 pages of love, seduction and intrigue.

Available from September 1998

*Available at most branches of WH Smith, John Menzies,
Martins, Tesco, Asda, and Volume One*

 WORD LINK

We are giving away a year's supply of Mills & Boon® books to the five lucky winners of our latest competition. Simply fill in the ten missing words below, complete the coupon overleaf and send this entire page to us by 28th February 1999. The first five correct entries will each win a year's subscription to the Mills & Boon series of their choice. What could be easier?

BUSINESS	**SUIT**	CASE
BOTTLE	_____	HAT
FRONT	_____	BELL
PARTY	_____	BOX
SHOE	_____	PIPE
RAIN	_____	TIE
ARM	_____	MAN
SIDE	_____	ROOM
BEACH	_____	GOWN
FOOT	_____	KIND
BIRTHDAY	_____	BOARD

Please turn over for details of how to enter ⇨

HOW TO ENTER

There are ten words missing from our list overleaf. Each of the missing words must link up with the two on either side to make a new word or words.

For example, 'Business' links with 'Suit' and 'Case' to form 'Business Suit' and 'Suit Case':

BUSINESS—SUIT—CASE

As you find each one, write it in the space provided. When you have linked up all the words, fill in the coupon below, pop this page into an envelope and post it today. Don't forget you could win a year's supply of Mills & Boon® books—you don't even need to pay for a stamp!

Mills & Boon Word Link Competition
FREEPOST CN81, Croydon, Surrey, CR9 3WZ

EIRE readers: (please affix stamp) PO Box 4546, Dublin 24.

Please tick the series you would like to receive if you are one of the lucky winners

Presents™ ❏ Enchanted™ ❏ Medical Romance™ ❏
Historical Romance™ ❏ Temptation®

Are you a Reader Service™ subscriber?   Yes ❏   No ❏

Ms/Mrs/Miss/Mr ....Initials............................
(BLOCK CAPITALS PLEASE)

Surname...

Address ....

....

....Postcode.........................

(I am over 18 years of age)   C8H